PRAISE I

"Always hilarious on page one, JJ Knight delivers romantic comedy like no one else. Each book is an irresistible seduction and a tale of connection that pulls you in and leaves you smiling."

—*New York Times* bestselling author Julia Kent,
author of *Shopping for a Billionaire*

"Every time I finish one of JJ Knight's steamy, hilarious books, I think this is the best one yet—then she writes another one that becomes the best! Slapstick comedy combines with heartfelt romance and some sultry scenes that will have you fanning yourself like it's summertime. JJ Knight is always the best."

—*USA Today* bestselling author Blair Babylon, author of *Rogue* (*Billionaires in Disguise: Maxence*) and other thrillers that bang

"JJ Knight is delightfully funny in an incredibly creative way. She will make you laugh so hard you will cry, and then wrench your heart until you shed real tears. Each new book has me wondering, what is she going to come up with next?"

—*USA Today* bestselling author Olivia Rigal,
author of the One Favor series

"Funny, romantic, sexy, sweet. And lots of pickle jokes! JJ Knight wrote a real winner!"

—*New York Times* bestselling romance author Lynn Raye Harris

OTHER TITLES BY JJ KNIGHT

THE
WEDDING
Confession

USA TODAY BESTSELLING AUTHOR
JJ KNIGHT

Text copyright © 2023 JJ Knight
All rights reserved.

No part of this book may be reproduced, or stored in a retrieval system, or transmitted in any form or by any means, electronic, mechanical, photocopying, recording, or otherwise, without express written permission of the publisher.

Published by Montlake, Seattle

www.apub.com

Amazon, the Amazon logo, and Montlake are trademarks of Amazon.com, Inc., or its affiliates.

ISBN-13: 9781662512063 (paperback)
ISBN-13: 9781662512056 (digital)

Cover design by Hang Le
Cover image: © ViewStock / Getty; © Julia Garan / Getty; © katarina_1 / Shutterstock; Africa Studio / Shutterstock

Printed in the United States of America

THE WEDDING
Confession

Chapter 1

ENSLEY

I can't believe what I'm seeing.

I've heard about situations like this at weddings.

In viral videos. Social media rants.

But this is the first time I've seen one right in front of me.

I glance over at my best friend, Ronnie. She's the bride, dressed in a beautiful but simple knee-length sheath.

Her mother's dress.

The mother who died only two years ago, before Ronnie's engagement.

The wedding was supposed to be a small event at the park where Ronnie's mom used to push her on the swings. She wanted to honor this amazing woman who had been a mother figure to all of us in the bridal party.

Well, the original bridal party.

Now there are ten bridesmaids and ten groomsmen. A country club. A swing band. And a seated dinner for four hundred.

This wedding got hijacked.

And now this.

The guilty party is the person right in front of me. Her arrival has left all the bridesmaids in shocked silence, piled up in the corner like a bushel of peaches in our strapless, puffy dresses that flatter no one.

Ronnie lets out a whimper. I know that sound. She's trying to control herself to avoid an outburst.

I can't believe it. I just can't.

The center of the attention is Felicia, Ronnie's new stepmother.

We don't know what came over Ronnie's dad when he married her. But Felicia is a firestorm. She commandeered their lives, using those big pouty lips to convince Ronnie's dad to sell their thirty-year family home for a McMansion near this country club.

Felicia is a trustee of the club, and once Ronnie announced her engagement, Felicia insisted the wedding should mirror their *elevated station*, whatever that means.

I felt helpless during the last few months, watching Ronnie's charming dream wedding unravel.

But not today.

Not with this.

Because Felicia has entered the room, not in the stately blue dress we thought she was wearing as stepmother of the bride.

But in a full-length beaded white gown. She even has baby's breath in her hair and a tiny white veil over her eyes. All that's missing is a bouquet.

Next to her, Ronnie looks like a flower girl.

She's been in the room a full minute, and no one has spoken.

"Well?" Felicia asks. "What do you think? It's the dress I always wanted to wear to an affair like this."

I see how it is. Felicia married Ronnie's father in a weekend getaway to Vegas that probably involved vodka and edibles, and she's making up for everything she missed.

Ronnie tries to get a few words out. I can tell how much it's killing her to say something nice. "It's a lot."

Felicia strikes a pose, fanning out her dagger nails. "Of course it is. An original Vera Wang. I would have nothing less for my dear new daughter's wedding."

Does she really think she's doing Ronnie a favor here?

"I like Vera Wang," Ronnie stammers. Her dress was off the rack at Dillard's. In 1991. "Where's Dad?"

Felicia examines a nail. "Your father's leg is bothering him. It's why I changed. I was going to save this gown for the reception, but it seems, my dear, that I'm walking you down the aisle!"

"What?" The word explodes out of me before I can stop myself.

Felicia gives me a sidelong glance. "You should be happy for us, Ensley." She says my name as if it leaves a nasty taste in her mouth.

I step close to Ronnie. "You want me to do something real ugly?" I whisper.

Ronnie leans close. "Remember your positivity training. You're all sunshine now."

Right. I can't afford therapy, so Ronnie paid for us to get training to cultivate the sunshine demeanor I've always wanted since moving past my difficult childhood. "I'm *positive* that I should do something ugly."

For the first time since her stepmother invaded the dressing room, Ronnie cracks a smile.

I glance back at the rest of the bridesmaids. Ronnie's older sister is serving as the maid of honor, but she's watching us in astonishment like the rest of the puff-dressed observers. Aren't we supposed to have Ronnie's back?

Ronnie and I have been best friends since we were children. She was there when my mom died when I was five. And I was there when she lost hers. There is no tighter bond than that.

I have to do something about this stupid dress and prevent Felicia from ruining Ronnie's entrance.

I glance around the room, searching for something that will help. I spot the fireplace tools. Is violence the answer?

No. I might get blood on my dress.

And then I see it. The perfect solution.

I hope someone is videoing it, because I'm about to be a viral sensation.

I can see the caption: *Perfect bridesmaid saves wedding.*

It's a tray filled with crystal goblets. Champagne. White wine.

And *red*.

I keep my voice casual as I walk over to the tray. "Felicia, may I offer you a glass of wine?"

Felicia smirks, her lurid lips glossy. She thinks she's won me over. "Champagne, please."

Ronnie watches me with concern as I pick up a glass of champagne for her stepmother, then choose wine for myself.

Red, of course.

Ronnie's eyes go saucer wide as she watches the next few seconds unfold. I think it's one of my finest moments.

I step closer, the glasses held out in front.

I trip, stumbling over nothing.

Then I toss both glasses straight at Felicia's pristine bodice. The wine soaks her, staining the white satin before the goblets crash to the floor and shatter.

"What have you done?" Felicia tries to step out of the way, but she's far, far too late. She looks like a zombie bride after a snack.

"I guess you'll have to wear the blue dress after all," I say. "Sorry."

I glance back at Ronnie. She mouths, *Thank you.*

See, I told you I'd save the day. I might aspire to be sunshine, but I can *burn*.

Except—the moment isn't over.

Felicia's face turns redder than her stained bodice. She makes two fists like a toddler refusing to go to bed and lets out a terrifying shriek.

The wedding planner bursts into the room. "Oh my God, what is it?"

"Call security!" Felicia yells. "Call them right now or you'll never work another wedding again!"

The poor woman nearly drops her phone. "What happened?" Then she sees the front of the dress. "Oh."

"Get security now!"

The woman scampers off.

Felicia turns to me. "You did that on purpose. I want you out of here."

"I'm here for Ronnie, and I'm not leaving," I say.

Her eyes narrow, and the pure evil aimed at me almost makes me shiver.

An oversize man in a brown uniform races into the room. "What's wrong?"

"Her," Felicia says. "Jeremy, get her out of here."

Uh-oh. She's on a first-name basis with the security guard.

"No!" Ronnie cries. "She's my best friend!"

"Take her in the hall," Felicia says. "She doesn't belong here."

The guard hesitates a moment, but Felicia's voice gets more strident. "Jeremy! Take her in the hall!"

That's actually a good idea. Ronnie's seen enough. "I've got this," I tell her. "Don't worry."

And before the big lug can put his hand on me, I walk ahead of him into the gold-wallpapered corridor, my puffy peach skirt swaying around my knees with my swagger.

Felicia closes the door to the bridal chamber and faces the hall. "This woman intentionally ruined my dress," she says to Jeremy.

"I tripped," I say. "I'm a bridesmaid."

Jeremy looks back and forth between us, taking in the ruined dress. "If she just tripped—"

"Jeremy," Felicia snarls. "I need her gone. I'm a trustee here. You should listen to me when I say she's a threat to our club."

Jeremy sighs. "Let's go." He reaches for my arm.

"No!" I spin aside. "I'm not leaving my friend!"

"Don't let her make a fuss!" Felicia hisses. "Take her the back way out!"

I wave my arms so Jeremy can't grab hold. "That woman is crazy! I tripped!" But I'm not entirely convincing. I *did* do it on purpose.

"Just follow me," Jeremy says. "It will be all right. Let's cool off."

He doesn't seem like he's going to actually throw me out, his face more annoyed than angry. He starts down the hall.

I hesitate, but Felicia says, "Go!"

All right. I'll go. We have some time before the wedding anyway.

When we're sufficiently far from Felicia, the guard says quietly, "Look, Felicia's been around this club a long time, and this isn't her first fit. She'll get over it. Just take a walk, let her calm down, and we'll let you return in half an hour."

"Half an hour!" I reach for my phone, then remember it was confiscated by the wedding planner. All of ours were, so that they wouldn't accidentally make noise during the ceremony. "The wedding is in fifteen minutes!"

"Whatever," the guy says. "Don't come back for fifteen minutes."

"Fine."

We continue down the hall. "Where are you taking me?" I ask.

"Out the back. You can walk on the golf course. Sit on a bench. I don't care. Just stay away from here for a little while."

I blow out a long, annoyed breath. I'm supposed to be sipping wine and hanging out with my best friend. Damn Felicia and her white dress.

A roar of male laughter bursts from an open door ahead. It must be the men's dressing room. I plan to peek in as we pass, but before we make it there, a groomsman steps out. "I'll make sure Ronnie hasn't sent a spy," he calls back into the room.

I almost smile. Ronnie did threaten surveillance if she thought they were drinking too much before the ceremony.

Based on the laughter, she was right to worry.

He glances the other way first, but when he looks toward us, my breath catches. It's Drew Daniels, and he's gorgeous in a tux. Like, unbelievably delicious.

I knew him well growing up. He and my older brother, Garrett, played football together, and I often sat in the window mooning over Drew as they practiced in the yard.

Seeing him dressed like this reminds me of all the fantasies twelve-year-old me used to dream up about Drew and prom and our very own wedding one day. Dashed, of course, because he was sixteen to my twelve and thought I was a twerp.

Unfortunately, today's bridal party lineup does not have him escorting me, so we haven't so much as shaken hands. But from the flutters in my belly, that girlhood crush is far from over.

Drew takes in the guard, then me, his face darkening. "What's going on here?"

I hate to admit anything. I almost say I'm the spy, but end up with the truth. "Felicia kicked me out," I say. "I have to go wander around while she cools off."

"Where?"

Jeremy speaks up. "Just out on the green."

"What did you do?"

I hate that he's finally talking to me, and it's about this. "I got wine on Felicia's dress."

"That would definitely get her riled." He falls into step beside us. "But I don't like them escorting you out of here. What if they lock you out?"

I glance up at the guard. "He assures me that I'll be able to get back in."

Drew's beautiful lips press into a firm line. "I think I should come along to make sure."

My heart swells. Drew has no idea how often I imagined him saving me whenever I got into tough spots as a kid. His family might not come from money, but they had a beautiful brick house, two parents, and the sort of home life I longed for. I always knew he would sweep me away from the dark, sad, dirty house with no mother and a father who rarely spoke to any of us after she died. My father still doesn't.

And here he is. Drew. It's hero time.

We enter the bowels of the club. The offices are dark on a Saturday night. At the end of the hall, we turn into a large room filled with rows of stacked chairs. There's a huge set of double doors on the back wall, which I assume is where deliveries are made. We seem to be heading for that.

This feels weird. There should be dozens of random exits to a sprawling building like this. Alarm bells start to ring. "My punishment is only for fifteen minutes, though, right?"

"Sure," Jeremy says.

Drew must also start to feel concern, because he says, "So you're certain we can walk around for a while, and then she can come back in?"

The guard smiles again. "Sure."

He unlocks one of the double doors and opens it to the cool night air. Outside is a concrete ledge that juts over a pit. Just as I figured, this is where deliveries arrive.

Jeremy angles me toward the door. "Go on now."

"But—"

"Out you go." He gives me a hefty push.

I stumble forward onto the concrete ledge. There isn't much space before the sharp drop where trucks pull up.

"Watch that!" Drew shouts.

I hear nothing else. My heel snaps, caught in the ridge between the concrete and the metal edge of the loading dock. I wave my arms, trying to sidestep and move toward the stairs I see to the right.

But I'm off balance. I can't find my footing on the broken heel.

I tilt forward to stare into the concrete hole.

Then, like a big ol' peach careening off a grocery store display, I start to fall.

Chapter 2

Drew

I lunge forward to grasp Ensley around the waist. "Gotcha."

She lets out a startled cry, so I turn her around and pull her against my chest. I'm going to cream that guard. I hold on to her, the funny peach skirt ballooning out behind her. She hiccups against my tux jacket.

Jesus. I remember her growing up. She often bugged us when I was over at her house to toss the ball around with Garrett. She was a serious pest, a tiny package of pure nonsense, spying on us from the windows.

Once she insisted on making us lemonade by stealing lemons from the neighbor's prized citrus tree, something that's hard to grow in Alabama. We ended up having to fetch her kicking and screaming after she got caught. I still remember chucking her tiny frame over my shoulder to haul her home.

She's not so little now. Her hair smells of flowers and beauty products. The strapless bridesmaid dress shows off her tan shoulders. It's March, and no time for sunbathing. I start to picture her naked in a tanning bed when a loud thud makes me turn.

The guard has shut the door, followed by the unmistakable sound of a bolt turning.

Ensley pulls away from me. "He locked us out."

I straighten her so she can stand. "You all right?"

She bends down to look at the broken shoe. "I won't be running a marathon in these."

I pull on the door handles. They don't budge. No sense banging on them. That clown will be long gone. "Not going back this way."

"We can walk around front."

I glance down at her shoe. "In that?"

"I'll be fine."

We move toward the stairs. Ensley clutches the rail, trying to compensate for the broken heel. Finally, she pulls both shoes off. "I'm fine barefoot."

I'm not so sure. It's a long way around.

I'm ambivalent about missing the ceremony. It was always going to be the Felicia show. When I signed on, I was the best man with only one other groomsman. The wedding was supposed to be small and informal, made up primarily of longtime friends. Franklin and I were roommates at Georgia Tech.

Then Felicia forced her son into the best man role and insisted on ten groomsmen. Ronnie and Franklin hadn't wanted to make waves. With such a huge wedding party, they might not even notice we're missing in the parade of tuxes and balloon dresses.

The back of the building is paved, and security lights help us navigate in the dark. The air is chilly and smells of rain. Yeah, that's coming. The thunderstorms were supposed to start an hour ago.

Franklin was glad the bad weather held off so that the wedding could get underway before the deluge, but it won't be long now.

Ensley walks fast, determined to get back in there. I glance over at her. She shoves a chunk of hair aside. Her updo has loosened after nearly falling. She was always trouble, but when I last saw her, she was barely in a training bra.

She's definitely out of it now. Her chest heaves in the strapless dress as she struggles to keep up with me. The puffy skirt bounces around her knees.

She yelps, and I slow down. "You all right?"

She knocks a pebble off her foot. "Of course I am. I'm Ensley, everyone's ray of freaking sunshine." She walks even faster, as if her pace proves the point.

Franklin mentioned this facet of Ensley's personality. Apparently Ronnie has been coaching Ensley to put a positive spin on everything. But I'm not buying it. Ensley was always a spunky, hardheaded tornado when we were kids. I would never have called her *sunshine*. But maybe she's changed. I'm certainly no longer in her circles now that I'm here in Atlanta and she's still back in Alabama.

We approach a small parking lot filled with neat rows of golf carts. I spot a small awning covering a door that is likely where golfers are given their carts before riding onto the green.

"We'll try this door," I say.

"It's going to be locked."

"I thought you were this big optimist."

"That was before I got tossed out on my butt."

"Did you have a plan for what might happen after you ruined Felicia's dress?"

Her face draws into a pout. "No."

"Didn't you know that poking the Felicia bear was going to go badly for you?"

"Probably."

"Were you maybe sure you could win her over with your fabulous smile?"

"Go to hell, Drew."

That's the Ensley I remember. I approach the door. But before I tug on the handle, I already see Ensley's right. The golf pro shop is closed up and dark.

"We'll have to keep going," I say.

The stone wall is unbroken for a while, not even a window. It might be the ballroom.

I pause, listening. There's a faint sound of music.

Ensley leans in beside me. "Is that the wedding march?"

"Yeah. See? No point in hurrying."

She presses her ear to the bricks. "No, it's just the sit-down music. We can make it!" She speeds up. At the corner, the pavement ends in scraggly grass bordered by a line of trees. She only takes one step before yelping again.

"Jesus, woman."

"I'm fine. Just stickers. I won't quit." She takes two more steps before she's forced to lean against the wall and pick more grass burrs out of her feet.

"Ready to give up yet?"

Her jaw clenches. "No." She storms off again, this time refusing to stop for the stickers. "I won't think about the pain. I'll focus on the positive, the—"

I shut her up by lifting her by the waist and throwing her over my shoulder.

"Drew! God! Stop it! You'll wreck my hair!"

"Already wrecked."

"My skirt will go flat!"

I adjust my hands on the back of her knees to make sure I have a good hold. "It's a ridiculous design."

She hammers her fists against my back. "But the pictures!"

"Just shut up while I get you there."

She goes quiet, her billowy skirt tickling my cheek as I hurry along the side wall. If the only unlocked entrance is the main door, we'll have to rush to make it. This place is huge.

"I'm sorry I got you into this," Ensley says, her voice bouncing and breaking as I jostle her along.

I grunt.

"But Felicia wore this awful white dress."

"So you decided to ruin it?"

"It was a wedding gown. She had netting over her face."

"Like a veil?"

"Exactly like a veil!"

Franklin had complained about his future mother-in-law many times. She's a real piece of work. When Ronnie's dad first started dating her, we were concerned. Ronnie took losing her mother hard, and Sheila had been a mother figure to us all. The whole wedding crew grew up together.

And we were right. Felicia turned out to be every bit as bad as the stereotype. With her big hair and short temper, she's a dead ringer for Cinderella's evil stepmother.

The building goes on forever, and soon, fat drops of rain hit my face. I stop, peering into the sky. Great. The storm has arrived. We need to make it to the front.

The rain pelts us as I break into a run. We won't be soaked if we can get to the front of the building. There's an overhang where cars pull in. We can tidy back up and hurry inside. I don't know exactly what Ensley will do about her shoes, but that's not my problem.

Lightning flashes across the sky and a clap of thunder shakes the ground, causing Ensley to squeal. The rain intensifies, and Ensley hammers my back. "Set me down!" she yells, her poof dress deflating in the onslaught. "We're too big a mess to go in there now!"

I do as she says. The grass here is better, less scraggly. Hopefully it is sticker free.

Ensley turns, her dress clinging to her, arms tight across her chest. Water streams down her face. Her hair is a clump of hairspray and pins.

"Now what?" she cries. I can barely hear her over the pounding of the downpour.

"Hell if I know!"

Ensley turns in little circles, her voice a singsong. "This problem has a solution. I am capable. I can handle what comes at me."

Lightning flashes again, and her eyes go wide.

"How are those mantras working for you?" I ask.

She grabs my arm. "There's a building in the trees," she says. "I saw it in the flash."

I ignore her, looking back at the country club. We still have a long way to go to make it to the next corner, and that might not even be the front.

Ensley takes my arm. "Come on."

She tugs, and I follow her. We enter the tree line and the storm gets quieter, the rain lessened by the canopy of branches.

"Up there." I can barely see her finger pointing in the darkness of the woods, but there's a paved path ahead. We reach it, a swath cut out of the trees.

We follow it and the building appears, a single weak light over a door. It's surrounded by dozens of golf carts in varying degrees of disrepair—flat tires, broken seats, missing tops.

"A golf cart graveyard," Ensley says, almost reverently, as if we should respect the dead.

I speed up, striding past the mass of carts. This must be a maintenance shed. At least we can ride out the storm.

The door is secured with a simple padlock. I pick up a rock and break it easily. Another peal of thunder booms, much closer this time, and Ensley squeals, jumping into the air.

"Come on," I tell her, yanking open the door.

The inside smells of oil and cut grass. I fumble for a light switch, but find none. Ensley steps timidly inside, shivering. Her balloon dress is a drooping mass of satin and netting.

I leave the door open so that the meager light over the entrance will give us something to work with.

"Is there a switch?" Ensley asks. She sets down her useless shoes.

I move to the other side of the door. "Looking for it." Something bites into my skin, and I realize it's a gardening tool. Lightning flashes, and I see that this side of the wall is hung with shears and rakes and shovels.

"I thought I saw a string for a bulb," Ensley says. Her shadow dances as she waves her hands in the air, trying to snag it. She jumps, and in the silhouette, I see the top of her dress fall, a clear outline of naked breasts with tight nipples. She gasps and drops her hands, pulling up something stiff, like a strapless bra maybe, and then the dress.

My body stirs in a way I don't like, not with an annoying woman I'm half pissed at and who was always a pain in my side when I knew her as a kid. But damn, that was a beautiful rack. I can already feel that nipple crossing my palm.

Down, boy.

She reaches with only one arm, the other across her chest.

I take a moment to clear my thoughts. There has to be a light in here somewhere.

I'm about to express my doubts that there's a hanging bulb when she chirps, "Found it!"

With her yank, yellow light fills the shadows. It's not much, but at least we can see what we're doing.

"Nice work," I tell her.

Her face flushes. I wonder if she thinks I didn't notice the moment with the dress, not in the dark. But my thoughts are right back on it, and I have to force myself to keep my gaze on her face.

She smacks at the soaked fabric near her thigh. "Stupid dress gets heavy when it's wet," she says.

So maybe she does know I saw.

My traitorous body stirs again.

"Can you manage it?" I ask.

"I'm fine."

My tux is no better, sticking to my skin. I strip off my jacket and bow tie and lay them over the handle of a mower.

Ensley circles the room, her hands holding on to the top of her dress. She's clearly struggling to keep it up.

"I assume you already gave up your phone," she says.

"Right with everybody else."

"So nobody knows where we are or if we're even coming back."

I pick up a fallen rake and lean it against the wall. "Nope."

One corner of the space is filled with hand mowers and edgers, filthy with mud and clumps of grass. The back wall has a long counter covered in engine parts and tools. Both front corners contain large built-in cabinets. "You check that one," I say, pointing across the room. "I'll check this one."

"What am I looking for?" she asks.

"Folding chairs. A blanket, maybe. No telling how long we're stuck here."

The rain lashes the building as the wind shifts directions. Water comes in the door, so I close it now that we have a light. There are no windows, so nobody will see we're in here, not that they'd be headed to the shed in this weather.

"Score!" Ensley says, so I turn to her. She drags out what first appears to be a folding chair, but when she opens it, it's a cot.

Interesting.

She scoots the cot to the center of the room as best she can with one hand. "Better than sitting on the floor."

I open my cabinet. It's nothing but paint cans, oil, and more maintenance tools. I head over to hers.

This cabinet has tarps, rope, and stakes. The large section at the bottom held the cot, but there's more hidden back there. I stoop down.

There's a plastic bin. I almost ignore it, but it's out of sync with the rest of the items in the shed. Too colorful, too new. I drag it out.

"What did you find?" Ensley asks, leaning over the bin as I pop off the top. "Score again!" she cries.

It contains a bottle of bourbon, a sheath of plastic cups, and two bags of Doritos.

"Looks like we're not the only ones using the shed after hours," I say.

"But why the cot?" she asks.

She's about to sit down when I say, "It's probably a hookup spot."

She stands up straight, looking dubiously at the canvas surface. "*Eeeew.*"

I snatch the bottle of bourbon and a cup. This will take the edge off.

Ensley opens a bag of chips. "I was too nervous to eat all day. I'm starving."

"Want some?" I ask, holding up the bottle.

"Definitely." She crunches a handful of Doritos.

I pour a healthy amount of bourbon and give it a sniff. "Not total rotgut." I pass it to her.

"I'll drink anything at this point." She takes a delicate sip and shivers. "This'll hit me like a brick."

I pour a couple of inches for myself and down it, then pour some more. The fiery warmth is the first good thing since I spotted Ensley in the hall. "This whole thing is bullshit."

Ensley examines the cot again, then sits on the edge. "I know. I'm sorry. But Felicia was going to make Ronnie walk down the aisle with her instead of her dad. She was so upset. I had to do something. I figured a red wine accident was better than bloodshed."

"I would have opted for murder."

Her shoulders droop. "I hope it was a beautiful ceremony."

More thunder booms, but we can't see the lightning anymore. Wind rattles the roof.

"It will hold up, right?" Ensley asks, eyes on the ceiling.

"It's old. Been through plenty of storms."

She holds out the bag of chips, and I take a few. I'm hungry, too.

"You were trying to help me, and now you're missing it all." Her voice is a lament. "I'm so sorry, Drew. It's like I lived up to all the times you called me a brat growing up."

I freeze, a chip halfway to my mouth. "I said that directly to you?"

"Pretty much every time you came over." She sips her drink, watching me over the rim. "You and Garrett hated it when I followed you around."

"We were punk kids, for sure." I toss the chip in my mouth.

She reaches up to touch her hair, and my gaze drops to the strapless dress, wondering if it's going to hold. The bodice is definitely drooping from being drenched.

That's a temptation I don't need. I walk to the door and open it to peer out. The rain is coming down in sheets, and a cold wind races through the room. The temperature has dropped twenty degrees, easy. I peer through the trees to see if I will be able to tell when the cars start to leave after the reception. It's impossible to know right now with the storm so intense.

I shove the door closed again. The shed is noticeably colder. I shouldn't have opened it.

When I turn around, Ensley is huddled in a shivering ball as if all her strength has finally run out.

Damn.

Chapter 3

ENSLEY

It's too much. Too, too much.

I'm cold. My hair is ruined. I'm pretty sure the boy I crushed on as a kid just saw my boobs.

The Dorito bag crunches against my belly as I crumple over, overcome with shakes. The thought of wrecking the only thing I've had to eat today makes tears squeeze out of my eyes.

I'm crying over Doritos.

Drew stands by the door like a gorgeous gargoyle. I can't make out his face. My fake eyelashes are coming off. I tug at them and let them fall to the floor. I'm a mess. A drowned-rat, mascara-running, strapless-dress-losing disaster.

And it's my own fault.

I had to be dramatic. Really sock it to Felicia.

Well, she showed me. I'm sure she changed into her backup dress and my little act did nothing. She probably forced her arm around Ronnie's and marched her down the aisle. And she's sitting in the middle of the family table at the reception right now, bossing the servers around and drinking champagne in a warm, dry room.

Ronnie probably wonders why I didn't return after my ejection to the hall. Felicia most certainly made up a lie. Ronnie must assume

I became yet another lost cause at the wedding, surrendering to her stepmother's will like all the other details that got changed.

I hiccup-cough, my nose running so badly I have no choice but to wipe my hand beneath it like a sniveling kid.

Drew hasn't moved from the door. I'm sure he sees me as a weak-kneed ninny who can't handle a storm. I'll forever be a snotty brat to his glorious king-of-the-world football star.

I extricate the bag of Doritos from where my belly crushed it and set it beside me on the cot. My cup of bourbon is on the floor, so I reach for it, slamming the whole thing like Drew did.

The fire rips down my throat and makes me sit straight up, like my spine has turned to steel.

"Whoa!" I see stars, then rivers of lava. Then my stomach feels warm and good. Oh yes, that shocked me right out of my pity party. I want more.

Drew steps forward, a crease of concern on his brow. "You okay?"

I hold out the cup. "I need another one of those."

His jaw ticks, his eyes on my chest.

"My eyes are up here," I tell him.

Drew clears his throat. "But your dress is down there."

I glance at my lap. The peach satin bodice lies in a heap around my waist. Great. I try to pull it back over the strapless bra, but it's a wet, twisted mess.

I fight with it until it at least covers my bra. The clingy satin outlines my belly and legs like a shiny second skin.

My empty cup has fallen sideways on the cot. I snatch it up and hold it out to Drew. "Get me a damn drink."

His jaw moves back and forth as he works it. But he takes the cup and pours another inch. "Take it easy."

I probably should. But if I'm stuck with Drew for hours, I'm going to need all the liquid courage I can get.

I take a gulp.

"You might want to hang up the dress so it can dry," he says.

I might be bullheaded, but I'm on the shy end when it comes to skin. I don't flash mine around. "I'm not getting naked around you. I know about your reputation. Franklin told Ronnie about your ridiculous number of one-night stands. That you're worse than a rabbit. Did you know a male bunny can bang a girl in less than five seconds?"

"I'm aware."

"Oh, right. You're a veterinarian. Ronnie said you can seduce the humps off a camel."

His eyes bore into me. "Trust me, seducing you is the last thing on my mind."

Oh, is it? Now he's pissed *me* off.

I let go of the bodice, and it falls to my waist again. I don't have to look to know the white bra has gone sheer with the wetness.

He growls and turns away to pour himself another shot of bourbon.

I'm mad enough to be crazy, so I decide to do as he says. Let the dress dry. I stand up and unzip the back, shimmying until it hits the floor.

He acts like he's not looking, but even though his back is to me, I can see the side of his face.

He's definitely looking.

My throat feels thick as I take the dress to hang over a mower handle like Drew did with his jacket. I move quickly, feeling self-conscious about the panties, which might be see-through from being damp.

When I turn around, Drew has stripped off his shirt. He kicks off his shoes and peels off his socks. Then his pants drop. Soon he's in nothing but shiny black boxers.

"Seemed fair," he says.

All right, then. I guess this is his way of being chivalrous.

My breath catches. His chest is broad and muscled, leading to wide shoulders and bulging arms. I remember seeing him without a shirt once, back when he was Garrett's friend and they were playing football on the front lawn during summer. Sweat had glistened on his skin, and I'd fallen off my perch at the window, knocking over a lamp and making the boys laugh.

But that moment is nothing compared to this. I'm on fire. I want to touch him, and for him to touch me. This pull is like nothing I've felt before.

He brushes past me to spread his pants and shirt across the mower handles.

I plunk down on the cot, trying not to shiver. The warming effect of the bourbon is wearing off, but I'm afraid to drink more. I'm a lightweight, and I need my head on straight for this.

Drew takes his time arranging his things, as if he's avoiding turning around. What's that all about?

Then I wonder—does he have a woody?

A giggle threatens to erupt. Did I have an effect on Drew? The twelve-year-old girl in me who would have died to know says I have to find out.

I stand up again, heading to the opposite cabinet to see if I can get a good angle. "I don't guess they have a heater in sheds like this," I say, pretending to look around like there might be one somewhere.

He's spent way too long making the long sleeve of his shirt lie across one of the mower handles.

It has to be what I think it is.

I peer around the edge of the door, trying to catch the shape of his boxers in front. Is it there?

Lord, I'm juvenile. But it's the most fun I've had since getting thrown out of the wedding. I bite my lip, imagining the scenario in Drew's head as he stands there trying to control his body parts.

I spot a jar of screws and plan to shake it to see if he will turn at the noise, and then I'll know for sure. I pick it up but don't expect the glass to be coated in something sticky.

"Ick!" I drop the glass, and it shatters near my feet, screws flying every direction.

Drew turns. "Don't move! You'll cut your feet!"

I forget all about checking his boxers as I realize what I've done. I'm stuck in my spot, broken shards all around me.

Drew circles the opposite side of the cot and shoves his bare feet back into his shoes. He stomps across the shed, crunching glass.

He's so mad, I actually tremble. When he reaches for me, I manage to say, "What are you going to—*eeep!*" He lifts me into his arms.

"You get into more scrapes than a baby ferret."

Carrying me this way is a far cry from the sack-of-potatoes method he used to haul me around the building. I'm cradled against his bare chest, his skin warm on mine.

I want to sink against him. The few steps to the safety of the cot are all too short, and soon I'm dumped onto the canvas surface like a bag of rocks.

"There's a broom here," he says. "I'll sweep it up."

I pull my knees to my chest as he fetches the straw broom from the garden tools. I'm a thousand shades of embarrassed and want to cover up.

When he turns with the broom, though, I see it. Tenting the black silk like the arm of a construction crane, Drew's rather impressive member is at full mast.

So maybe I do feel better.

Chapter 4

DREW

This woman is making me crazy.

And not because she shattered glass when she's barefoot.

Ensley has a way about her that is irresistible, like a puppy licking your face.

If that puppy had a rockin' bod in see-through underwear.

I sweep the glass and screws into a corner. When I set the broom aside, Ensley is curled into a tight ball, arms wrapped around her legs.

"Cold?" I ask.

"Not too bad," she says, but a quick chatter of her teeth exposes the lie. She won't meet my gaze.

"Hopefully our clothes will dry."

"Not with the rain," she says. "The humidity is too high."

I sigh. "Let me look around. If there's a cot, there might be a blanket somewhere."

I head back to the cabinet and rummage through the tarps. They're plastic and useless, but my hand grazes something softer. I shove the tarps aside and find a pair of men's coveralls, the big one-piece kind the maintenance people wear. They're tan with a patch over the breast pocket.

I drag the coveralls out and shake them, sending dried grass flying. There's a long tear down the back, which is probably why they're in here. But they seem serviceable. "Here," I tell her. "You can put this on."

She wrinkles her nose, but accepts the outfit from me. I turn my back as she unzips the front. It's probably going to be awkward getting into them.

"At least it's not navy blue," she says.

"What's wrong with navy blue?"

"It's for police officers and pilots. And I look like death in it."

I grunt and lift more tarps to see what's underneath. I don't find a normal blanket, but there is a softer covering, the kind you lay over plants during a freeze. I spread it over the cot to make a more comfortable place to sit.

Ensley zips up the coveralls, so I figure it's safe to turn around.

But I have to hold back my snort. She looks like a kid playing dress-up. The pant legs cover her feet, which is good, I guess, for keeping warm. The sleeves fall long past her fingers. The waist is somewhere midthigh.

She tries to pull out a hand to roll up the sleeve, but the sheer bulk of the uniform makes it difficult.

"Here," I say. "I'll do it."

I think she's going to jerk her arm away, but she doesn't. I unsnap the cuff and roll the heavy fabric until her hand appears.

"Thanks," she says. "I can manage the other."

I shrug and turn away, pouring another cup of bourbon. I'm not bothered by the cold. I sit on the cot and watch her struggle with the cuff while I drink.

Her dark hair fluffs out as it dries. It was always naturally curly when she was a kid. A few pieces are stuck in place by pins. She's a mess, but a cute mess, like she's just gotten out of bed after a busy night.

I shift my thoughts. The silk boxers give far too much away.

"So what's that blanket you found?" she asks.

"Something to cover plants."

She runs her hands over it. "It's pretty rough."

"Better than whatever might have been on the cot."

"That's true."

I pluck the unsquashed package of Doritos out of the plastic bin and open the top. I angle the bag toward her, and she takes a handful.

"Take two on the fancy dinner," she says. "This time as Mike." She points at the patch stitched onto the chest of the coveralls.

I grunt, the closest thing I have for a laugh. I've used up my allotment of patience for the evening. It takes a lot of effort for me to exchange inane pleasantries, and I'm done.

We crunch on Doritos, and I pour each of us more bourbon. Now that she's covered up, the tension drops significantly.

"Here, we can arrange this better." She hops up, unfolding the blanket so that there's an extra length, and settles it over my knees. "I don't want you to freeze."

Every response I could give her—*fine* or *I'm not cold*—seems wrong, so I shove another chip in my mouth. The bourbon is doing its work, and I feel relaxed, especially now that Ensley is more or less taken care of. She's stopped shivering and stares into her plastic cup like she's reading tea leaves.

"So." She can't seem to go more than ten seconds without talking. "Do you talk to Garrett anymore?"

"Nope." I crunch a chip to make clear I do not plan to elaborate.

There's nothing to tell, anyway. Garrett was in my friend circle in high school. But while Franklin and I got into Georgia Tech, Garrett stayed home to work maintenance at the city bus barn. I didn't mean to lose contact, but life happened.

Ensley picks at the frayed edges of the coveralls. "I guess it might have been different if Garrett had been able to go to college."

My stomach sinks, and I can only stare into the bag, not wanting another bite. Ensley's family was seriously poor. All the kids struggled. But they were a friendly brood, and those of us who hung out with them were more than happy to bring over snacks, or leave behind a wayward baseball glove or football so they'd have more things around. It was an unspoken promise.

"I hear he's doing all right."

"He is," Ensley chirps, seeming to have recovered now that she's clothed and dry. "The supervisor is set to retire, and Garrett thinks he might move up."

"That's great." I pass the bag to her.

She takes a chip. "I got promoted at my bank last summer. I'm assistant head teller."

"Good for you." It sounds surly, and I shift on the cot, uncomfortable with Ensley's expectation that I will be all rah-rah over work stuff. I don't do small talk.

She doesn't seem to notice. "I was so glad Janet didn't get the promotion. Everyone thought she would since she's been there longer, but honestly, she's such a pill that nobody wanted her to be in charge of anything."

She doesn't seem to expect me to speak on this topic, so I sip the bourbon while Ensley prattles on about her coworkers and the problems with the bank's software interface.

If I'd been anyone else, I could have chimed in about how we're always having trouble with the updates to our veterinary software as well, and how these specialized programs are a racket. And that I used to have a Janet on staff, too. I scared her off.

But I don't. I never do. Even at work, I manage the animals, listen to them, let them show me what's wrong in the privacy of the treatment space.

My techs manage the human conversations unless I'm specifically called out. It's how I work best.

"Tell me about them," Ensley says.

"About what?" I intend to avoid more discussion by eating Doritos, but we've cleaned out the bag.

"The animals you work on. I've always admired you being a veterinarian. You must really love critters."

I grunt.

"Is that a yes? Can you say anything more, or has one of those cats taken off with your tongue?"

"It was torture."

Ensley huffs. "It's torture talking to me?"

"No, the phrase. It's from torture."

She thinks a second. "So 'cat's got your tongue' is about torture?"

I nod. "Tongues were cut out and fed to cats."

She holds up a hand. "Forget I said it. So do you have the urge to adopt every sad, bedraggled baby that comes into your clinic?"

"No."

"No? Just no? Why not?"

"I'm never home."

"Huh. A veterinarian who doesn't own any animals."

"I help them. I find them homes."

"But never yours." She stares up at the roof. "Still coming down."

"Probably will through the reception."

"Great." She lies back on the cot, legs folded so she only takes up her half. "So tell me something about you I don't know."

I'm stuck with a chatterbox. I put her off for a moment by removing my squishy shoes again. They need to dry. "I don't talk about myself."

She feels her head for pins and plucks them out, dropping them to the floor. "Why do you hate talking?"

Probably due to questions like this. But I just grunt.

She crosses her arm over her forehead, staring at the ceiling. "If I'm around you long enough, will I be able to tell the difference between your grunts and growls? Is there a code?"

"No."

She sighs. I get about ten more seconds of blissful quiet before she comes up with a new topic. "I've been wanting to be something more than a bank teller. But I don't know what it would be. I don't have a lot of options."

I sip my bourbon.

"I guess I would rather work someplace that matters. I mean, I know banks are important. And I'm good with people. I could talk to anyone, really. But moving money around, it's not very satisfying. Do you get that?"

I do, but I have no words for it. I can only grunt.

"You're easier to talk to than I thought," Ensley says. "Everybody's always full of bad advice or telling me I should be grateful for what I've got, given how I grew up."

This comment cuts my silence. "I hated how much your family struggled," I say.

"He speaks!" Ensley sits up. "Did you really? Hate it?"

"I hated that you guys were hungry all the time."

Ensley tugs at the collar of the coveralls. "I missed out on a lot. I didn't get to go to prom. By the time my baby sister was a senior, they had fairy godmother programs for dresses. But I had to skip."

I didn't know that. "I would have taken you." As soon as I say it, I force the cup to my mouth. *Shut up, Drew. Shut the hell up.*

She grins. "Maybe if Mom had been around, she could have figured out something for me to wear."

My vow of silence evaporates. "I would have bought you a dress." And I mean it. But her prom was the same time as my college graduation. I wasn't talking to Garrett anymore. I had no idea.

She closes her eyes, her face dreamy. "I would have died and gone to heaven if you asked me to prom. But the age gap was bigger then."

I can only grunt at that. It's definitely less now that she is twenty-six to my thirty.

"I had the hugest crush on you," she says. "Oh, that's a terrible confession. Never mind. I didn't. I hated your guts."

This is new. My gut tightens. "A crush?"

Her gaze meets mine and I expect my dick to stir again, but it's something else I'm feeling. Something closer to what comes over me when a wounded rescue is brought to the clinic.

"I did. I got this crazy notion that you were going to save me. Big strong Drew would swoop in and carry me away from my misery and let me live in his big brick house. We'd go to prom and have a big fancy wedding like in movies."

Jesus. That hungry twelve-year-old had pinned her hopes on me, and I hadn't even noticed. "My house wasn't that big." And it had misery of its own.

"But your house is what started the fantasy. I went there once to find Garrett. Your mom let me in. The living room was so clean. I could see the floor. And the kitchen! It was bright and there were freshly baked cookies on the stove. It was heaven."

My throat gets tight. "I hope Mom gave you one."

"She did. I remember holding it, not wanting to eat it. I'd never had a warm cookie before. Sometimes we got a packaged one in the free lunch at school. But never one so fresh."

I can't stand it. "Ensley, you should have all the cookies you can eat."

"Oh, I do now. I have my own apartment, and there is always cookie dough in the fridge." She flashes a smile. "See, you had an impact on me, without even knowing it. Cookies make me think of safety. Of your house. Of that wonderfully naive idea that someone like you would show up and carry me out of my hard, stupid life where there was never anything to cook, and four kids to feed, and a dad who never noticed we existed."

We fall quiet, the rain pounding the roof. Thunder booms, but the lightning is invisible to us.

"Does Drew Daniels have a care in the world? A single one?" She gazes up at me, her hair a halo of curls now that it's mostly dry.

How easily she went back to her happy status quo. Her face is upturned, all the makeup washed away. She's young and beautiful. And apparently, at one time she thought I could be a hero.

She must see something in my expression because hers goes serious.

"There *is* something wrong in Drew's world!" She leans over, her hand covering mine. "I confessed to you. It's your turn. Tell me one."

I don't think I will say it, but then the words tumble out. "I've never been in a relationship." It comes out like a bark, and she recoils as if I've yelled at her.

"Whoa," she says. "No need to holler." She faces me, straddling the cot. "But you go on dates. Franklin says you do that, like a *lot*."

"One each. That's enough."

"No second dates. Hmm. Why is that, Drew Daniels? No woman lives up to your standards?"

I've said too much. Now this minx wants an explanation.

I reach for something to say. She's definitely not getting the truth. "It doesn't work out."

She leans in. "Who decides? You or them?"

A low growl forms in my throat. "I scare them."

She isn't the least bit surprised. "Of course you do. You growl more than a hungry bear."

It's true.

"I don't remember you being this bad in high school," she says.

I shrug.

"What made Drew become a grump?" She taps a finger on her lower lip, and I have to tear my gaze away from that pouty mouth. "Did some girlfriend break your heart when you were young? I don't remember you dating anyone long term."

"I did not."

"Do you compare these women to your mom?"

"No."

I stare at the door, but Ensley is all ready to analyze me. "Face me, Drew Daniels. Look me in the eye and tell me why you don't do second dates."

I clamp my jaw. When I don't turn my face, she puts her damn hand on my chin to force me to meet her gaze. Her touch is electric. The solitude, the sight of her, the storm—it's adding up to something I better resist.

I want to lash out at her, to growl.

"Drew, are you afraid to look at me?" Our knees bump, and my body reacts, bringing back all the visions from this night. The fallen dress. The sheer bra and panties. Her terror when the glass fell. Her body cradled against me.

I let her turn my face to hers, keeping myself under tight control as her shiny gray eyes meet mine.

"What is it, Drew? Are you scared of little ol' us? Teensy weensy girls you could break in half?"

"Of course I am." My voice is a surly rumble. "All my best buds fell one by one, forgetting anything existed but their precious girlfriends. Everything that mattered before. Gone."

Her face shifts instantly. "But you're here for Franklin. For his *wedding.*"

"It's what best buds do." I can't explain it. I shouldn't even try.

"So you decided never to fall for that," she says. "And even if you go on a first date and like the woman, you don't let it go any further."

She's doing exactly what I didn't want, examining my motives.

"Shut up, Ensley."

"So why do you go out with them at all, then?" she asks. "Why not focus on your work and leave us evil vixens alone?"

I refuse to look at her. I'm done with this conversation. I'm having trouble managing this talk with her body so close to mine.

"I want to know, Drew. Why do you mess with us at all if we're so dangerous to your status quo?"

Thunder peals, so close that it rattles the spare parts on the counter. But Ensley doesn't yelp this time. She doesn't move at all.

She wants to know what draws me to women. What makes them worth it.

I'll show her.

I drag her body against mine for a kiss she will not easily forget.

Chapter 5

ENSLEY

I'm falling for the third time tonight.

First, I faked falling to spill wine on Felicia.

Then I very nearly fell off the loading dock.

And now, it's happening. I'm weightless, flying off a cloud.

Drew Daniels is kissing me. His mouth is frenzied, hands on my back. His body is hard against mine, his chest a strong place to cling to. Both arms hold me so tightly that I trust he'll never let go. I will stay here as long as I want.

He tastes of bourbon and darkness and need. I can't pull away, don't want to pull away. My arms encircle his neck, matching his lips, his tongue. Our heartbeats slam against each other.

He shifts my body so that my legs straddle his waist. I can feel him, even through all the heavy fabric, hard against me. His hands move to my hips, grinding me down on him. I want to get rid of these stupid coveralls, to be skin to skin. I want every inch of him.

I kiss him back, reveling in his closeness. I want to learn him, his back, his shoulders. I can touch it all. For this moment, he's mine.

We break the kiss, and his mouth moves to my jaw and my throat.

The coveralls really do cover it all, but he pulls back, fingers on the zipper, yanking it down.

The shoulders fall down my arms, and his lips are hot on my skin. I arch to him, hanging on to his neck as he works his way down.

He shifts our position, laying me back on the cot, and the cool air hits my belly as the oversize uniform opens wide. His hair tickles my neck as he works his way along my chest, pressing his face into the hollow below my ribs.

I'm on fire, hands on his head, his shoulders, his back. He's a monster, all muscle and sinew. I feel a release of tension and realize he's unhooked the bra. He tosses it away, and now his mouth is on a breast, drawing in the nipple.

Am I doing this? Is it real? He sucks hard, and I cry out. My God, it is totally real. How far will it go? Do I want it?

I do. How can I not, this long-held dream finally realized?

He's told me no second dates. So this will be it. A onetime tryst. A wedding fling.

I'll take it. I wrap my legs around his waist, encouraging the grind of that hot erection against the mass of fabric of the coveralls. Damn it all, I want them gone!

But Drew is content to linger, touching, kissing. He takes his time, occasionally a low rumble of a growl escaping as he moves into fresh territory. He returns to my mouth, his kiss deep and penetrating. His hand slips along my body—collarbone, breast, belly—then slides inside the coveralls where the zipper ends, finding my damp panties.

He caresses the outside, making me writhe beneath him. My breathing is labored, hot around his mouth. I'm like a clock wound too tightly, ready to spring.

A finger slips inside the panties, the contact making my body lurch. He pulls his face from mine, the barest inch. "May I?" he asks, his voice low.

"Yes," I say, and then he's on me, mouth pressed on mine, fingers delving into me. I want to cry out, to scream. He works me so quickly, so fast. I'm spiraling out of control, gasping, rising to the precipice.

But then he stops, cocking his head to listen.

I want to groan with frustration, but then I hear it, too. "What is that?"

We go still. The rain is only a light patter on the roof. But the sound becomes clear. The slam of a car door. Then another. Then the rumble of an engine starting.

"It's over," he says. "We have to catch them before they all leave." He stares down at me, my body exposed in the open zipper of the coveralls. "Damn it." His jaw ticks. "We have no choice."

I nod, dropping my legs so I can move off the cot.

I glance back at the dress. Should I try to get it back on?

"We have to hurry," Drew says. He lunges for his pants and shoves his legs inside. He's barely thrown his shirt over his shoulders and shoved his feet in his shoes when he's out the door.

I zip up the coveralls and stand in the doorway, watching him dash down the path. Lights pierce the trees in a dozen directions, cars coming to life. I wait a few moments, wondering if I should change. But then the other bridesmaids are there, holding out my purse and phone, hugging me.

Ronnie's sister, Becca, gathers my dress and shoes. She doesn't notice the bra, thank God. "Let's get you to the hotel," she says. "And don't worry, Dad is spitting mad. He's going to deal with Felicia."

Another bridesmaid brought flats for the dancing, so she passes them to me to wear as we walk out of the shed. When they've gone a few steps, I say, "Hold on a second," and race back into the building.

I gather Drew's jacket and bow tie and socks. I shove my bra into my purse and look around a moment. Things happened here. I feel different. Missing the wedding was horrible, but this loss seems worse.

I felt something, and it's over before it even began.

I pull the light cord. In moments, I've joined the bridesmaids, and we're dashing around the corner of the building. There was a side door so close the whole time. Just a few more steps in the storm, and we would have seen it. Drew is standing inside it, nodding at another groomsman, his face serious. He doesn't look up.

We huddle in the warm limo, and all the talk is about Felicia. My phone buzzes, and it's Ronnie: I can't believe this happened!

I tell her to have a happy honeymoon and tuck my phone in my purse.

Drew appears in the door, and I pass him his things. He gives me a quick nod and takes a seat at the other end of the car.

"She made you miss the wedding!" Becca says. "Thank God her daughter decided not to ride with us. I'd kick her in the shin!"

"She's probably as big a victim as the rest of us," I say, feeling terribly self-conscious in the oversize coveralls.

"Just look at you!" Becca says. "Stuck out in the storm, drenched like a dog!"

She goes on, but I tune her out. I watch Drew on the other side. He drops his socks in a trash can and folds his wet jacket on his lap. He looks as handsome as he did before the disaster, with only a slight curl to his hair. I ache for him, even if I'm shocked at how far things got.

He meets my gaze with a grim press of his lips, but then he turns to accept a bottle of beer from one of the groomsmen and the moment is gone.

All that's left is going home.

Chapter 6

DREW

Monday comes all too soon after the excruciating wedding weekend. Franklin's on his honeymoon, so beyond what I heard in the limo on the way back to the hotel, I'm clueless to any fallout of our ejection.

I probably should have talked to Ensley when we got back. Things did get out of hand. But I will not give her any false hope. I made very clear the sole reason why I seek women out. Even if we got cut off, she can't be an exception. I'm not the man for her. I can't be.

"Dr. Daniels?" The voice is timid, almost fearful. It's Jenny, the new receptionist. The last one quit after only three weeks, saying I created a hostile work environment.

The techs took Jenny aside to avoid a repeat situation. The side effect is that she's terrified of me.

I almost bark, "What!" because I'm in the middle of treating a weak, dehydrated kitten. She's a three-month-old Persian who was abandoned in a parking lot. Her hair is matted and dirty, but we can't wash her until she's been assessed. Maria already fed her a bit of wet food.

I don't wish to be disturbed. And yet, here is Jenny.

But I think of Ensley, an irritatingly common intrusion since Saturday, and picture her seeing me act like a caveman. I adjust my tone. "Can it wait until I'm done with this kitten?"

"Mrs. Evers is on the phone. She thinks Bennie has parvo."

I let out a long, slow breath. "Bennie got his parvo shot. Last week she thought he had distemper. She does this every time she adopts a new dog." I stroke the kitten's slender back. "Have Maria talk to her. She's good at calming Mrs. Evers."

"B-but she asked for you." The poor thing is quaking in her shoes.

"So?" My voice is a boom.

Jenny yelps, and once again I picture Ensley during the storm. I have to get that woman out of my head.

I grit my teeth to make my voice come down. "Give it to me."

Jenny brings me the cordless phone and races out of the room.

I pick up the call on hold. "This is Dr. Daniels."

Mrs. Evers sounds breathless. "Oh, Doctor, poor Bennie has parvo. He's only been here a few weeks, and I'm already losing him."

I hold back a sigh. "What are his symptoms?"

"He's lethargic and he won't eat. Those are two of the signs! I looked on Google!"

"We gave him his parvo shot," I tell her. "It's very unlikely he has contracted it. Has he been going to the bathroom?"

"Well, sure, right on my rug. I'm still housebreaking him."

"Anything unusual there?"

"I don't think so."

"Did you change his food recently?"

"Well, I ran out of the big bag the rescue sent with him and started feeding him what I had."

"When was that?"

"Yesterday."

"And when did he stop eating?"

"Yesterday."

She says it without hesitation. She doesn't even hear herself.

I stroke the kitten's head. She blinks at me blearily. "Mrs. Evers, Bennie's not used to the new food. Try to buy a small amount of the old one, mix it in with the new one, and gradually transition him. You probably wouldn't like it if you ate pizza every day, and somebody suddenly made you switch to brussels sprouts."

"I love brussels sprouts."

I squeeze the phone so hard, I'm surprised the plastic doesn't crack. This is why I don't talk to people. "I will have Maria send you my instructions. Okay?"

"Okay, Dr. Daniels."

I end the call.

I'll brief Maria later. I need to return to the kitten.

She has fleas, which I pick off her by hand. She barely flinches as I examine her throat, chest, and body.

"You'll feel so much better here," I tell her, stroking her tiny ear. She almost purrs, the faintest crumbly sound, but falls asleep.

My lead vet tech, Maria, enters the treatment space, wiping down her blue scrubs with a wet paper towel. One of our patients must have gotten her good. "How's the kitten?"

"I picked off fleas, but when she's more stable, we'll want to treat her to get any eggs."

Maria nods. "Poor thing."

"Write up something for Mrs. Evers. She switched food and Bennie won't eat. Just how to transition a diet."

"Will do."

"Oh, and I scared the new girl. Be nice to her."

Maria peers at me over her glasses. She's ten years my senior and great at handling the staff. "We already are. You, my friend, are the problem."

I grunt in acknowledgment as Maria heads back to an exam room.

We're nearing the end of the day. A quick look at the schedule on the wall monitor shows that there's only a couple of vaccinations that the techs will handle unless something goes wrong.

I pull a tall stool next to the exam table where the Persian kitten lies on her side, her perfect little paws stretched out in an elegant cross.

No telling how long she's had to survive on her own, or how she got into this circumstance.

Humans don't deserve these creatures.

The treatment space remains quiet. We don't have any surgical cases in the recovery kennels today. It's only the kitten with me in the long room of exam tables. I watch the slow rise and fall of her chest until my irritation starts to ease.

Todd, another tech, passes through to the storage room. He gives a quick nod in acknowledgment that I'm there, nothing more.

That's the level of interaction that works best for me.

The kitten stirs, turning her white head to look at me. When I lean close, she lifts a paw, claws out, and gives a wee hiss. Now that's an excellent sign.

"I had a feeling you might perk up once you were warm and fed."

She stumbles to her feet, looking around. When I reach out to keep her from leaping off the exam table, she curls around my hand, biting my knuckles.

"I see how it is." I laugh and pick her up. "You were waiting to see if I'm friend or foe."

Now that she's in the air, she clings to me, her blue eyes watching my face.

"Hmm. Should we see if you'll drink?"

I carry her to the counter and fill a small dish with fresh water. "What do you think?"

She sniffs at the dish and takes a few delicate licks.

Good enough. She's going to be fine.

I wait a moment until she's finished drinking and wiping her whiskers, then pick her up. "Let's get you in a kennel before you escape, then we'll set up your flea bath."

I walk her over to one of the larger cat cages, already prepared for her with a litter box, a scratching post, and a bed. She wanders her surroundings, sniffing, a paw reaching out to bat the fuzzy ball attached to the post.

I can finally relax. Amazing how they bounce back. I watch her a moment, and for some reason I think of Ensley's mom. She died when Ensley was young, but I remember her. She had a fierceness to her, a tough layer beneath her loveliness and grace.

"Why, of all the cats I've seen, do you make me think of Sasha?" I ask the kitten.

The ball bounces on the end of the string and hits the pretty Persian in the face. She backs up on her hind legs to fight it. I can't help but laugh. "Right. You're like Ensley, too. The qualities she and her mother shared."

Maria reenters the space. "Everyone's checked out. Jenny is heading home. Vera is closing out the pharmacy space and diagnostic. Todd left ten minutes ago. You need me to help with the kitten?"

"Blood draw. Flea treatment. She's perked up."

Maria heads over to the kennel. "Look at her now. I'll take care of it. Did you give her a name?"

Before I can think if it's wise, I say, "Sasha."

"Perfect," Maria says. "Just as luxurious as her long white coat. At least once we've cleaned her up."

I grunt in agreement and head to my office. I have paperwork to do.

When I'm seated at my desk, I sort through the mail, tossing half of it. Nothing important there.

I pull up my email and scan the subject lines. Most of it is pure junk, sales pitches and vendors.

But my gaze pauses on one.

Sender: Ensley James

Chapter 7

ENSLEY

I shouldn't have done it.

But Drew's address was right there in the group email about the wedding.

He thinks he can blow me off after what happened, but I won't let him. Maybe all those other women he humped and dumped could let it go, but not me.

I'm like a Chihuahua with a stuffed rat in its mouth.

I'm gonna hold on like it's my very last rat.

I crafted my first message to him carefully, considering his known caveman communication style. I made it sound like we've been talking all along, and I expect it to continue.

Drew,

How did the rental place handle the return of your drenched tux? I had to give up on saving my dress. I cut out a square to put in my memory box for Ronnie's wedding, not that I have any memories of it, and tossed the rest.

And I know you think I'm a bastion of positivity, but really—let's plot revenge on Felicia.

Sincerely,
Dangerous Vixen Chick

I'm quite proud of it. It's lighthearted and nonthreatening, and it ends with an invitation to work together for a common goal.

I head to work in one of my favorite pick-me-up outfits, a gold lamé jacket over a chic black dress I found on clearance. My gold boots click on the concrete as I cross the bank's parking lot.

I live in an apartment with my baby sister, Tillie, who never gets up before noon because she's a bartender. And I own the coolest vintage and thrifted clothes a girl could ask for.

Life is fine.

Even better if Drew Daniels writes me back. I got too close to putting the finish on my childhood crush to let it go now.

Farm to Market Bank and Trust isn't open for customers yet, so I enter through the employee entrance, buzzing my way in with the code.

My supervisor, Cindy, is already there, getting the computers booted up.

"Morning," she says. "Nice jacket."

I take a saucy spin. "I hope it's not too much."

She shakes her head. "I'm pretty sure our customers come into the branch just to see what you're wearing." Her approving smile gives me that squishy warm feeling that I assume daughters get with their moms.

Cindy is in her late fifties, so it's perfectly logical that I could be her daughter. I hadn't known my own mother for very long. She died of a brain hemorrhage when I was five.

I take Cindy being here as another sign that I am exactly where I belong, despite what I told Drew. Sure, bank telling isn't a super rewarding job. I don't save animals' lives like he does.

And I have to deal with Janet, who is even more difficult to work with since I got promoted over her. But given the way my life started out, and my inability to go to college, and my mediocre grades—I feel pretty lucky.

"Can you set up the cash drawers?" Cindy asks. "I'm a little behind due to the system update."

"Not a problem. Janet isn't here yet?"

Cindy rolls her eyes. "She said she would be late because her car needs an inspection, and she can't go to any of the places near her because they're always rude to her. So she has to drive across town and will probably get stuck in traffic."

"Jeez. She can't do that on a Saturday?"

Cindy shrugs. "I do not question the ways of Janet. I might go mad. We'll manage fine."

"We will. We are competent. We are enough."

"You know it," Cindy says. She likes my positivity mantras. Most of the time, they get me through.

Last weekend was definitely an exception. Felicia. The rain. My shoes.

But then there was Drew.

I head to the vault to collect the cash trays. This is one of my special tasks as assistant head teller. I do not take it lightly.

The morning settles into a happy rhythm. All the Monday regulars come through, depositing their small business receipts from the weekend.

Clyde opens the door and stamps his boots before entering. He owns a feed store, and he's eighty if he's a day.

"Aren't you a ray of sunshine this morning?" Clyde leans his elbow on the counter as he pushes a pile of cash and checks under the window.

"Why, thank you, Clyde. Weekend go well?"

"Had a bit of a wild moment yesterday."

He pulls a round snuffbox out of his back pocket. The denim is bleached white in the outline of a circle where he carries it. I never see Clyde without a snuffbox.

44

"What happened?" I thumb through the cash, swiftly turning each bill to face the same way.

"One of my regulars, old Mary Myrtle, owns a chicken farm. She decided that my feed had gone bad because several of her chickens keeled over."

"Oh no."

"She piled all those dead chickens in a box and brought them up to the store as proof that my bagged feed caused them to kick the bucket."

"She brought them into the store?"

He pinches a bit of snuff from the canister and slides it in between his cheek and gum. I carefully avert my eyes.

"She shoved the whole smelly lot of them in my face, and I told her to get her dead hens out of my establishment."

"Were other customers there?"

"Quite a few."

"Did they seem worried?"

"Nah. They're all regulars. Deb Steiner happened to be right there. Told Mary Myrtle it was clear as day that those chickens had the pox, and she better get them out and have the rest of her flock checked over."

I line up the bills in the currency counter. "What did she do?"

"She sputtered and spit like she done come out of a sewer tank. She insisted that wasn't what was wrong with them."

"Was it true?"

I move on to the checks, feeding them through the digital scanner.

"Darn tootin' it was. Marlon O'Malley said you could tell from the spots and scabs."

"So did she leave?"

"She said they were all ganging up on her because she was a woman farmer. Like we care who raises chickens. And then she dumped that box on the floor and stomped right out."

"Oh! What did you do with the chickens?"

"Had to take them to the incinerator. If they've got the pox, you can't have them sittin' around."

"I'm so sorry that happened."

He straightens, shifting his feed store gimme cap on his head. "In another week, she'll run out of feed and show up like nothing ever happened."

I slide his deposit slip across the counter. "You're all taken care of. Hope this week is easier, and there's no dead chickens you have to burn."

He touches his hat brim. "Thank you kindly."

When he's gone, the lobby is empty again. Cindy sidles over. "Is it me, or does he have a story like that every Monday?"

I nod. "Every Monday."

"You didn't say how that wedding went."

Right. I hesitate. Cindy and I have good camaraderie at the bank, but I'm not sure how she would take the knowledge that Ronnie's stepmom kicked me out of the country club.

"There were a few disasters, like you always expect, but my best friend is happy and that's what matters."

"Did that strapless dress give you any trouble?" Cindy opens the cabinet near me to grab a stack of deposit slips to refill the table in the lobby. "I know you sure were worried about how loose it seemed."

For a moment, Drew flashes through my mind. *Your dress is down there.* I can still see his smoky eyes and feel the heat of his stare. I wonder how he'll respond to my email.

"Somebody's miles away." Cindy hesitates at the door to the lobby. "Did you meet a man? I love wedding meet-cutes."

I so want to tell her. Drew is too good a secret to keep all to myself.

Surely mentioning him is safe enough. "I might have reconnected with a guy who played football with my brother in high school."

Cindy pushes on the door. "Hold on to that thought. Let me get these out there and then we can talk all about him."

I sort through what I can safely say, but we get a boatload of customers, and a line forms. By the time the rush dies, Janet has arrived, and I don't want to talk about Drew in front of her.

Throughout the day, my thoughts keep turning to him. I check my email on my phone periodically, but I don't expect an answer so soon. I'm sure someone like Drew goes to work early and is super focused on his job the whole day. If he sees my email, it probably won't be until evening.

But just thinking about having contact with him sends a little zip through me.

He's the most exciting thing that's happened to me in a long time.

Chapter 8

Drew

Rather than wrestle with Ensley's email, I pay some invoices and place orders. Normally, my receptionist also serves as the overall office manager, but I haven't had a solid one since Cathy retired six months ago.

First we got Dana, who Cathy trained, but she left for a different job after only four months.

Next came Brittany, who seemed promising, but then she quit over my *hostile work environment.*

And now Jenny. I have a bad feeling she'll fly away the moment she finds something else. Her personality definitely isn't a fit for mine. Maria should have seen that, but she wouldn't let me interview anyone after I scared off half the candidates when we got Dana.

I exit the office to make my rounds. Everything has been closed up for the night. The lobby is dark. The exam rooms are cleaned and prepped. Maria is gone. We have no overnight boarders or fosters in the kennels.

It's just me and Sasha.

I head to her cage. Maria has moved her to a new one now that she's been treated for fleas. She sleeps in a white fluff ball, pushed up against a soft blanket.

I don't want to wake her. She's still in recovery from her ordeal. But as I step back, her white head pops up, and she peers at me, her blue eyes gray in the dark. She lets out a tiny hiss.

I open the latch. "Come here, you little hellcat."

I don't pick her up, but hold out my hand. She sniffs at it, then bats it with her paw.

Maria has left a bag of treats and a catnip banana on the shelf over the kennels. I extract a treat with one hand and feed it to Sasha. She quits attacking me to sniff it, then gobbles it down.

I don't have any pets at home. My work hours are too long and there's no one to comfort an animal left alone all day. Sasha sniffs the finger that held the treat, then bites it.

I laugh. "You're a nippy one. You must not have been around your siblings long enough to learn how to play." I pick her up. She curls around my hand like before, but this time, she doesn't hiss. I bring her to my chest, and she climbs onto my shoulder, digging into the lab coat with her claws.

I pet her head as I check the other rooms, the pharmacy, the lab, and storage. Everything is as it should be. Maria has taken over many of the duties of manager. She's quite possibly more important to this clinic than I am.

"Okay, Sasha, time for night night." I try to pull the kitten off my shoulder, but she has dug in. "Come on."

I finally take off the coat, setting it on the exam table so I can disentangle the kitten. She lets go and tries to crawl up my shirtsleeve.

"To your kennel, little one." I pick her up, holding her outstretched so she can't get stuck on my shirt.

But when I set her in the kennel and close the door, she climbs the metal bars, mewing pitifully.

I've been firm in my five years of veterinary work to avoid falling for homeless pets. My situation is not conducive to taking one in, and the vet techs sometimes adopt our lost creatures. For the rest, we have rescues and foster homes.

But something about Sasha has done me in. She's been here only a few hours. She's all alone. I didn't plan for her, so Betty won't come in for a night check.

I stick my finger through the bars, and she bites the tip. She shoves her paws through the bars and wraps them around my hand.

I can't leave her.

"All right, you little snowball." I open the kennel and hold her in my palm. "Come on." I set her on my shoulder, and this time she digs into my shirt.

I pack a soft-sided kennel, a litter tray, and some food.

I guess I have a houseguest for the night.

This has got to be Ensley's fault.

~

It's late by the time Sasha is sacked out on my bed, the litter box and water dish on the floor of my adjoining bathroom. I lean against the headboard, planning to read a few articles on my phone, when I remember Ensley's email.

I can picture her, tapping her hand on a table, waiting for me to reply. I know damn well I won't be able to simply ignore her like the random women I've engaged with.

I can't get her out of my head anyway.

I pull up her email on my phone. What did she want?

Oh. Revenge on Felicia.

I'm not interested in indulging her on this. For one, if I'm getting revenge, something's about to get set on fire.

And second, women like Felicia aren't worth my energy.

But I'm not going to say anything like that. My thumbs hover over the letters, wondering what the hell I can type.

Finally, I snap a quick picture of the kitten and send it with only two words. And one of them is a lie, because Ensley can't know I named the kitten after her mother.

Meet Snowball.

That's enough.

Chapter 9

ENSLEY

When an email comes through from Drew, I'm lying on the sofa watching reruns of *The Bachelorette*.

I sit up so suddenly that my sister Tillie looks up from her laptop, a pencil holding her dark hair in a pile on her head. "Everything okay?"

"I got an email from Drew."

Now she's interested. "He wrote you back?"

"Yes." I told her everything that happened. That I got kicked out of the dressing room and carried over Drew's shoulder. Then we were stuck in a rainstorm, and I darn near banged him in a shed.

But not that I've been obsessing about him since.

She probably already knows that. She remembers how I used to follow him around as a kid. Even though I'm the oldest sister and tried to keep my life private from my younger sisters Lila and Tillie, my crush was too juicy not to notice.

I close my eyes. I want to hold on to this happy feeling that he's written me back.

I half expected him not to. I picture the set of *The Bachelorette*. Me in a long, sparkly black gown. Drew in his tux, unbuttoned at the throat. I'm holding the single red rose.

Yes, reading it is going to be just like that.

But when I click on the email, there are only two words. Meet Snowball.

And a picture of a cat.

The kitten is cute and all, sure. But I don't get it.

"What did he say?" Tillie asks.

"He sent me a picture of his cat."

She closes her laptop. "But you said he didn't adopt animals. His work hours are too long."

She's right.

I pull my phone closer to my face. The cat is clearly on a bed. I can see the edge of it, and a hardwood floor below. That is not a veterinary clinic.

And he's introducing her. Like she's new.

He adopted a cat?

Did I influence him to do that?

This might be better than a rose. Better than the slinky dress and the beautiful set and that heartrending moment when two people declare that they belong together.

Because this is Drew we're talking about. He's never going to be in any bachelorette situation.

But he's changed something about himself.

Just two days after we spent time together making confessions!

I blow up the picture and study every inch. In the corner is a bit of the dresser. I see a wallet and a set of keys. A folder. And the bottom half of a framed photograph.

Who would Drew be sentimental enough about to have a picture of on his dresser?

It can't be a girlfriend. He was very clear about that.

His parents? His family?

It's definitely people. There are legs. No one wears a skirt.

I wish I knew. I want to know everything about Drew. I want to talk to him. To ask.

"Dang it!"

Tillie laughs. "Now what?"

"I'm stalking his bedroom based on the picture."

She leaves the table to sit beside me. She just got in from the bar, so her slashed off-the-shoulder T-shirt smells of beer and fried food.

"Let me see. I'm a class A stalker." She peers at the image. "He's neat. This furniture is nice. And the cat is on a real bedspread. The bed is *made*." She nudges my shoulder. "You don't even make *your* bed."

"I can change."

"Looks like he could make it for you."

I nudge her back. "He insists he doesn't date. We vixens ruin men."

"He also insisted he didn't adopt pets."

I pet the kitten's head on the screen. "She's cute."

"So what are you obsessing over in this picture otherwise?"

"The photograph on his dresser. He didn't strike me as sentimental."

Tillie peers at it, squinting her eyes. "The pants on everyone are colorful. I bet they're scrubs. It's his veterinary clinic staff."

"On his dresser?" I lean in again. She's probably right.

"Maybe opening day of his clinic or something. That's kind of a big deal."

That's true. And not very helpful in learning more about him.

Tillie sits back against the cushion. "What will you write back?"

"I have no idea. He didn't give me much of an opening here."

"You can talk about the cat."

"I could. Oh, I don't know. I should wait till tomorrow, anyway."

Tillie drums her hands on her thighs, a concerned expression on her face. This isn't like her. Tillie doesn't get nervous. She's a hellcat. She has to be to survive at that Podunk bar.

"What's up?" I ask.

"Our lease is almost up," she says.

This doesn't sound good.

"And I've been worried about Lila. I'm thinking about moving in with her to help with the pregnancy now that she's alone."

"Oh." I won't have a roommate. I can't afford this two-bedroom on my own. "Why can't she move back here?"

"I've tried. She won't do it. She thinks Dodge is coming back, and she should be there."

"He better not."

"I know." Tillie rests her head on the cushion, chin thrust toward the ceiling. "My boss said he's got a friend with a bar not too far from her rent house. I could work there."

"You already have a job there?" Panic flashes through me, hot and prickly.

"Ensley, you've got this. You can get your own place, a smaller one. You know you can."

"But I've never lived on my own."

"It's about time. We're all grown." She drags me close, her arm around my shoulders.

My mind is already racing. Who else could I ask to move in with me here? So many of my friends are already settled down.

Of course, there's Janet at work. Ha.

I could do an ad. Or maybe Tillie is right. I can find something smaller. I did get a raise when I was promoted.

Do I want to live alone, though? I go crazy if I don't have anyone to talk to.

"It'll be all right," Tillie says. "You've been here for me, and I want to be there for Lila. The bigs and the littles all do their share." She's quoting Mom, even though she only learned the phrase through me.

My throat gets tight. She's right. I'm being greedy.

"Tillie?"

She turns back to me.

"Can you bake some cookies?"

Her gaze rests on me a moment. She knows what this means. I'm afraid. And when I have fears, warm cookies remind me that there is a safe place, like Drew's kitchen. Like Drew. It's so wild how life has circled back.

"Sure."

I start typing a response to the kitten picture.

> I have to admit, I'm jealous of Snowball. Not because she's on your bed—ha, ha. Okay, maybe that, too. We have unfinished business, don't you think?
>
> But she's all taken care of. My younger sister lives with me and just announced she's moving to help our other sister. So now I have to find a roommate! I don't guess Snowball has a friend . . .

I press send before I can overthink it.

Chapter 10

DREW

Tuesday is another crazy day at the clinic. I've brought Sasha with me to work. Maria sets up a bed for her on top of the cabinets, far from any of the animals that come in.

She's content to be up there and only hops down to pop into her kennel for a snack or a litter box break.

"Looks like you've got yourself a cat," Maria says, stroking a bunny in labor. A little girl named Lindsay, maybe seven years old, and her mother are sitting in chairs next to the exam table.

"Is her baby coming out yet?" Lindsay asks.

She's asked this approximately every ninety seconds since they arrived with the pet bunny. The mother got concerned when the bunny started having difficulty breathing after laboring all night. We've already done a sonogram and determined that there is only one baby bunny coming.

I push aside the straw and bunny hair lining the nest and check the birth canal. "Almost time." I glance up at the mother. "You want her to see this?"

Mom nods. "I'm relieved it isn't a big batch. Isn't it rare to be only one?"

I don't want to say that there were many unviable sacs in there. "Bunnies sometimes know what they can handle. You'll spay her?"

The mom nods. "As soon as it's safe."

"I see something!" Lindsay says, leaning closer.

A tiny bit of pink starts to show under the bunny's white fur.

"That's the baby," I say. "Remember not to touch. Baby bunnies are extremely fragile. You shouldn't handle it for two to three weeks."

Lindsay's eyes grow big, and she pushes a long lock of brown hair out of her face so she can see better. "Is Frolic pooping the baby out of her butt?"

Maria bites her lip to avoid laughing.

"No," I say. "Girl bunnies have a special place in their tummy where the babies grow until they are big enough to be pushed out of a special canal."

Lindsay looks up at her mom. "I'm glad it's not coming out of her poop chute."

Now I'm the one trying to hide a smile.

"There it is," I say as the baby lands in the nest. I'm saying a small prayer that it's alive. Many bunnies deliver nonviable kits.

Frolic turns around in the straw and begins licking the bundle of pink.

"It's naked!" Lindsay says. "Where's the fur?"

"It will grow," I assure her. "All bunny babies are born without any fur."

The placenta and sac start to come out, and I decide this might be too much for a seven-year-old. "Mom, I'm going to take Frolic to a quiet spot so she can tend to the baby without stress. You and Maria can go fill out some paperwork to get her spayed."

"Do we get to take her home tonight?" Lindsay asks.

"Of course," I say. "Feed her some parsley and herbs and a bit of her favorite treats. She'll be pretty tired."

I carry the box with the nest into the surgical room so that Frolic can do her business with the afterbirth, and I can tend to the empty sacs. If Frolic rejects the kit because it's cold or having difficulty, I'll intervene. Most bunnies will accept a lethargic kit if you help it along.

After a few minutes, Maria pops her head in. "Clinic's shut down other than these two. How's the kit?"

"Looks good. Frolic has accepted him."

Maria peeks into the nest. "Oh, good. That little girl is very attached already. She's going to name him Harper."

"Kit looks good. They don't need to come back in other than for the spaying."

"I told them." Maria glances back into the treatment space. "I think I'll go through the shutting down procedure and look in on the dog we had to splint."

"I guess Sasha could stay here tonight, since the dog will be here and Betty will check in," I say.

"After you gave her a warm, comfy spot last night?" Maria clucks her tongue. "Don't be mean."

I head for the door. "I'm going to process payroll. Can you give Frolic and Harper back to Lindsay once she's done with the postbirth process?"

"Sure. They're in the lobby."

I nod. "Good. Let me know if you need me."

"Will do, boss."

Sasha sees me head into my office and makes her way down from her perch, hopping to a shelf, then a table, then the floor. She winds her way in and out of my feet as I walk.

I watch my legs so I don't step on her. "Seems you've changed your tune since you hissed at me this time yesterday."

Sasha pays my words no mind as I sit down. She hops onto my desk and spreads herself over my keyboard. Of course.

"I'm going to need that."

She lays her furry white head on her paws.

I shake the mouse. I don't need to type anything yet. I find the accountant's files to approve. Most are direct deposit, so I check the amounts and send them on. There are also several vendor checks, so I send them to the printer and sign them manually.

Now for email. I open the list. Sasha is pressing on the space bar, so I scoot the keyboard out from under her. She opens one eye and scolds me with an aggressive meow.

"Sorry, Sasha. I have to work."

She turns in a circle, presenting her tiny white butt to me, and settles in the space under the monitor.

Another day of mostly junk email that I can quickly delete.

Then Ensley.

I knew she'd written me back right away. I heard the notification before my phone went into do-not-disturb mode last night. But I hadn't read it, and the morning went swiftly, as they do, my home routine and getting to the office.

I open it.

> I have to admit, I'm jealous of Snowball. Not because she's on your bed—ha, ha. Okay, maybe that, too. We have unfinished business, don't you think?

> But she's all taken care of. My younger sister lives with me and just announced she's moving to help our other sister. So now I have to find a roommate! I don't guess Snowball has a friend . . .

My body stirs at the idea of Ensley on my bed. We definitely have unfinished business on that score. But she's in Alabama, a good three hours away. That's pretty far for a hookup.

But the vision of her intrudes, lying on the cot, her hair a wild mass of curls. The open zipper revealing miles of skin. I can feel her in my hands.

Meow.

Sasha peers up at me, as if she's sussed out that I'm thinking about some other female. "That reminds me," I tell her. "You're almost old enough to spay."

Her blue eyes peer up at me as if daring me to say it again.

"What should I say to this woman?"

Sasha sashays over, her head rubbing against my arm. Her fluffy tail twitches, knocking pages aside. I hurry to catch a check before it falls, and the sudden movement startles her. She hisses and bites my elbow.

I barely feel it through the lab coat, but I scoot her aside. "No, Sasha. No biting."

She plunks down on her butt, unhappy at my tone. A plaintive *meeoooow* fills the office.

I sigh. "Come here, then." I pick her up and set her in the cradle of my arm. She tucks her head into my elbow as I stroke her back. After a moment, she pulls out and crawls up my arm onto my shoulder.

"You know, you won't always be small enough to do that," I tell her. She digs in, her head against my neck.

At least I can type the email again. But what to say?

Maybe I should cut this off. I shouldn't encourage her.

But Ensley is safely away, ensconced in another state entirely. The image of her returns, looking up at me on the cot. I can picture her body, almost feel it in my hands again.

Heat rises in me, words I've never said aloud forming in my head. I start to type.

I picture you in my bed. No coveralls this time. But we can keep the rain. It will block out the world as I touch every part of you, learn exactly what makes you cry out. Can you scream? I bet so. I will find a way.

I stare at the words. Yeah, that's about the heart of it. The sort of thing you might write a long-standing lover. Certainly not someone you mainly knew as a kid.

Time to delete it. I reach out to highlight the whole thing, planning to suggest she find a rescue kitten of her own. But a new incoming message makes my computer ding, and somewhere along the way of the cat tromping my keyboard, the volume has maxed out. The noise reverberates in the small space, startling me.

Sasha flies off my shoulder in fright, landing on my desk. Her back paws hit the keyboard, making it shift on the desk, knocking off more papers. She yowls and jumps away.

I try to grab her, but she shoots across the room. Thankfully, the door is closed so she can only huddle between the wall and a filing cabinet.

Another loud *vrooosh* sound sends her scrambling farther back. Good grief. I punch the button to lower the volume, ignoring the new alert while I fetch the kitten. Something in the back of my mind sends alarm bells about the sound, but the kitten comes first.

I kneel on the floor, my hand outstretched. "Come on, take a good bite of my finger," I tell her in low tones. "It's your favorite thing to do."

It takes a while, but eventually she does indeed latch on to my thumb, and I pull her out. I tuck her in my lab coat pocket, my hand petting the scruff of her neck as I return to my desk. Time to close out the day. Ensley can wait. I'm done.

I'm about to shut down my emails when I notice my draft message is no longer on the screen.

Realization starts to dawn as I scan the icons, looking for where it has been minimized. It's nowhere.

Oh no.

Ensley's message to me has an upturned arrow beside it, signaling that I have replied to it.

No, no.

I hold my breath as I switch to my outgoing folder.

And there it is. My dirty, dirty email.

Message *sent.*

Chapter 11

ENSLEY

Tuesdays are Tillie's night off. Normally she hangs out with her work friends, but I guess she's feeling guilty about abandoning me soon, because she decides to stay in.

She agrees to watch *The Bachelorette*, even though she despises shows that treat either gender like a piece of meat.

I torture her with two episodes, and then we switch to one of our comfort movies, *The Princess Bride*. We didn't have a lot growing up, but we did have an ancient DVD player and this movie. There was a scratched spot on the disc when you got to the scene where they drink the wine with the poison, but we kids knew it so well that we could act it out while the laser tried to free itself.

My copy doesn't have this problem, but even so, when we get to the iocane powder, we pause the movie and recite the lines in a fit of laughter.

Tillie makes fruity cocktails, and by the time we get to the last scene where Westley kisses Buttercup, I'm seriously sleepy. "What did you put in this?" I ask her. I skipped the giggly phase and went straight to knocked out.

"Ketel One," she says. "It's a lemony vodka."

I peer into my empty cup. "It went down easy."

She takes the glass from me. "You're a lightweight."

Tillie makes Marion from *Indiana Jones* look like a lightweight. She can knock back shots of whiskey like nothing I've ever seen. She says it's necessary for her line of work.

But not me. The warm, gooey feeling takes me back to the wedding on Saturday, that lightheadedness of drinking straight bourbon on an empty stomach.

I glance at the clock. It's after nine. Did Drew write me back? My phone is on the charger in my room.

Tillie cuts the lights. "You all right?"

"Sure." I pad to my bedroom to check my phone.

There's a notification that I have a new email. This jolts me awake. Could it be Drew?

I quickly open the app.

Yes. It's Drew.

I gasp as I read the lines. I mean, I did say something a little risqué in mine, but this is an entirely different order of magnitude.

I fall back on the bed. He wants to figure out what will make me scream?

My whole body buzzes with heat. This must be the Drew that lures women into one-night stands.

I can see why.

Now I can't think about anything but him in the shed. The rain on the roof. The unzipped coveralls. His mouth. His hands.

I'm completely taken over, electrically awake. What do I say back? Do I act shocked? Do I not dignify it with a reply?

I lie there for a while, then decide to try a different tactic entirely. If he can spill these feelings out to me, why can't I do the same to him? I'll double down.

We'll see who's dying for the one-night stand after this.

> You unzip my coveralls, your hand sliding inside them to touch me. The panties are a thin barrier, separating your skin from mine.

I gasp, arching my hips to meet you. You slide your fingers inside me, curling one at just the right angle. I suck in a breath. You've figured me out, learned me. My hands grip the side of the cot.

But you're not done. You want more, lying over me, your face hovering near mine. Your hips grind against me, the silky boxers sliding against my body. I reach down to take you in my hands.

That's enough. I feel the wicked smile come over my face. I skip a line and say one more thing.

Should I go on?

And hit send.
Oh my God. I'm going to hell.

Chapter 12

DREW

For the first hour after the accidental email, I can't even leave the office. I pace the room with Sasha in my pocket.

Right. Sasha. I named the cat after her mother. I already see that lie coming back to bite me in the ass.

I consider ways I might retrieve this message before Ensley gets it. But only comedy scenarios run through my head. Break into her house. Steal her phone. Hire a hacker.

But Ensley may have read it instantly. That's the beauty of emails. They are immediate.

Should I send a follow-up email? Apologize?

These mistakes don't happen to me. I'm in control of my life. I'm the boss.

What came over me? Why had I even typed those words?

Sasha stirs in my pocket, and I pet her head. "I'm calling you Snowball from now on."

I sit at my desk, trying to come up with a proper message to Ensley. What if she forwards it to Franklin? Or the board of ethics for veterinary medicine?

No. She won't do that.

It's very simple. I'll compose an email with a clear apology. Let her know that it won't happen again.

Then I will delete her from my contacts forever.

Sasha—Snowball—emits a loud meow. I try to concentrate, hands over the keyboard, gathering my thoughts.

But the mewing is incessant.

I pull her out of my pocket and set her on the desk. "Are you hungry? Do you need the litter box?"

Snowball sits primly, her tail curling around her body. She watches me solemnly, like she's trying to figure me out. She looks so small on the vast desk. It's hard to imagine that she's caused this huge debacle for me.

No. The blame for that is solely on me. I didn't have to write that message.

Meow.

Something's up with her. I will have to compose this at home. I shut down the machine.

"Okay, come on." I tuck Sasha, dang it, *Snowball*, in my pocket and head to the treatment space. I set her in her corner with her litter box and food dish and check on the dog whose leg we set.

He's quietly sleeping.

I walk the clinic, making sure the lights are out and everything is locked. When I return, Snowball waits by her now empty food dish.

"Okay. Let's go."

When we get home, I get Snowball settled and order some Thai to be delivered. I composed a hundred emails in my head during the drive, but none of them feel right.

> Ensley, I would like to apologize for the most egregious email that was accidentally sent to you by my cat.

No, no. I must take the blame.

> Ensley, this evening I wrote a few paragraphs of inappropriate commentary.

No, no.

I pace the condo, the kitten tottering after me, trying to attack my shoelaces.

I sit on the sofa. "I need to get you some toys." She jumps in my lap to go after a shirt button.

Another email forms in my head.

> Ensley, I take full responsibility for the incredibly inappropriate email that was sent to you a few hours ago.

That's a good start, but what do I say next?

Maybe I can leave it at that.

With this set in my head, I open my laptop and pull up Ensley's email to form a new reply.

I've only just begun to type when the doorbell rings. My food.

I pay the delivery driver and set the bag on the kitchen table. I won't even eat until I've dealt with this issue. With any luck, she's busy tonight, and she hasn't read the email yet.

I look over the words again.

> Ensley, I take full responsibility for the incredibly inappropriate email that was sent to you a few hours ago.

It feels unfinished. Maybe I will eat after all and think about this more. I shut the laptop to avoid any more keyboard sends.

Sasha—Snowball—sniffs at the bag as I pull out my red curry. "You don't want any of this," I assure her. "It'll singe your whiskers off."

She lies back on a place mat, content to fight the plastic handle of the bag.

Maybe it's the email format that's the problem. If I could text her, perhaps I could get away with something short.

I don't have her phone number, but there was a group text some-where along the way. Ronnie sent one back when she was first planning the wedding, before Felicia got her hands on it and everything went to the coordinator.

That's smart. Since she hasn't replied, she probably hasn't seen it yet. A text might get seen first, whereas another email would only come after the first one.

I dump rice into a bowl and top it with the curry. As I take my first bites, I thumb through my history of text messages.

I locate it. Almost a year ago.

Ronnie: Hey everybody! If you're in this text, that means you're part of our wedding! The ceremony will be March 5 in Atlanta. Save the date!

There's a stream of congratulations and excited comments after that. I run through them until I spot Ensley's.

Okay, so I have her number.

I take a few more bites and type in the sentence I came up with to see how it looks as a text.

I take full responsibility for the incredibly inappropriate email that was sent to you a few hours ago.

I like it.

"What do you think, Sasha?" Now that I feel this chapter will close, my kitty can keep her name.

Sasha rolls on her back, all four paws swiping at the plastic bag monster she's fighting. I rattle the bag, and she hisses.

Good enough. I hit send.

Unless Ensley is asleep, I probably won't have to wait long for a response. If I'm really, really lucky, she'll get the apology before the email.

And sure enough, within a minute, comes a one-word reply.

Ensley: Oh.

Me: ?

Ensley: I already sent you an email back.

I open my mail app. Because I get so much spam, my phone is not set to notify me about each message. But one arrived from Ensley ten minutes ago, after I sat down to eat.

I read the first line, and the spoon I've been holding in my mouth clatters to the table.

> You unzip my coveralls, your hand sliding inside them to touch me.

I can't stop reading. Whoa.

Whoa, whoa, whoa, whoa.

I have to adjust my pants. I've never gotten an email like this before.

Of course, I hadn't sent one like this before, either.

What do we do now?

I take a cue from her playbook and reply very simply.

Me: Oh.

Ensley: Sorry.

Me: I started it.

Ensley: Technically, I may have started it with that first email?

She's right. There was that saucy line in there.

Me: It's the shed all over again.

Ensley: Unfinished? Or just hot?

My body stirs. I'm ready to drive for three hours to get to her. I clamp it down.

Me: The wrong moment.

Ensley: Definitely.

A full minute passes. I have nothing else to say. The conversation may have already played itself out.

But then she writes again.

Ensley: Is Snowball around? A cute kitten pic solves most problems.

And I don't know what comes over me. Maybe I want to be honest with her after this bizarre conversation.

Me: Actually, I named her Sasha.

Ensley: For my mother?

Me: Yes.

Ensley: That's so sweet.

Me: There's something about her that's like your mom.

Ensley: I barely remember her.

Me: She's very clear in my mind.

Ensley: So weird to think you remember her better than I do.

Me: I was older. And very sorry when she died.

Ensley: We all were. Life never seemed to make sense after that.

Me: It got hard.

Ensley: It did.

My gut churns, and it isn't the curry. This conversation doesn't seem right over text. It's too personal. Too sad.

Me: You home?

Ensley: Yeah. Tillie and I were watching TV, but she's gone to bed.

So she's alone, and I've jerked her around plenty this evening, between my lusty email and my reminder of her mother.

My thumb hovers over her phone number.

Then it lands.

It rings.

"Drew?" Her voice is timid, like maybe she should fear me.

"I don't like texting about hard things." My voice is gruffer than I'd like.

"But you don't enjoy talking."

I grunt.

She laughs. "Now there's the Drew I know so well."

It's tough to swallow over the lump in my throat. "I really am sorry. I don't know what came over me when I wrote that email."

Her voice is mischievous. "I have an idea of *exactly* what came over you."

I laugh. It feels strange. I don't laugh often. "Well, I would be lying if I said I hadn't thought about the shed."

"Me, too. Obviously. Since I wrote you about it."

I laugh again. What is this witchery? "I got your number from the group text."

"That's right. Before the evil one took over the wedding."

"Did you hear from Ronnie before they got on the boat?"

"She texted me from her limo saying she was devastated that I wasn't there. But her dad did walk her down the aisle. They did it quickly while Felicia was changing. So that probably *was* the wedding march we heard through the wall."

"I'm glad he walked her."

Sasha has fallen asleep, one claw entangled in the plastic bag. I carefully pull it off and ball up the bag to avoid her suffocating in it.

"Is Sasha with you?"

"Sure."

"Would it be too forward of me to ask you for a pussy pic?"

I laugh again. "It's a pretty pussy."

"Send it to me."

I snap a quick shot of Sasha and send it through.

"Oh, look at her!" Ensley exclaims. "So beautiful. You adopted her?"

"Apparently."

"But what about your work hours?"

"I take her with me. She's got a spot on top of one of the cabinets. The other animals don't even notice her."

"I love it."

I hear a beep of a text notification. It's from Ensley, a photograph of Richard Nixon with meme text that says, *Your Dick pic.*

Another laugh escapes. "We got those out of the way."

"Mm-hmm. I guess I could ask what you're wearing."

I glance down at my shirt and pants. Then I realize what she's talking about. Phone sex clichés. So I say, "A red thong and matching pasties."

"Oh my God!" Ensley's choking laugh is so loud I have to hold my phone away. "Drew! You're the worst! And the best! I love you!"

Interesting how easily those words spill out from her. I'm not sure I've ever said them aloud, not even to my parents.

But she goes on. "Oh no! I just said 'I love you'! I'm so awkward!" I can practically see her slapping her hand over her mouth.

I have nothing to say. I can only grunt so that she knows I'm still there.

Her voice is squeaky. "I've set you back to your caveman vocabulary!"

"It's fine."

"I tell everybody I love them! Even my bank customers!"

"Even Janet?"

"You remember!" She sounds utterly astonished. "You were listening!"

"You were wearing coveralls by then. I could focus." I shouldn't have gone there, but I did.

"Oh. Gosh."

We've come full circle.

I clear my throat. "I really did want to apologize."

"It's okay, Drew. But I guess you know from my reply that I was happy to play along."

My body stirs again. "I can see that. You were quite adept with your descriptions."

"It was fun."

This is the longest conversation I've possibly ever had, other than maybe with Mrs. Evers when she's worried about her dogs. But I've exhausted my ability to be chatty.

"You have a good night, Ensley."

"You, too, Drew."

I end the call.

I'm not sure what I've done. But my step is extraordinarily light as I pick up the remnants of my dinner.

And my step? It's *never* light.

Chapter 13

Ensley

Wednesday is slow at the bank. Cindy and I eat an early lunch together while Janet covers the teller stations. My outfit is a shiny red jacket over a red-and-black-striped dress, all in honor of Drew's thong and pasties comment last night. I don't tell anybody that. It's a joke for myself.

Cindy pulls her frozen lunch out of the microwave and sits down next to me. "You look like the cat who ate the canary."

I stir my Styrofoam cup of Good Noodles. "It's been a great week."

"Does this have to do with wedding boy?" She peels the plastic film off an awful gray mush.

"Maybe. What are you eating?"

"Cauliflower rice and mushroom sauce."

"Good lord, girl. Somebody throw you some mac and cheese."

She shrugs. "Don't think you're getting out of telling me about this guy."

I sort through things that are safe to tell her. Dirty emails? Probably not. My relationship with Cindy doesn't go quite that deep, not like Ronnie or my sister. But I do say, "He called me on the phone last night."

She sets down her fork. "Like a phone call? With your voices?"

Cindy is Gen X, and she believes that all the younger generations consider phone conversations against their religion.

"We young whippersnappers *do* know how to use them."

She aims her plastic fork at me. "As long as they don't have rotary dials."

I have no idea what she's talking about. "We were emailing, then we moved up to texting, and then he called me."

Cindy takes a bite, then grimaces. She pushes the frozen meal away. "Are you going to see each other? Isn't he in Atlanta?"

I pass her my extra granola bar. "He is. I don't know. It's a three-hour drive."

"That's nothing for true love." She accepts the granola bar and peels back the package.

I fiddle with my noodles. They're getting cold. "One of my sisters lives in Adamsville. It's on the outskirts of Atlanta."

Cindy's painted-on eyebrows lift. "So you should go visit your sister."

Should I? Tillie has already dropped the bombshell that she's moving there. Maybe the two of us could make a trip down. Soon.

"You know what? I think I might."

Cindy aims the granola bar at me. "Don't wait for good things to manifest. Make them happen. You taught me that."

It's always funny when one of my newfound positivity mantras is pushed back at me. But she's right.

Janet pokes her head in the break room. "I've got a customer in the lobby and one just pulled up to the drive-through. I need help."

I push back my chair. "I got this," I tell Cindy. "You eat."

Cindy nods. "I'll be out there in a minute."

I'm about to leave when she stops me with a "Hey."

I turn back around.

"Do you remember that reorganization I told you about? How the bank is absorbing another regional bank?"

"Sure."

"We'll have some changes. Good ones. We'll get another teller."

That's good news. "More help is always great."

She nods. "Don't tell Janet yet. I'm not sure how the titles are going to shake out."

"Mum's the word." I push through the door.

Interesting. Another new employee will help when we take breaks, for sure. I return to my post, but beyond what Cindy said about getting a new coworker, I think about her suggestion to visit my sister. It'll put me within reasonable distance of Drew.

I just might do that.

~

Tillie is working tonight, so I stare at my phone while I heat up my second cup of Good Noodles for the day. Should I call him? Text him? Email? How do I reach out?

Dang. This is harder than usual to figure out.

I sit at the table with my Styrofoam cup. Steam rises from the noodles, and I breathe it in. A billion rules I've picked up along the way compete in my head. How women should act when dating. How men should respond. Who takes the lead. Who waits. How long between contact.

I need to write my own rules. Manifest the future I want, like Cindy reminded me to do.

And I want Drew. At least to talk to him.

So I text him.

The cat is always safe.

Me: How's baby Sasha today?

I glance at the clock. It's eight, earlier than when we talked yesterday. His clinic closes at five. I checked the hours. But I know he probably stays late. That's just who Drew is.

It takes a moment, but I get a text back with a new picture. Sasha sits on the bedspread I remember from the first image.

Me: Is she fluffier?

Drew: She got a wash and a blow dry.

Me: She's beautiful! Is she tough, too?

Drew: Just like her namesake.

Mom. We've gone there again. I figure he's softened toward me, so it feels comfortable to click on his name and send through an actual call.

"Ensley," he says, and I have to admit, my body shivers at the sound of it.

"Drew." I hear a meow in the background. "And Sasha!"

"She's a talker."

"Then you two are the perfect pair. She will fill all the silences." I realize my hands are sweaty, and I rub them on my skirt.

There's silence for a moment, but I can't let it go on. My compulsion to talk is too strong. "So I have a new confession."

"Oh?"

"I thought we could continue our theme from the shed."

"We had a lot of themes in the shed."

My face gets warm as I realize he's thinking of the other activities we could continue. But I stumble on. "Remember, you confessed you aren't relationship material. And I confessed I crushed on you when I was twelve."

"Right."

"I told you about Janet. She's a piece of work. Well, I've been pulling pranks on her for quite some time. It might be driving her mad."

"Oh?"

"She's one of these organization freaks. There's six of us in the office. The tellers, the branch manager, and then the bankers and loan officer."

"Sure."

"Janet got annoyed that the refrigerator was always a mess. So she designated zones. She marked her zone where her food goes. I got mine. My boss has hers. Et cetera."

"What did you do?"

"I felt like putting the squeeze on her spot."

"You moved the zones."

"Tiny, tiny bits at a time. She put masking tape around them, so I made her zone smaller and smaller every day."

"That's pretty evil."

"I can be evil."

"How long did you move the zone on her?"

"I'm still doing it."

His laugh is like music to me. "And she's never said anything about it?"

"I'm not sure she's figured it out. Sometimes she shoves her paper bag in there and tilts her head like—huh."

"When will her bag not fit at all?"

"Probably in about four more moves. I might pause before that happens, let her work on making it fit for a while."

"Remind me to guard my fridge when you're around."

"You better!"

Of course, I'll never be around his fridge.

Another silence falls.

I rack my brain for something else to say. I don't want to get off the phone. "Do you have a confession for me? It can be small."

He grunts.

"I'll give you some space to think about it." I go quiet. To distract myself from butting in as the silence gets uncomfortable, I count slowly down from twenty-five.

I get to about eight when he finally says, "My receptionist is going to quit."

That's not what I expected. But I can totally work with that. "Has she been there long?"

"A couple of weeks."

"She doesn't like it there?"

"I scare her."

I stir my cold noodles. "Yeah. I can see that."

"Right."

"Has she given notice?"

"She said as much to Maria. I think she's scared to tell me. Maria thinks Friday will be her last day."

"But it's not official?"

"It sounds like she plans to leave her keys on the desk and disappear quietly."

"Drew! Were you a real caveman with her?"

"I'm a caveman with everyone."

"You're talking to me."

Silence.

"What's her name?"

"Jenny."

"I know you can be nice to Jenny. You can fix this."

"It's probably too late."

"You've got to try. Unless you have a lead on a new one."

"No. She's the third one this year, and it's only March."

I nearly knock over my noodles. "Drew! Did you scare them all off?"

"Maybe."

"I think yes!"

"The last one said I created a hostile work environment."

"Drew! What will you do?"

"I don't know. I am what I am."

"You're not Popeye!"

This makes him laugh. "You watched Popeye cartoons?"

"And the movie. I wanted to be Olive Oyl when I grew up."

"That's an interesting figure to aspire to."

I'm about to start singing the "He Needs Me" song, but I stop myself. I have to hold back my core freak, at least for now. "So tomorrow when you see her, I want you to practice replacement."

"Replacement of what?"

"Replace your negative thoughts and actions with positive ones. Think of something good before you talk to her, and that will lead to good behavior."

"I'm not sure I should be a subject for your positivity whatever-it-is."

"But you have to try!"

His voice is deadpan. "Sure."

I want to come up with more ideas for him, but he breaks in with, "I should go."

So soon! But this was how he was last night. It's like he just gets done.

"Thanks for your confession, Drew. It makes me feel better."

He grunts.

"And thank you for thinking about my mom. I like that someone else remembers her."

More silence.

"Good night, Drew."

He must be out of words, because he simply ends the call.

Chapter 14

DREW

I consider what Ensley said last night as I approach Jenny Thursday morning. Think good things and you will do good things.

Jenny looks up at me with big doe eyes, like I'm a wolf about to attack.

"Good morning, Jenny," I say. "How are you today?"

She grips her pen so hard her fingers are white. "I'm okay, Dr. Daniels."

She's trembling. I realize I should have done this every morning. Said hello. Talked to her when we were not in a difficult situation. Ensley is right. You have to find positive things to say in positive moments, because when things are hard or busy or stressful, it's too easy to reach for negative words.

"Veterinary work is very stressful," I say. "I apologize if sometimes I am rather abrupt."

She nods, her blonde ponytail swinging.

"It's my understanding that you're feeling uncomfortable here. I would like to fix that."

Her gaze drops to her notepad.

"Jenny? Do you think we can fix this?"

Her voice is barely audible. "I already got another job."

The confirmation of my suspicion hits me so hard that I forget to modulate my voice. "You can't do that!"

She startles backward, making her chair roll into a file cabinet. The jolt knocks over a jar of treats sitting on top, and it falls to the floor with a smash.

Jenny jumps up. "Oh my gosh! Oh my gosh!"

I see red. "Sweep that up before any patients arrive. Make sure you get every shard. We can't have those poor animals cutting their paws."

"Yes! Of course!" Jenny runs in circles, then dashes down the hall toward the maintenance closet.

Maria steps out of an exam room, holding a stack of patient folders. "That went well."

I brace my hands against the counter to the reception desk. So much for good thoughts and good actions. "I guess the next one needs to have more mettle. Can you manage that?"

"So I get to interview them again?" She drops the folders on Jenny's desk. "In my spare time?"

I draw in a breath to say something, but she cuts me off.

"Don't pull your bullheaded act with me. Remember that I understand you. And don't get mad when we fall behind because I'm having to hire another new employee because you keep scaring off the people who work for you."

She turns around and heads back to the exam room. I sense that Jenny has found the broom, but she doesn't want to come back into the lobby until I'm gone.

Fine. I cut through the second exam room to avoid bumping into her in the hall or Maria on the other side.

This day is great. Just great.

~

I wasn't planning to call Ensley tonight. But most of the staff gave me the cold shoulder today, and I could use someone on my side.

Sasha kneads her paws on my legs as I sit against the headboard and click on Ensley's name.

"Hey, Drew!" Her cheery voice immediately brings my brooding down a notch.

"Hey."

"So I have to tell you what Janet did today."

I pet Sasha's head and listen as Ensley goes on and on about Janet's attempt to rearrange the cabinets beneath the teller windows. She doesn't care if I don't comment or add to the conversation. Gradually, the knot in my belly loosens.

Finally, she runs out of stories. "So," she says. "Did you talk to Jenny?"

"Yeah."

"And?"

"She quit. A day early."

"Drew! What did you do?"

"The usual."

"What happened?"

"I tried to be nice. I failed." I stare up at the ceiling. "I thought treating animals meant I'd be left alone. But it's still too full of people."

"I'm sorry." The words hang in the air. She seems all out of mantras. I'm a hopeless case.

But I like the quiet. We sit with it a minute, and then she says, "So I have a new confession."

"Okay."

"Do you remember that football jacket you gave Garrett because he lost his and the team only issued one before you had to pay? Your name was stitched inside."

"Maybe."

"It was a long time ago. It saved him. We definitely couldn't afford to replace his."

"What about it?"

"I took it. Not until the season was over. But I took it."

"From Garrett?"

"Because it was yours. I told you I had it bad."

"You dated in high school, right?" I'm hoping she didn't pine for me or anything. She already said she didn't go to prom.

"I did. That's how I got decent meals." She laughs. "I finally got over you when I kissed Finley Martin."

"Delaney Martin's little brother? That twerp?"

"He wasn't a twerp by then!"

"If you say so."

"He was a great kisser."

I definitely don't want to hear about her kissing Finley Martin. "Glad you recovered."

"I did! It was a jolt to see you on that wedding list. Ronnie said she hadn't seen you in years."

"Franklin wanted all the old friends at the altar, since it was Ronnie."

"Did you have a falling-out with him?"

"Nope. He was more into Ronnie than his buds."

"Oh, right. That again." She goes silent, and I know that's bad.

Before I half shout a response, I take a breath and lower my voice. "What does that mean?"

"Oh, the whole just-one-date thing. I guess you haven't seen anyone recently, uh, since, well, since we, you know."

I get it. She's asking if I've slept with someone since the wedding. "It's only been five days."

"Are you this weekend? Going on a date, or whatever you call it?" Her voice is tremulous.

"No."

Her release of air creates a wind-rush sound on the phone. "Okay."

Two feelings war within me. First, who the hell is she to ask me if I'm going on a date? Second, what are we doing here? Am I getting involved with her? There's a reason I don't do relationships. I told her this. I was very clear, and I can't afford to go back on that, not even for her.

"Gotta go," I say.

"Sure. And hey—I'm sure you'll find a new receptionist. There's got to be someone out there who can handle Drew Daniels, even at his worst."

It's not looking good. But I say, "Thanks," and end the call.

Chapter 15

ENSLEY

I think I screwed up.

I pace my apartment after getting off the phone with Drew. I *had* to bring up dates, didn't I? Ugh! I couldn't stop myself from asking if he was going to have another hookup. I *had* to know if he was getting naked with somebody.

Stupid!

On Friday, my grumpiness is an excellent impression of Drew. I keep my head down. I don't talk to anybody. I don't even move the masking tape on Janet's refrigerator zone.

I listen to my customers' crazy farm stories with scarcely a nod.

And that night, Drew doesn't call.

I don't call him, either.

Then it's Saturday.

I'm so disgusted. I had to act all jealous. I have no claim on Drew in any way. He told me his parameters on dating. I'm just being stubborn, thinking that somehow I can save him from himself.

Still, as Saturday passes, I wonder what he's doing. Did he go out after all? He said no, but then I may have made him mad enough he had to sock it to me by doing his thing with some Tinder bait.

By evening, I can't take it anymore, so I head up to the bar where Tillie works. It's crazy there, but I find a stool where the bar meets the wall, and I can hang out mostly unobserved until I decide if I want to retaliate for Drew's imaginary date with a hookup of my own.

"What's got you all riled up?" Tillie asks as she shakes a margarita.

"I screwed up with Drew."

"You're still worrying about when you asked him if he was going out with someone this weekend?" She knows the whole story.

"He hasn't called or emailed or texted since then."

She fills margarita glasses and sets them on a tray. When she pulls out a bottle of blue curaçao, I know she's making a drink for me. I love a good Blue Hawaiian.

Rum. Vodka. Simple syrup. Pineapple, lemon, and lime juices.

No one makes them like Tillie.

She sticks an orange on the rim and slides it over. "I need to catch up on orders. But I'll be right back."

I don't see how. The bar is packed. But I sip my drink, sitting cross-legged on the tall chair, my back against the wall. It's interesting to watch the patrons trying to connect.

People who appear to barely know each other sit at a proper distance, shouting over the noise. Other couples clutch each other on the dance floor. Some argue. A few try to ignore each other, turned away, watching the dancers go by. The entire spectrum is here.

I consider letting random guys hit on me so I feel better, but nobody's noticed me all curled up in the dark corner.

A second bartender comes on shift, and Tillie finally has time to return to my end. "Ensley, if you want to talk to him, just talk to him. In fact, do it right now. If he doesn't respond or answer the call or whatever, then you know it's pointless to pine."

"But I want to pine." The very idea of Drew's gorgeous face buried in some other woman's cleavage is making me absolutely crazy.

"Get your answer. There's no sense freaking out over nothing."

A man walks up to the bar and raises his arm, so Tillie heads down to take his order.

I hold my phone in my hand. I can't call Drew from here.

But I could text. Something simple.

But what to say? I've used the kitten too many times. I can't think of another good confession off the top of my head.

But there's the receptionist issue. I could at least ask the very ordinary question if he's found a new one.

That should be perfectly safe.

I send the text and set my phone on the bar to wait.

The drink is heavenly. I want to chug it and see if I can get my giggles on. But Tillie hates it if I drink too much at her bar. I become a liability.

So I nurse it like a good sister, hoping my phone will light up.

Nothing.

"This seat taken?"

I look up to find an appealing twentysomething leaning his elbow on the bar. He's not my usual type, farm boots and jeans. He's more like the customers at my bank than someone I'd date.

But he runs his hands across his scruffy chin, and his eyes seemed to light up when he looks at me.

Will this make me feel better?

Maybe.

"Not taken," I say.

He sits down, and Tillie heads over, her gaze bouncing between the two of us. "What can I get you?" she asks, but her tone is hard. She's playing the big sister even though I'm the older one.

He glances at my blue drink. "I'd say I'll have what she's having, but it might be too fruity for me."

"It's her favorite drink," Tillie says. "Don't insult her."

This is amusing. I sit back against the wall to watch their interaction play out.

But the man holds up a hand. "I'm sorry. I meant no offense. I just mean I don't like sweet. And it looks sweet."

Tillie cocks her head. "The drink or my sister?"

Now he's the one looking between the two of us. "Yeah, I can see the resemblance."

Tillie turns to me. "You like him? Or should I get him out of here?"

My phone lights up. It's Drew. I snatch it to poke at the message.

Tillie doesn't miss a thing. "Is that who I think it is?"

I nod.

"Okay, farm boy, other end of the bar. My sister and her sweet drink aren't for you."

Dude-in-boots lets out a huff. "What a pair of bitches." He pushes away from the bar and heads out to the tables.

I look up at Tillie. "Dodged a bullet."

"I could've told you that. I can read 'em from across a crowded bar. Total asshole material."

"I sure didn't see it."

She shrugs. "Comes with the job." She leans down. "What did Drew say?"

"I asked him about his receptionist." I angle the phone toward her. "He only answered the question. The temp agency didn't get back to him Friday, so he'll have to manage Monday without one."

"Hmm." She spots another person down the bar. "Hold that thought."

I stare at Drew's words. I don't know where I can go from here.

Maybe an apology?

I sip my drink. I tap out the words.

Me: Sorry I asked about your dating last time we talked. Not my business.

I chew on my straw while I wait for him to respond. He won't ignore that. Drew might grunt like a caveman. But he'll recognize someone's making an effort.

Drew: I figure as far as things got last weekend, I probably owe you something.

My stomach settles. Maybe things will be all right.

Me: So will a temp do for your job?

Drew: Not really. But at least the phones will be answered.

This is easy. Talking about work is nice neutral territory.

Me: How many employees do you have?

He must not be busy tonight or he wouldn't be texting me so quickly.

Drew: Three full-time techs. One part-time. Plus the front desk.

Me: That's a lot.

Drew: The receptionist is key to the flow of the office.

Me: Will you be able to manage Monday?

Drew: No choice.

Tillie drifts back down the bar. "How's it going?"

"Good. Work talk."

She's about to head away when I stop her. "Tillie? When were you going to go see Lila next?"

She shrugs. "Hadn't thought about it. Maybe not until I move at the end of the month."

"When is your next day off?"

"Monday and Tuesday as usual. But I'm a short-timer now. Nobody expects me to play too nicely."

A plan forms. "Do you have to work the late shift Sunday?"

"I don't close. But I probably won't be done till nine."

"Is that too late to go to Lila's?"

"I guess we could drive down that late. Makes more sense to go Monday morning, though. Don't you have to work?"

"I think I could swing some time off. We have a floater who can go between the bank branches."

Tillie shrugs. "Sure. We can head out Sunday night if you want. What's this about?"

"Just wanted to go to Adamsville and see my sister."

She narrows her eyes. "Never mind that Adamsville is close to Drew."

"He seems like he could use some help Monday."

"You're going to work for him?"

"Maybe for the day."

She wipes down the counter. "There are about a dozen ways this could go south."

I shrug. "I'm a kindhearted girl helping a friend."

She shakes her head, but a group of laughing women approach the bar, so she has to head over to get their orders.

Drew hasn't typed anything since his last message.

Me: I hope it works out. Good night!

Drew: G'night.

Now to look up where his veterinary office is.

Chapter 16

DREW

I brace myself for a Monday morning of chaos. Friday was a surgery day with few regular appointments, so Jenny's absence mattered a lot less.

But Mondays are always brutal, as many stressed-out pet owners will try to work their way into our schedule for whatever happened over the weekend.

I pull Vera from diagnostic to run the front desk. Our retired part-timer Betty will pop in for a couple of hours to manage prescriptions and handle phone inquiries.

I take over diagnostic plus handling all the emergency cases that come in. It feels like I've worked for hours, exhaustion already hitting when I look up and realize it's only nine.

Vera approaches me cautiously at the surgical table. "Dr. Daniels, you have a visitor."

I don't even glance up from the fourteen-year-old cat I'm having to stitch up. Well into her golden years and still getting into fights. "If it's some industry rep, tell them to come next week."

"It's a young woman, actually. Says she's Ensley James."

My head snaps up. Ensley's here? In Atlanta?

"Put her in my office and tell her I'll be there when I'm done with this suture. Fifteen minutes."

"Sure." She walks away with a surprised look, as if she expected that conversation to go worse than it did.

I have the entire staff on edge. I need to hire a receptionist and quick. I realize I haven't followed up with the temp agency. If I don't do that shortly, I won't have anyone for tomorrow, either. Hopefully, my reputation hasn't preceded me there.

I draw in a slow breath. Focus on this cat.

Maria comes to the surgery bay door. "All the exams this morning have gone fine, but we have three diagnostics in kennels. We need Vera to handle them since you're running ragged."

"Can Betty do them?" I finish up the stitches and tie them off.

"She tried, but all the machines are new since she was last here full-time. Vera can't leave the lobby to show her."

"Can Betty do the phones and Vera do the diagnostic?"

"That would only help us for another half hour. Betty has an appointment of her own and can't stay."

This is ridiculous. Mondays are always all hands on deck, but with one less employee, we're completely strung out.

"I'm going to move this one to her kennel before we wake her. She's pretty wild. Can you grab a warming blanket?" I deflate the intubation and pet the sleeping cat's head.

"Will do." Maria hesitates. "You know Vera is not super great on the phone."

"I know."

"She gets frazzled kind of easily if there are many people in the lobby."

"I understand."

"Todd ran both of the exam rooms while I helped you."

"I hear you."

When the cat starts to twitch, I gently remove the tube and slide her into the kennel her owner brought, adjusting the warming blanket around her. It's not a bad way to wake up. I scrub down at the sink while Maria quickly sanitizes the surgery bay.

I have zero time for Ensley. What the hell sort of surprise is this? I'll have to be quick. And then call the temp agency. And then come back and see where we are.

I realize at the last minute there's blood on my coat and whip it off. I have a clean one hanging by my desk.

The door to my office is mostly closed. I straighten my shirt as I prepare to go in, then pause. Ensley's talking.

"Daniels Vet Care. How may I help you?"

I peek through the crack. Ensley's on my desk phone.

"Oh, that does sound scary! Dr. Daniels and the techs are in exam rooms. Can I take down all the details and have one of them call you?" She glances around for a piece of paper, then pulls a blank one from the printer.

"Got it. Yes. And which patient? How old? Do you know how much Sissy weighs? Oh good. I've got it all down. We'll get back to you. Think all the positive thoughts until then!"

She punches the button and picks up another call. "Mrs. Evers, I'm back. I'm so sorry. Please continue your story." She listens, tapping the pen on her desk. "So you talked to Dr. Daniels last week? What did he say?"

She nods as if the other person can see her. "Oh, I can tell you really love that sweet Bennie. You know, I'll leave him a quick note about this, but it sounds like Dr. Daniels gave you some wonderful advice last time. If you try it a bit longer, I bet you'll find Bennie is gobbling that kibble down."

Another pause. "Oh, I did enjoy talking to you, too, Mrs. Evers. Kiss Bennie for me!"

She punches the button and scans the lights. She seems satisfied and moves from my chair to the small chair in the corner.

I step inside.

She stands up. "Drew! Surprise!"

I lean against my desk, arms crossed. "Were you handling some of the calls?"

"I was. The woman out front seems to be struggling with the phone system." She grimaces. "I thought I could take a bit of the load off while I waited for you. Is that woman the new receptionist? Is that why she's having a hard time?"

"No. She normally runs our diagnostics and pharmacy."

"Any leads? It seems so easy. All the callers care so much about their pets!"

Light dawns. One of Ensley's wedding confessions was that she didn't find her work at the bank meaningful. She wanted to do something that mattered.

And she's trying to show me how well she can do here.

Plus, her sister lives nearby. Didn't she mention she was about to have to find a new roommate?

She's making a bold move. She wants to transfer to Atlanta and take a job here, something with a higher purpose, the care and health of animals.

I'm proud of her.

"It's yours," I say.

Ensley tilts her head. "Mine?"

"The job. It's yours. You're obviously great. You're used to customer service. Bank work means you can handle our invoices and payment processes. You're perfect."

She watches me a moment with those sparkly eyes. I try to force myself not to take in any more of her, not the slender plum dress and black tights. Not the dip of the cut of her neckline, showing a hint of those breasts I could easily recall if I just slip into memory.

Eyes up there. On her face.

She presses her hand to her cheek. "I wasn't expecting that. Oh. Wow."

I've overwhelmed her. "I have to get back to the exam tables. We can talk more about it later. But welcome aboard."

"Thank you," she says, still seeming shocked.

Relief floods through me. The situation is taken care of. Ensley has a bright, sunshiny personality, at least when she's not backed in a corner.

She knows how to maneuver around me. And she has the experience necessary to dive right into the primary tasks. She can pick up the veterinary-specific skills as she goes.

She sits back at my desk, answering another phone call. I turn on my heel, realizing I don't even need to tell her what to do. She's already helping.

And only when I get back to the exam tables, Todd leading in a dog who ate three chocolate Easter bunnies and needs to have vomiting induced, do I realize having Ensley here will involve one distinct problem.

I'll have to keep my hands off her.

Chapter 17

ENSLEY

What have I just done?

I continue to take calls from Drew's desk. Since I have no other duties, there are long lulls where I ponder the ramifications of my spontaneous action.

I already have a job. And I haven't given notice. Do I even want to? Cindy will kill me.

But let's say I take this job. Drew will be my *boss*. My brain skitters into the explicit emails we sent each other. What about those? I can't date him if he's my boss!

I text my sisters in a panic.

Me: Drew hired me as his new receptionist. What do I do?

Tillie: What?

Me: I was helping out. He thought I wanted the job permanently. So he hired me!

Tillie: He did not.

Me: He did!

Lila: We'll all be together again! Isn't your apartment lease up soon anyway?

Tillie: It is.

She's right. I was planning to take a one-bedroom in the same complex. The leasing agent said they had some. I simply had to look at the floor plans and choose.

But I haven't yet.

I pace Drew's office, trying to think this through. I make the half circle several times before the phone rings.

The woman out front must pick it up, because the light goes solid, then blinks out. She accidentally hung up again.

This drives me crazy. This is Drew's clinic!

Drew hasn't told me to go out front or to do anything beyond help as I have been, but I open the door to peer into the hall. I don't know my way around. But I retrace my steps back to the lobby. The woman slams down the receiver in frustration. "I can never figure this thing out."

There are two people standing by the desk, waiting to be checked in.

I come up beside her. "Hey, Drew suggested I answer the phones today to help. Don't worry about them at all. I will pick up every line."

She spins in her chair. "Are you from the temp agency? I thought they hadn't gotten back to him."

"No. I knew Drew growing up. He needed help, so I said I could fill in."

"Praise the Lord," she says. "I'm Vera. I normally run diagnostics. Phone systems are not my thing."

I glance at the people patiently waiting. "You check them in. I'll get the phones. We'll work on transitioning me to the front desk completely once this rush is settled. Maybe during the lunch hour?"

Vera nods. "That would be great."

I hope I'm not saying anything out of turn. But I sense that the entire staff is winging it at the moment.

And I *am* an assistant head teller. I can take charge.

I go back to Drew's office and answer calls until Vera pokes her head in. "No one should come in the front door for the next hour. I can show you around the desk and how to check people in. I talked to Dr.

Daniels. He says you're an amazing self-starter and our new receptionist. I'm so relieved."

Oh no. Now Vera thinks I'm staying. "We haven't ironed out the details yet. But show me everything."

I'm hoping to speak to Drew soon. I sit in Vera's chair as she runs me through some of the basic operations.

She punches on the keyboard. "Don't ask me what to do for everything, because I don't know. This isn't a spot I ever sit in. Maria might know more."

"Maria?"

"She's the head tech. She knows everything about this place. Possibly even more than Dr. Daniels, since she's a holdover from the vet who owned this clinic before. Maria will be the one who can get you up to speed."

Good. I'll learn everything, and then I can train the new person without disrupting the rest of the staff's duties. It will be an easy transition of power, considering the chaos Drew is experiencing. He'll appreciate me. He'll recognize how much I've gone out of my way to help them.

And then we can explore our unfinished business. He claims he ends every romantic encounter with a single hookup. I'm not so sure. I think Drew Daniels has more to him than he lets himself believe. In fact, maybe I could take my full vacation at work right now. If I can be around him for a week or so, maybe I'll figure out if I'm right about him, and then, if we have any lasting chemistry. If not, I go home, back to my job, get my smaller apartment, and close the door on this sidenote to my longtime crush.

As lunch passes while I take a crash course on the front desk operations, I'm grateful for the granola bar I always keep stuck in my purse. I don't see Drew. He never comes up from the back, and when the clients start arriving again at one o'clock, it's a steady stream of work.

I answer the phones, take down detailed messages, and transfer calls. Check in the clients, pull their folders. I clean up poop and pee accidents in the lobby. I meet Todd, the other vet tech. And eventually Maria checks on me to welcome me aboard.

I know I need to speak to Drew quickly and correct his assumption that I'm here permanently. But I see no way to do it. There's no opportunity for me to go to the back, and judging by the flow of pets, he's too busy to talk to me.

I stay straight through to five, my stomach rumbling. It's much harder work than the bank already, and I haven't even learned all my duties, including filing pet insurance claims and dealing with the flood of emails that come through. A couple of vendors show up, and I have to turn them away, hoping I did the right thing.

But finally Vera crosses the lobby and flips the lock on the doors. "Last pet out." She sighs. "This was definitely a Monday. We would've fallen apart without you, Ensley."

I stand behind the desk. "Happy to help. Is Drew free?" I might make him take me to dinner. I'm starved.

Vera twists her bottom lip. "Let's have you talk to Maria first. I know you know Dr. Daniels. But do you *really* know him? He can be pretty difficult."

"I know Drew very well," I say. "I tried to help him figure out how to handle Jenny. But apparently my advice wasn't enough."

Vera looks relieved. "Okay, good. No one knows why the good Lord made Dr. Daniels the way he is, but when he's angry, the ground shakes."

"I've seen it since I was a kid. I'm not afraid."

"What a blessing you are, girl. I'm behind on diagnostics. I'm going to run some more. Normally you can get to billing and things in between check-ins and phone calls. But Mondays are always a little extra."

"I get it," I say. "Mondays are always crazy at the bank where I'm assistant head teller." I don't know why I try to tout my experience. I guess I want to feel competent. There's no telling what these people would think of me if they learned that the real reason I came to Atlanta had to do with a series of dirty emails.

Maria arrives from the back. "Ensley, let me show you how to shut down the system, and then Dr. Daniels will be ready to have a chat with you about your duties."

I sit back down in the chair as she moves the mouse on the desk. "There are a few tricky bits to this application," she says.

"Understood." I take a few quick notes as she runs through a series of clicks until the screen goes dark.

"All right, let's take a tour." Maria straightens, and I follow her down the hall.

This is my first time all the way to the back. During the course of the day, I stepped inside the two exam rooms, ran to the maintenance closet for a mop, popped into the diagnostic and pharmacy area to fetch prescriptions, and of course spent time in Drew's office. But I haven't been this far.

She gestures to two tall steel tables jutting out from a long counter filled floor to ceiling with cabinets. "This is the treatment space where we bring the animals when we need to work with them away from their owners."

We walk farther into the large room. "Those are our recovery kennels outside the surgery bay. Always know that there's a webcam on the cages, so anything you do in this area is being recorded." She laughs. "It's no place to pick a wedgie."

My cheeks bloom warm. "Noted." It would also not be a place to make out with the boss.

Not that it's going to happen.

But I hope it happens.

She leads me to a side door. "Over here, we have a storage room with most of the feed and supplies. This table at the end is what we use for a break room, not that we sit down to eat for long. Those cabinets are good for personal items, although you can keep yours up at reception. Food goes in this fridge. Don't use the med fridge for human things."

I nod.

I haven't seen Drew. Past the stock shelves is a door that leads out to a parking lot and a stretch of grass and trees.

"It's nice," I say.

Maria nods. "It is. It's a great small practice."

"Where's Drew?"

"He was just back here, but I'm guessing he's gone to his office. I'll drop you off there."

My belly quakes. I have to figure out exactly how to explain to Drew what my intention is here. And of course, there are all these unknown factors, like taking my full vacation, if Cindy will even let me.

Maria knocks on his door, then opens it.

"I have Ensley," she says.

Drew is behind his desk, Sasha on his shoulder.

"Does she always cling to you like that?" I ask.

"It's apparently her thing," Drew says. "Thank you, Maria. Set Ensley up for the full managerial position. She's perfectly capable."

Maria nods. "She definitely impressed everyone. Vera couldn't stop talking about her."

Really?

Maria leaves and closes the door behind her. I drop into the chair in the corner. "This has been quite a day," I say.

He continues to rapidly sign several pages. "Mondays are hard, and being shorthanded makes it worse."

"Everyone was super nice. I could tell that Vera was uncomfortable on the phones, so I'm glad I could help."

"You seem to have fit in almost immediately."

"I think so. I didn't speak much to Todd."

His jaw tenses at that. What is that about? Does he think I'm interested in him?

I set that aside. I have more important things to convey. He needs to know I'm only here to help temporarily.

His phone buzzes. Maria comes on the intercom. "Hey, I was talking to Mrs. Jennings, the owner of the cat we spayed last week. Callie. The calico. She got her cone off and she's had some complications. Can you pick up line two?"

Drew leans in. "I will. Thanks." He looks up at me. "Tomorrow is our dental day, so we have long periods of working on dogs under anesthesia and less traffic. It will be an ideal day to learn the ropes. I have every confidence that you will be in full control of your duties in no time." He pushes a folder toward me. "All the forms are in here. If that salary is inadequate, we can negotiate. I took a moment to look at commensurate numbers for bank tellers and think you'll be pleased. The usual government forms are in there as well. Thank you."

I haven't explained the situation, but he gives me a dismissive nod and picks up the line. "Mrs. Jennings. What's this about Callie?"

I pick up the folder and head out the door. What have I gotten myself into?

Chapter 18

DREW

I arrive at the clinic early Tuesday morning feeling well rested and calm.

There were no chatty text messages or phone calls to navigate. The only email last night was the one with her paperwork filled out. Ensley is now safely ensconced in a specific slot in my life. Employee.

Sasha clings to my shoulder as I walk into the clinic and flip on the lights.

I check on our two overnighters, emergency cases from the day before. Betty already reported that they were fine at her midnight welfare check, and I woke up twice in the night to watch them on the webcam.

Both seem groggy, so I open their cages and give them some pets and a bit of medicated food.

It's dental cleaning day, so the load will be light in the morning, other than checking in the patients we will put under anesthesia to work on their teeth. Cases will pick up in the afternoon when we see regular well checks and vaccinations.

It's a good morning for Ensley to officially start. She'll have plenty of time to make sure everything goes well with each patient, and we can take her through the entire process and make sure proper steps are followed.

All is well.

Maria comes in not long after me. "Looks like everyone's recovering. How many dentals do we have today?"

"Four," I tell her.

"We will have some calling to do with the diagnostics that ran late yesterday," she says.

"I'll handle them."

Maria's eyebrows lift. "You will? You will voluntarily make some phone calls?"

I shrug. "I can do that."

"Someone's in a good mood." She heads for the storage room. I wonder about this observation of hers. I *am* in a better mood. No doubt this is because I have the receptionist position squared away, and I know it's someone who is competent and not afraid of me.

A niggle of doubt in my belly reminds me that I find this new employee outrageously attractive, but I push it aside. I am a man of control. This will not be a problem. I've never consorted with my employees before.

But then, Ensley was never my employee. I've put myself to the ultimate test.

Nothing I can't handle.

I set up the surgical area, and Maria arrives to assist. Ensley should be the next to come in, and I hear the jingle of the front door, which is likely her. Everyone else arrives through the back.

I glance up, and Maria catches my eye. "I'll tell her. Park in the back, come in through the back."

I nod, arranging the cleaning instruments and creating packets for each dog we will treat today.

Ensley and Maria talk amiably, their voices filtering down the hall. Soon, both of them are in the room. Ensley is dressed interestingly. Her black pants are faux leather, and her bright-orange shirt is topped with a shiny silver bolero jacket.

She's definitely got a style of her own. As she walks past me, her pants fit precisely the way pants should, and my eyes can't help but be drawn to the shimmer of the fitted jacket.

"I wonder if we shouldn't put a lab coat over what you're wearing," Maria says. "I have a feeling that your shiny jacket might be extremely inviting to every cat with claws today."

Ensley looks down at her outfit. "Oh! Sure."

I shouldn't have worried. Maria has everything well in hand. My attraction to Ensley might not even be a factor. If she's good at her job, and she surely will be, she won't require as much of my time as the previous receptionists. They always seemed to need one thing or another. The day goes smoothly, as far as I can tell. I have back-to-back dentals, so I don't even lift my head until almost noon, with Maria at my side the whole time.

Todd goes in and out occasionally, handling specialty food purchases and managing two big deliveries.

Vera catches me between the cleanings to let me know about a few diagnostics.

Only when I've scrubbed myself out and I'm headed to my office to grab a quick lunch do I think to stop in the lobby and check on Ensley.

She's tapping on the computer while eating a granola bar.

"Ensley?"

She about jumps out of her skin. "Drew!"

I glance around the lobby. There's no one there. "It might be best if you call me Dr. Daniels around patients."

"There's no one here right now."

"I'm aware. Just a reminder."

She stares at me for a second, then seems to shake it off. "Sure. Fine. I was going through the invoices and matching them up with the paperwork. It might take me a while to sort it all out."

"We've been through some chaos. I'm glad you're here."

"About that," she says, but then the phone lights up. "Sorry."

She answers the phone with the perfect voice, authoritative but friendly. I watch her listen to the caller, nodding as if they can see her, which makes me smile inside.

"And when was his last veterinary appointment?" she asks. She writes more things down. "Let me see what we have available."

I realize she's scheduling an appointment. I wait a second to make sure she knows how, but when she pulls up the application and scrolls through the empty squares with total competence, I step back into the hallway. I should let her do her job. She's clearly just fine.

Maybe missing the wedding was a lucky break. It wasn't clear at first what role Ensley might have in my life, but now it's perfect.

I no more than sit down when she buzzes me on the phone. "Dr. Daniels, I have Alina Carmichael on the line. She's the one with the dog whose leg you set last week. She has some concerns about his limp. Do you want to speak to her, or should I simply make an appointment?"

She already gets it. She intuitively knows how to work the office. "I'll talk to her, thank you."

"Sure thing. Line one."

I sit back in my chair. All is well at Daniels Vet Care.

As long as I can stop picturing my receptionist in unzipped coveralls.

Chapter 19

Ensley

I've gotten myself into one hot mess.

By the end of the day, though, I have my vacation worked out. I told Cindy I wanted my full eight days, which means I have to drive back to Alabama next Wednesday night to be at work on Thursday.

Or else quit my bank job.

Without notice.

Which is not something I have ever done. Not even when I worked at the chicken place where the owner would chase me around the butcher table.

Cindy approved my leave and worked out a rotating round of help from the other branches. Janet is annoyed.

Which is a nice bonus.

But now I have to figure out what I want and where I want it in just over a week. One night with him to finish out the wedding debacle? The start of something more? *One thing at a time, Ensley. Don't get ahead of yourself.*

My sisters think this whole situation is hysterical.

"Ensley is going to be banging her boss by the weekend," Tillie says, shoving a pizza box at me.

Lila manages a small smile. She's struggling with all-day morning sickness. "Just be safe."

I wonder exactly what she means. With protection so I'm not unexpectedly pregnant like she is? Or with my heart? I do have a soft spot for Drew.

I have no idea how to be safe in my current circumstance. I feel like I'm teetering on the edge of a pit, like at the wedding. Everyone at the office thinks I'm staying. And I don't know how to make any inroads with Drew when I only see him for a few minutes at a time. He's gotten very formal with me.

This might be my worst scheme ever.

I only know that I think about him all the time. I picture him in the shed. Stripping out of his tux. Carrying me to the cot.

And of course hovering over me, his head dipping down to the unzipped coveralls.

Something's shifting. My kid crush is growing into something decidedly adult. Lila's right. I definitely need to be safe.

But I also have to act. Eight days isn't much, even if it is tacked on to a long history.

On Wednesday morning, I come out of the bathroom to find that my sister Lila is already up. She's often awake early in the mornings, because she starts puking the minute she rolls over.

She lies on her sofa, which is still made up as my bed. She's got an ice bag on her head and a bucket in the crook of her arm.

Thankfully, it's currently empty.

There's only one bathroom in her rent house. "I'm sorry I took too long," I say. "I didn't realize you were up and sick."

She waves her hand at me. "I can always puke in the kitchen sink. Or this bucket."

That's Lila in a nutshell. Practical. Unassuming. She never likes to make a fuss. If I had a deadbeat boyfriend who knocked me up and took off, heads would be rolling. Even thinking about it, my whole body gets hot with anger.

No. Think positive. Manifest your perfect future.

If only I could manifest one for Lila. She won't stand up for herself. Not even when she's left alone with a baby.

Although, we were both left alone with a baby when Mom died. I was five. Lila was three. Dad seemed to go into a grief trance that he's still stuck in twenty years later. Even though Garrett was the oldest, he wasn't much help. He practically lived at friends' houses.

I was in kindergarten and had to take up the mantle of raising the little ones. We all went to this tiny church school and day care where, I later learned, they paid our tuition as charity. Those were better years than later, because at least when we were little, the church ladies made sure we had clothes and sent food home for dinner. I carefully portioned it out to last over the weekends.

Summers were the worst. Dad didn't always remember to get groceries. I learned to hoard what we had to string it out. Garrett would eat elsewhere most days. We could go for a week without seeing him.

When we aged out of the church and got dumped into public school, we created strategies to stay fed and clothed. Garrett would lower Tillie into the donation dumpsters to find us things to wear. I was the one who raided our neighbors' gardens to find vegetables to throw in a pot with Good Noodles. I only got caught once, trying to filch lemons from a potted lemon tree.

Drew saw that one, of course. He hauled me home. I never should have tried it during the day, but I wanted to make lemonade for him. I had it as bad for him then as I do now. But this time I've taken a *job*. That's quite a leap from a stolen lemon.

Lila rubs her eyes with the heel of her hand. I have a few minutes before I have to leave for the vet office, so I sit on the floor beside her. "How long have you been this sick?"

"Since the week I found out. Random throwing up is what clued me in."

She lifts her bucket, and I prepare myself for the visual and audio of her puking, but then she sets it down again. "False alarm."

"I'm proud of you, doing this on your own," I say.

"I won't have to. He'll come back." Her voice is firm on this matter, as it always is. She's the only one who believes that scumbag of a boyfriend will return. He was exactly the sort of man you hate to see your sister hook up with. He laughed too loud and often at her expense. He spoke sweet to her when he had to, but mostly he was gruff, the definition of a toxic male.

He forgot her more often than not, preferring the company of his beer-swilling friends. She delivered pizza to pay the bills. He pitched in randomly when he got work building an engine here and there. Said his back was too bad for full-time employment.

Probably he had a girl on the side.

But I say none of this, checking my bag for granola bars. I'm here for her. And Tillie will be, too. It's like she said. We have to take care of each other.

And speaking of that, I should go to the grocery store. It's been a lot, the new job, my sisters, figuring out my next move. I'm absolutely jonesing for a cup of Good Noodles, and we should buy things that Lila can keep down.

Lila touches my shoulder. "Anything new with you and Drew? Any sparks flying?"

I shut my purse. "I hardly see him. And he treats me like an employee, one hundred percent. This might've been my worst decision ever."

"When will you tell him you're only there until the middle of next week?"

"I don't know."

"Do you like the job? You could always keep it. Then you can be around Drew all you want."

I don't say this aloud, but that's the whole problem. Drew has put me in the employee zone, and I'm not sure how to get out. And I do want out. I want more of what we stirred up in that shed. What led us both to write racy emails. I didn't even get my one-night stand!

But the stakes are high. What if I find out that Drew is going on a date this weekend? What if gossip of his conquests gets to me?

I'm not sure how professional I can be if that happens, not even for eight days.

But I don't want to put any of my worries on Lila's plate. She has plenty.

I put on my brightest smile. "I have time to decide. I'm going to make an extra effort to be around him today. Yesterday was a lot of learning curves. Today will be better."

"I'm glad you're here," she says. "Ronnie did a good job helping you be more positive about life."

I almost frown at the reminder of my former brooding, obsessive self. "Me, too." It took Ronnie going into the pit for us to find a way to get us both out. It had been her idea, shortly after her mother died, for both of us to do positivity training. When I saw my sweet, happy, caring friend turn into, well, *me*, I knew we both had to make a change. Her mirror of all my ugliness about how the loss of my mother ruined my life was too much for me to bear.

We played with crystals and opened our chakras, attended special yoga classes, and even consulted with a guru since Ronnie paid.

Ronnie was far more into the tangible positivity methods than I was. She has all the totems, the worry beads, and the posters. When I started with the mantras—*all is well, I am enough, I choose to be at peace, I have all the time I need*—the words resonated with me. It's all I kept of our training. And it's actually helped, even if sometimes my pithy reminders are annoying to other people. *Love radiates from me.*

I hop up and straighten my skirt. Right now, I need to get to work. I'm also going to have to hit a thrift shop this weekend. I didn't bring a week's worth of clothes, at least not ones that are Drew-worthy.

"Can I get you anything before I go?" I ask her.

"No. I'm afraid to move. It'll settle down in a bit. Right now I can't even tilt my head."

I squeeze her hand. "Make that sister of ours take care of you."

"When she wakes up. She's used to crazy hours."

I nod. "I lived with her for two years. I hear you."

With that, I head out the door.

On the drive over, I rack my brain for something I can do to speed up the process of figuring Drew out. I want to do something for him, get him to talk to me.

I should have baked him cookies. Dang it.

I don't want to wait another whole day to find an excuse to seek him out, but then I have it.

I pull into a doughnut shop and grab a dozen doughnuts for the staff, plus a cup of coffee for myself and for Drew.

Between the vacation pay and the new job, I'm getting paid double. I can afford this small luxury.

When I enter through the back door, the storage room is empty. I set the bakery box on the table near the fridge, and place a doughnut on a napkin to take to Drew. This is it. Time to initiate part one of do-I-or-do-I-not get a night with my childhood crush.

Or even more.

Today's outfit is a brown suede skirt that falls below my knees and a gold button-down with big cuffs. I borrowed Tillie's brown boots to finish out the look. I think it's smashing, and certainly suits an office manager, even if I do sometimes end up on poop patrol.

Drew's office door is cocked open, so I bump it with my hip. "Coffee time!" I singsong.

Drew is peering at his screen. "What?" he barks.

Wow. That was ugly. No wonder Jenny ran for the hills.

"I brought you coffee, Mr. Grumpy Pants. The proper response is, *thank you.*"

He still doesn't look up.

Good gracious.

I set the cup in a blank spot on his desk, but can't find anywhere to place the doughnut. I finally set it on a chair and start organizing his piles.

"What are you doing?" he booms.

"Good lord, Drew! Did someone tie off your balls?"

His eyes go big. "You can't talk that way to your supervisor."

"Sure I can. The vet office isn't even open. Stop trying to be Mr. Boss Man and be a human."

He lets out a long breath, and Sasha, ever present on his shoulder, stretches out a long white paw to tap his cheek. See, even she knows he needs to calm down.

I continue to straighten the papers. "I'm not disturbing their order or location," I say. "I'm giving them right angles so they fit on the desk." I finish the job and move the doughnut to a cleared spot. "You look like you could use some caffeine and a snack."

And some manners. But I keep that part to myself.

"I don't eat sugar," he says but picks up the coffee.

"Okay!" I snatch the doughnut and take a hefty bite.

"Hey! That was mine!"

Oh my God. "Drew! You said you don't eat sugar."

"I was being difficult."

"You don't have to tell me!" I walk around the desk. "Here." I hold the doughnut near his mouth. "Eat something before you talk anymore. You obviously need some calories."

"You already took a bite."

"And you've already been all up in my saliva, if you recall."

Drew glares at me. Sasha sniffs delicately at the doughnut.

He takes the doughnut from me, turning the side with my bite away from his mouth. His shoulders relax as his teeth sink in. "That's good."

"Exactly. And plenty more where that came from. There's a dozen in the storage room on the break table."

"You brought these?" He takes another bite.

Doesn't eat sugar. What a crock.

"I did. I've enjoyed the challenge of the last two days, and I wanted to do something nice."

He swallows. "We should do something for you."

Now that he's not roaring like a bear, I feel bold. "I agree. I say you take me to dinner tonight."

He frowns. "I can't do that."

"Oh, I know. You're my boss. But I have some things to discuss with you. So I insist." This is great. I don't know why I didn't think of it before.

He finishes another bite before answering. "Why can't we have the conversation here?"

"Because I'm saving your butt, you got me mostly naked less than two weeks ago, and you owe me!"

He sets down his doughnut. "All right. But please keep this between us."

This is definitely progress. "Our secret is safe with me."

And before my perfectly manifested future can get derailed, I head for the door.

Chapter 20

DREW

This woman is going to be the death of me. She brought me doughnuts, looking far too adorable for veterinary work.

And now she's convinced me to take her to dinner even though she works for me.

It's downright irritating the way she can make me go back on my convictions with a toss of her curly hair.

The whole situation has me thinking about the movie *Bambi* from my childhood. I never understood the whole twitterpated scene. I felt the same way about my friends as Bambi did, watching his skunk pal take off with some skunk girl. And then there were the birds fluttering around to pick up mates. Bambi wandered around the forest in confusion as they all took off, wondering what had gotten into everybody.

I mean, I get that Bambi eventually meets the doe and they hook up. But the big takeaway for me was, Why is everyone abandoning their best friends for a random female?

But some of us aren't cut out for love like that.

Shortly after lunch, when things are quiet, I hear a bunch of oohs and aahs coming from the lobby, audible all the way to my office.

I head up front. Ensley is kneeling in front of a cardboard box that has apparently been brought in by a kid who can't be over twelve.

"What's this?" I ask.

"A stray mom and her kittens," Ensley says. She turns her gaze toward me, and the pure love there makes my heart skitter. "Just look at them."

I peer into the box. A scrawny young female cat, barely a year old, blinks up at us as three gray kittens poke around her belly. They are very tiny, three weeks old at best.

The boy, a hank of hair falling over his eyes, says, "She's been living in a drainpipe where me and my friends hang out. We bring her food. But when she had the babies, I figured I'd better do something."

"You did the right thing," Ensley says. "We'll take care of them."

"Mom said I couldn't keep them," he says. "I tried."

"We understand," I say.

The boy looks down at the box one more time, then heads out to where his bike is lying on the sidewalk.

"What do we do with them?" Ensley asks.

I pick one up. It's warm with a fat belly. They aren't in terrible shape, at least. "We'll give them an exam. Check out the mother. She probably needs shots."

Ensley nods. "They're so soft." She runs her hands along the babies' backs.

I tuck the kitten against her mother. "I can take these to the back."

I'm about to lean down to pick up the box when a woman with two yappy Chihuahuas opens the door. They quickly spot the box and dash to the ends of their leashes, climbing the side to peer in.

The mama cat hisses and jumps out of the box. She heads straight out the open door.

"Oh no!" Ensley cries. She dashes out after the cat.

"Whoa, there," I say, grabbing the leashes of the dogs and pulling them back.

"I'm so sorry!" cries the woman. "I had no idea."

I pick up the box and set it behind the counter on Ensley's desk. "There's no reason you would've known. Don't worry about it in the least. If you have a seat, we'll get you checked in."

The woman takes the Chihuahuas off to the side where a vinyl bench fills the wall.

I check on the kittens. They squirm around, but they don't seem to be too distraught by the sudden noise and the abrupt departure of their mother.

"I'll check on Ensley and see if she got the cat," I tell the woman. "We'll be right back."

"So sorry," the woman says, but I head out the door.

"Ensley?" I glance around the parking lot. I wonder how far away the cat got.

I walk to the road, glancing each direction. There are some pedestrians, but no Ensley.

I head back to the building. "Ensley? Where are you?"

No answer. I pause to listen. Between the swish of the passing cars, I hear the yowl of an unhappy cat.

I follow the sound to the side of the building, then hurry forward. Ensley has climbed a tree in her boots and suede skirt, clutching a limb with one arm and the mama cat in the other.

"Ensley?" I ask.

She doesn't answer. Her face is buried in the cat's fur.

I approach the tree. There is no way for her to get down with the cat in her arms.

"Pass me the cat," I say. "Then I will get you down."

She turns her head ever so slowly. Her voice is raspy, dark with fear. "I don't think I can move."

I pull out my phone and quickly text Todd to bring a stepladder. "I'm getting reinforcements."

Ensley hangs on to the tree. Her curls are a riot around her face. The cat is angry in her arms, yowling to be put down, but isn't biting or scratching.

"So you followed her up the tree?"

Ensley's big eyes meet mine. "I didn't think I was climbing as far as I was."

"Just hold on. Todd's on his way."

Todd emerges from the back side of the clinic with a ladder. "What's going on, boss?" Then he sees Ensley. "Oh."

"Set it here," I say, pointing at a spot below the cat. I climb up the steps, my lab coat flapping in the breeze. I reach up and carefully disentangle the cat. I pass it down to Todd. "Take her in through the back to avoid the dogs. There's a box with her kittens on the reception desk. Get them in a kennel and feed them. We'll do a full exam in a bit."

Todd curls the cat in his arms. "Gotcha." He shakes his head up at Ensley. "She okay?"

Ensley still clutches the tree, hiding her face in her arm.

"I'll get her," I say to Todd.

I wait until he circles back around the clinic. Ensley seems distraught.

I take another step up so that I'm level with her face. "Can you not get down?" I ask softly.

She shakes her head.

"Are you afraid of heights?"

"Not until now." When the tree quivers, she sucks in a breath.

"I can help you."

She nods.

Crazy woman, going up after a cat in a tree when she's this afraid.

I take in her position to determine the best way to get her down. If I can get her to let her legs fall, I could probably get her close enough to the ladder that she'll let go.

But I'm not sure. She's got a death grip on the limb.

"Ensley, look at me. We're going to do this together. Okay?"

She nods.

"No one can see us. It's just us."

She nods again.

"I'm going to bring your legs around and hold you tight, until your feet can find the top of the ladder. Is that okay?"

Another nod.

"Okay. Here we go."

I reach for her legs, my hand sliding along the smooth calf to her knee, trying to guide the leg closest to me down. My pulse speeds up, and it's not just the difficult moment. I'm touching her again. I realize how badly I've had to fight to hold back from doing this very thing the whole time she's been here.

"Your skirt is narrow, so we have to do this all at once."

Another nod.

I slide my arm underneath her other leg and guide it over to the ladder. She shifts on the limb, and I rotate her body, holding her steady until her boot grazes the step. "Right here. Put your weight down."

She follows my instructions, her belly quivering with fright.

I hold her firmly around the waist. "You can let go of the branch. I've got you."

She seems afraid to lift her head.

I need to brace her better. I keep one arm around her waist and the other one across her chest so she feels secure. The closeness of her is not lost on me as I pull her away from the tree, and finally she settles her weight onto me instead of the branch.

"Okay. We've got it. Down one step."

Once we're moving together, I'm able to let go of her with one arm and hold on to the ladder. Slowly, we ease down step by step, our bodies flush.

When I reach the ground, I lift her away from the ladder and set her down. "We made it."

She faces away from me, her arms trembling.

"Ensley? You okay?"

She turns around and clutches me, her head in my neck. I don't hesitate, but hold her close. "You're brave. It's not many people who will follow a cat up a tree."

She nods against my shoulder. The sunlight filters through the leaves. It's chilly out, but not cold. Ensley is warm and soft and feels perfect in my arms. Too many competing feelings roll through me.

Tenderness. Concern. Admiration. I give myself a little leeway for my behavior, since we've recently been so close, and slide my hand up her neck into her hair.

She lets out a soft sigh, and when she pulls back to look up at me, kissing her is the most natural action in the world.

This connection is nothing like the one in the shed. That one was mired in rain, bourbon, and anger.

This one is springtime and sunshine and relief. She did what I would do, only she got to it faster, at a greater risk to herself.

Our lips softly caress each other. I resist the temptation to take it deeper, to move out of this tenderness and into the passion I know we can fall into.

Not here. Not now. I do have that much self-control.

But I let myself touch her again, gently, her shoulders, her back, the curve of her waist. The tension drops. A level of relaxation that I rarely know comes over me. Normally to get here, I would have screwed some random woman senseless, and this is the quiet aftermath, a brief period when my body is content.

Strange to feel it now.

I want to touch her face, to draw my fingers along her jaw. But the kiss has gone on too long, and I have to be her boss.

Reluctantly, I pull away. "It's a natural reaction to danger," I say. "Proving we're alive."

Her gaze meets mine. There are leaves in her hair. I reach up to pull them out. "You going to be okay?"

She nods.

"Why don't you take some time to gather yourself?"

"The kittens are okay?" Her voice hitches.

"Perfectly fine. Todd's taking care of them."

"Can I go back and see them?"

"Of course. You rescued their mom. You've earned it."

It would be natural to take her hand as we walk around the front of the clinic, but I know I can't do that.

As I hold the door for her, the Chihuahuas already moved to the exam room by Maria or Todd, I know something's happened here. Something I didn't expect. This is nothing like the women I take out once and then ignore.

This is Ensley. My feelings for her cut straight to the bone.

And not only that, I'm taking her to dinner tonight.

Chapter 21

ENSLEY

I have no idea why I remain so shaken after the tree incident. I picture what I must have looked like, straddling a tree, a cat in my arms, refusing to even look at Drew as he pulled me down.

I was fine going after the cat. But not so fine once I had her. There seemed no way out, no safe way to get down.

But Drew had rescued me.

And that kiss. The way he held me. I had no idea that this grumpy, unyielding man could be so tender.

But now I do.

Maria sends me home early. There are only a couple of more check-ins, and they decide to handle it. I'm worried about agreeing to it, thinking Drew might try to get out of the dinner I insisted on. But about an hour after closing, I get a text message from him.

Drew: So where am I taking you?

Nobody's currently home. Tillie has taken Lila to Walmart to pick up a prescription for her nausea. So it's just me staring at my phone as I reply.

Me: You know Atlanta better than I do.

Drew: What do you like to eat? Italian? Cajun? Barbecue?

Me: Is there good Italian in Atlanta?

Drew: Of course.

Me: Let's do that.

Drew: Should I pick you up?

Me: Okay.

It's nice to have him drive. Something's happened to my nervous system. Maybe it was the last straw, heading up a tree after nearly two weeks of nonstop wildness. I got kicked out of a wedding, stuck in a storm, turned on by a childhood crush, sent wild emails, and started a new job in a new city, while keeping the old job in the old city. No wonder I'm falling apart.

I sort through my clothes. Thankfully, a date with Drew was something I planned for when I packed for a two-day trip that has become a ten-day stay. I pull out the red dress, wondering if it's too much for a Wednesday.

No, I need to go for broke. I have seven days left to figure out if I'm going to pursue this or take my ball and go home.

The dress is silky and slides along my body when I pull it over my head. It falls just below midthigh, so I pair it with black tights and knee boots I thrifted four years ago. They always make an outfit come together. They're my lucky boots.

Now the hair. I go for a half updo, long curls pulled into a twist, and the others gelled within an inch of their life to stay in pretty ringlets rather than frizzing into oblivion.

"Behave," I tell them in the mirror. "Don't make me hair spray you."

Red lipstick the color of the dress pops against my dark hair. I'm ready. Anxious. If Drew doesn't see me as something more than an employee tonight, then this whole experiment has failed, and the fates have decided.

A knock at the door makes me jump. I take one last peek in the mirror to be sure there's no lipstick on my teeth, then head to the living room, picking up my purse on the way. The weather is perfect, chilly but not so cold that I need to ruin the lines of the dress with my puffy coat. It has long sleeves, at least.

When I open the door, I take a step back. Drew wears a charcoal-gray suit, a white shirt, and a deep-blue tie. He looks even better than he did at the wedding.

"Wow," I say. "You're taking this dinner seriously."

His gaze touches on key points of my outfit. "So are you."

I turn in a circle. "Go ahead and gawk. I'm here for your perusal."

When I make it back around, his face is so serious that I think he'll surely say something about our professional relationship again, but he doesn't.

"Red isn't wasted on you."

I grin at him, but his expression is hard, almost pained. Good. I like making him uncomfortable. Knock him off-center.

"Is there any color you can't wear?" he asks.

"You've already forgotten. Navy blue."

"Oh, right. It's for police officers and pilots."

"And I look like death." I lock the door, and we head down the crumbling porch with broken steps. I feel no self-consciousness about the humble house or the fact that my dress cost seven dollars at a thrift store. This is Drew. He knew me when my family barely got fed, when the only clothes were dumpster dives.

For us, *rich* was new clothes, even from Walmart. Food in the fridge between meals. Lights that stayed on. A prepaid mobile phone with minutes left on it.

I'm rich now by those standards. I rarely buy new clothes, because I've adapted my style to my circumstances. But I can do it every once in a while. And I bought doughnuts for my coworkers today. That's super rich. Buying food for somebody else.

I follow Drew to his gleaming black SUV. I grin when he opens the door and realizes there's a cat carrier in the passenger seat and a pile of pet food samples on the floor.

I stand by as he quickly clears it all out with a mumbled, "Sorry."

I love it. Even Drew Daniels can be flustered, can fail to plan ahead.

Eventually I'm in the seat, inhaling the faint smell of dog kibble and the pine air freshener hanging from the rearview mirror. It's comfortable. Clean, but cluttered. The sign of someone with more in his life than being perfect.

"The restaurant is a bit of a drive, but it's worth it," Drew says, peering at the backup camera screen as he reverses into the street.

I settle against the leather. "I don't mind." More time with Drew.

"First time I've left Sasha alone at my place."

"You worried about her?"

"I'm worried about my house."

I can't help but laugh. "Think she'll destroy everything?"

"I think she'll find a million places to hide, and I'll spend half the night looking for her."

He really cares about that cat.

Sasha. For my mother. My heart turns over. "She won't come out when you return?"

"No idea. I've never left her. But she has the terrible habit of squishing herself into places she doesn't belong. This morning I found her sleeping in a tissue box."

"She fit?"

"It was half-empty. It made a great bed."

"If it fits, she sits." The streetlights whiz by as we head onto the highway. "What made you adopt her when you don't usually do that?"

"I don't think I did. She adopted me."

"Well, I'm glad. You two are perfect for each other."

I can barely make out his face in the low light of the car, but I know when he glances over at me. "Same as you and the clinic. I consider it a stroke of luck that you showed up when you did."

Oh, that.

Maybe I should hold on to the truth. It could be that I stay and it never matters that I originally never intended to take the job. I certainly don't want to disrupt this happy feeling. "You seemed to be in such a pinch."

"Did you up and leave your old job? No notice?"

I can tell from his tone that this concerns him.

"We have rotating tellers, so I'm easily replaced." This isn't a lie.

"I see why you wanted something with more meaning," Drew says. "You would be very hard to replace from where I stand."

I know he means at the clinic and not personally, but my silly heart feels hope anyway. I've talked with Tillie about this a million times. Am I confusing my girlhood crush for the man I see now? She thinks so.

But she isn't inside my skin. And that pure, naive love I felt for him when I was twelve rushed right back today after he pulled me down from the tree.

"I told you," I say before I realize it's slipped out.

"Told me what?"

Might as well barrel forward. "That you'd save me."

"From your mundane job in Alabama?" In the low glow of his dashboard lights, his eyebrows move together.

"From the tree."

"I think you would have come down, eventually. The cat would have insisted."

I fiddle with the hem of my skirt. "I suppose." It didn't feel that way at the time. The cat had been howling, clearly as upset as me. Her life was out of control, too. Knocked up, half-starved, babies born in a pipe. Finally in a warm, quiet place, then two barky wild things get up in her business.

"I guess the kittens are at the clinic?" I ask.

"A rescue came for them after you left."

"Oh." Already gone.

"They'll be back. I'm doing their shots and spaying the mother. I'll let you know when they show up, although you'll probably be the one to check them in."

"Good. Did they get names?"

"You can look up the rescue. They'll name them before putting them up for adoption, but that will be weeks yet. If you want a say, I can give you their number."

"That's okay. I just want to know how to refer to them in my mind."

He shakes his head. "You're a sentimental one."

"Says the grumpy vet who insisted he'd never own a cat."

"Touché."

The right turn signal blinks, flashing light into the dark car with a comforting ticktock. We head off the highway toward a lighted row of restaurants and businesses. Looks like the next phase of this date will officially begin.

I'm going to have to bring my A game.

Chapter 22

DREW

I better watch it, or I'm going to slip out of professional territory.

As the hostess seats us at a table tucked in a corner, partially set away from the main dining room by a wall topped with ivy, I wonder if I should have chosen such a romantic spot.

Ensley looks around as if she's never seen a place like this. It *is* upscale. Maybe I'm showing off. Our Alabama town had nothing to compare to this.

The sommelier in a red jacket arrives to discuss our wine options. Ensley rests her elbows on the table, her chin propped on her clasped hands as she listens.

He smiles at her attentiveness.

"Are you a red wine or a white wine person?" I ask Ensley.

She suppresses a giggle. "The last time I chose between red and white wine, I was about to throw it on someone's dress."

The sommelier looks scandalized, and I bite back my smile. "Certainly red is ideal for staining a dress. Is that your preference to drink?" I ask her.

Her long lashes curl against her eyebrows as she gazes up at me. "Sure, let's go with red."

"The bordeaux," I say.

"Very good, sir." The sommelier steps away to fetch the bottle.

Ensley glances around the table. "There's no wine menu. How do you know how much it costs?"

"We probably don't want to know how much it costs."

She shakes her head. "That's crazy."

"The occasional indulgence is fine." But I know what she's thinking. It's probably hard to escape the mindset that was pervasive in her childhood. And Ensley and her family had it hard.

"So we're celebrating you saving my clinic," I say. "In a professional capacity."

Ensley laughs. "I think we should straight up admit that our relationship, no matter what it will be in the future, will never be as professional as it would have been if we'd never known each other as kids, and never gotten trapped in a shed during a storm after being thrown out of the wedding."

The waitress arrives right then and stops short. "I see I have an interesting table over here."

A dark annoyance settles over me. I don't like random strangers knowing my business.

"Oh, Drew," Ensley says. "Don't worry."

She's figured me out. And I don't like that, either.

The waitress sets the evening's menu, artfully typed on a simple cream-colored card, in front of us.

"These are tonight's selections, curated by our chef. May I start you with our Italian escargot in wine sauce or perhaps a pesto bruschetta?"

"Bring them both," I say.

She nods and steps away.

Ensley leans forward. "Doesn't escargot mean snails?" Her face pulls into a grimace. "I used to pick those off the fence after a rain."

My dark mood lightens a bit. "Did you ever salt them and eat them? They're quite delicious."

Her mouth drops open.

"I kid. I kid. You've never had escargot?"

She shakes her head. "But I'm game. Isn't escargot French?"

"Usually. But you'll find all sorts of things on the menu here."

I can tell by her sudden frown that she thinks I come here often. "It's my mother's favorite place to eat in Atlanta."

She seems placated and scans the small card. "It's definitely not the menu at Olive Garden."

Now I'm back to smiling. What is this about her?

She turns the card over. "No prices on this, either. How can I order the cheapest thing on the menu to avoid looking like a gold digger if I don't even know what they cost?"

Her concern doesn't surprise me in the least. These were all things said to girls growing up where we did. If your economic circumstance was lower than the person you went out with, obviously you were doing it for the money. If you had more, you were showing off. You couldn't win.

"Nobody's judging you here," I say. "Enjoy yourself. Go with the flow."

She lifts her chin. "Did I just hear Drew Daniels, the grumpiest veterinarian in the state of Georgia, tell me to *go with the flow*?"

She's got me there. "Just trying to help."

Her finger slides along the edge of the card. "I'm afraid I need to google all these things to even know what they are. I don't want to accidentally eat candied brains or something. It's what happens on all the TV shows when a lowbrow girl like me steps into a joint like this."

"I'm happy to explain." I run down all the options, from sauces with admittedly complex Italian descriptions to the braised meat and seafood.

"What's the most decadent pasta on this list?" she asks.

"Tagliatelle alla bolognese. It's an egg pasta with a rich meat sauce. You'll swoon."

"That's it."

The sommelier returns with our wineglasses and the bordeaux. Ensley is rapt as he opens the bottle, pouring only a small amount in the glass next to me.

She frowns. "So only the *man* gets to sniff and swoosh? I watch TV. I know what to do."

I slide the glass across the linen tablecloth to her. "All yours."

She rotates the glass, lifting it high to watch the wine swirl. She brings it to her nose for a proper sniff, then takes a small sip.

Her eyes go wide. "Oh my God. That's better than sex!"

I have to hold back a snort, but the sommelier is not fazed. "Very good," he says.

Ensley sets down the glass, and he fills it, then mine. He rests the bottle, wrapped in linen, in a silver bucket and leaves us to it.

"I shouldn't've said that, huh?" Ensley asks.

"I think it amused him."

"I'm not exactly a twenty-year-old ingenue."

She's such a study in contrasts. In one moment, she's self-conscious about her upbringing, and the next taking over a wine approval and using words like *ingenue*. I could never get bored with her.

I lift my glass and hold it up. "To your new position at my clinic," I say.

She bites her lip as if something's wrong, but she clinks her glass against mine. "To the future."

We both take a drink, and she sighs in contentment. "This would probably set me back a day's pay, but it sure is good."

"I'm glad."

My treacherous eyes pause on places they shouldn't, not as her boss. The skin revealed by the wide neckline, her delicate collarbone, the fit of her dress. I endeavor to instead study the deep color of the wine in my glass.

When I look up, Ensley is watching me. "Do you think things will ever change for you?"

I have no idea what she means. "In what way?"

"The one-night stands. You said that's all you do. It sounds dumb to me. Why just one? Is it riskier to go out with them three times? Isn't there a point at which you can say, *Uh-oh, I'm falling for her fatal charms. Maybe I should quit before it's too late?*"

"Well, when you put it that way—"

"In fact, this entire thing seems ludicrous. It's as if you have no control over yourself." She uses a deep tone as if she's speaking for me. "I'm dating this woman. I see her a lot, therefore I can never call my male friends again." She taps her finger on the table. "From what I've seen so far, you don't even *have* any male friends. Your work schedule is absolutely insane. Who are you giving up relationships *for?*"

She has me there. It's been eight years since undergrad, and five since veterinary school. All the friends I played football with, or were my roommates, or even met at sports bars or billiards, have moved on.

I'm pretty much the lone bachelor in my circles.

Who am I doing it for?

The tiny thread of a notion that maybe it was because of her tries to wind its way into my thoughts, but I brusquely shove it aside.

"It's the principle of the matter—" I begin, but she cuts me off again.

"It's the cult of Drew Daniels, who shalt forsake all good women in the name of a bachelorhood life that no longer even exists."

Anger simmers forth. Who the hell is she to question my choices at this dinner she forced me to ask her on?

I harden my expression to show she's in the danger zone. But she holds my gaze and gives me a hard look right back. "I'm going to challenge you," she says.

"This better not be one of your positivity shticks."

Her eyes sparkle with mischief. "You're taking me on three dates. Not just one. Three. To break the spell. You can see that it changes nothing. You'll still go to work every day like you always did. You'll have the same conversations, watch the same TV programs. There will be only one addition to your life."

"What is that?"

She glances to the left and the right to make sure no one's coming, then leans forward. A good amount of cleavage pushes above the table, but I refuse to focus on it.

"We'll finish what we started. We can do it on every date, if you want. Or only once. But there will be three dates. You commit to three."

Something quivers deep inside me at the very idea. And I never quiver. "And if I don't?"

"I quit working for you. My job is over as of right now. You're back where you started."

"You wouldn't dare."

"I'm totally daring. I'm daring you to three dates with me in the next seven days, with benefits if we mutually choose."

Alarm bells ring in my head. I shouldn't do this. Not with her. Especially not with her. This is no time to test the rules that have kept me careful all these years. "This is completely unprofessional."

"So is hiring the chick you finger-banged at a wedding."

When I almost snort my wine, she shrugs, swirling her glass.

I manage to regain my composure. She can't really want this. What does this dare mean to her? What does she want from me?

She keeps her gaze fixed on my face, waiting on an answer.

I clear my throat as if none of this is important to me, the whole question a mere nuisance. "And what if, at the end of these three dates, your heart is broken? Are you going to be able to do your job?"

"Not an issue," she says. "My heart is not what's on the table." She leans forward again. "Just my lady bits."

All right, then. Maybe I have nothing to worry about. If Ensley James wants to finish our night in the shed, not once but up to three times, no strings attached, I'll indulge myself, same as I'm doing with this dinner.

I scoot closer to the table, because at the very thought of her naked beneath me again, my dick is not in my control.

It's probably that same part of my anatomy talking when I finally say to her, "You're on."

Chapter 23

ENSLEY

Well, that was a nutty proposition I made, but it solves all my problems.

I'll see Drew more often. It falls within my time limit.

And I put sex on the table.

I might regret that if we go there tonight, mainly because I ate so much pasta. By the time we go out to Drew's car after the meal, the wine, and the most outrageous Italian wedding cake, I feel done for.

As I strap the seat belt over my food baby, I wonder if I even want to get naked right now. I'm completely self-conscious.

And unsure.

Our crazy moment in the shed came naturally.

Anything we do tonight feels forced.

Did I really insist that our three dates could have benefits?

What am I doing here? What do I want?

But I know. I want the twelve-year-old dream for Drew to be mine, even if only for a little while.

We've been driving about ten minutes when his booming voice in the quiet startles me. "So does the end of dinner mean we're done with the date? Or should there be more?"

Does he mean sex? Or more normal date stuff?

My talkative superpower is failing me. I stare out the window at the passing lights streaking through the dark.

"Now whose tongue has been eaten by a cat?" he asks.

That makes me whip my head around. "So gross! I wish I never knew that!"

"Got you talking."

Harrumph. "Are you using my own tactics on me?"

"I'm learning from the master."

That placates me. "I think we should take a walk. Somewhere picturesque. What does Atlanta have?"

He glances over at me. "You might get chilly in that dress."

"Then you will be a gentleman and provide me your jacket."

"All right." He signals to change lanes, even though there are no cars anywhere nearby. I smile inwardly. Drew Daniels does everything by the book.

We exit the freeway and make a U-turn.

"Thought of a location?" I ask.

"Yep."

No more details are forthcoming.

I don't have long to wait. We exit again, and soon a park surrounds us. Wide expanses of green space end with a path along a small lake. Several people stroll under the streetlamps, mostly walking dogs. Drew finds a spot along the street and kills the car. "This work?"

"It looks beautiful."

We walk along a broad path. The lake reflects the lights of the cityscape of downtown Atlanta. It's breathtaking.

We haven't walked very far when the chill bites into me. I hide it for a while, but as we cross a wooden bridge over the water, a gust of wind brushes my hair back, and I wind up hugging my arms over my body.

Drew takes off his suit jacket and wraps it around my shoulders, buttoning the front. My arms are still inside.

"Like a straitjacket?" I ask.

"Like a straitjacket." His grin knocks me backward. It's so rare, and it lights up his face. A girl could totally fall in love with a smile like that.

The jacket smells of him. I breathe it in. Sandalwood aftershave. I only know what it's called because I used to rip cologne samples out of the magazines in the art teacher's room. She had tons of *Glamour* and *Cosmopolitan*, and there were always ads with little folded pages that gave you the beautiful scent of some expensive bottle when you pulled the pieces apart.

She mostly censored the magazines before giving them to the students to make collages or use for tracings. But occasionally there would be a survey about how many times your man had stimulated your clitoris. Ronnie and I were known to fold these up in our pockets when we encountered them so we could pore over them later.

Unlike me, Ronnie had a mom growing up. So when she asked her how to stimulate her clitoris, her mother immediately took her to the clinic to get on the pill. It was years before she needed it, but I distinctly recall being jealous that she had someone who had her back like that, no questions asked. All because of a stolen page from an art teacher's magazine.

I shouldn't think of clitoris and Drew at the same time. The smell of him all around me is definitely taking me back to the night in the shed.

The walkway is well lit, and a woman with two gray puffs of hair tweaked into springy ponytails brushes past us with a white poodle sporting a matching hairstyle.

We both turn to watch them walk away and manage to withhold any laughter until she is well out of earshot.

"You could dye your hair white to match Sasha," I say to Drew. My urge is to reach up and ruffle his hair, but my arms are imprisoned.

"It will happen soon enough."

"Has your dad gone gray?"

His expression falters immediately, and I wish I could take the question back. Maybe Drew has an irrational fear of going gray. Eventually, he says, "He has."

Note to self: don't bring up going gray.

We pass a tree that branches out low to the ground. It would be an easy step up. I point it out. "If only mama cat had gone up a tree like that. I wouldn't have had a problem."

Drew assesses the branches. "But she could have gotten a lot higher. Why did she stop? Is that how you caught up to her?"

I nod. "She took off in a dead run, but a car went by and scared her into stopping. I almost scooped her up in the parking lot, but then she darted toward the building. Thankfully, she hesitated on that branch, so I could snatch her before she got any farther. Otherwise I would've lost her."

"Did you know you had a fear of heights?"

"I don't think I do. I used to climb trees all the time as a kid. It was something about not being able to hold on with both hands. And fear of losing the cat. It triggered something in me."

"You did a great job. It's not a situation that will happen often. We rarely have loose cats in the lobby, especially if dogs will be arriving."

"It's surprising to me it was only earlier today when we were up a tree. It feels like days ago."

And he'd kissed me. Would he again?

I want my arms back, so I wriggle them until they slide inside the jacket sleeves. My fingertips barely come out at the ends. Crisp winter leaves litter the path, and they crunch as we walk over them. I wonder if I should just get it all out. Confess that I still have a job. Tell him I'm trying to figure out if we have chemistry.

The words are forming in the back of my throat when our fingers brush against each other, and I'm silenced by the electric jolt I feel.

He takes my hand in his, warm and large enough to envelop mine whole. "So we're on a date," he says.

I squeeze his fingers, my confession set aside. "It's nice." I hesitate to bring up the next topic, but I get the words out. "So how do your one-night stands go? Do you somehow manipulate the evening so that it's a sure thing at the end?"

He clears his throat. "This doesn't seem like the right thing to talk about."

"I'm curious. And I also want to watch for the signs. If you're steering me into your bed, I kinda want to know in advance."

"I am absolutely going to steer you into my bed."

Is he? My belly warms over, sparks of interest darting through my body. "Oh?"

"You said all three dates were with benefits. Change your mind?"

I swallow around my dry throat. "No."

"Good." Despite the intimacy of the conversation, his eyes remain on the path ahead.

"How does it normally go?" I ask. "You know, to get there?"

His jaw works back and forth, as if he's trying to explain it properly. "It starts pretty typically, like ours. I would probably lay it on heavier when I picked her up. Press her against the door when I kiss her."

I can picture it. My heart hammers. "And that works?"

"Sometimes it works right then. We never even make it to dinner and end up ordering in."

"You didn't do that with me."

"We hadn't established that it was a date. It was a boss and employee situation until the main course, remember."

"Right." I feel disgruntled that I missed out. "And then?"

"If that doesn't do the trick right away, often I will take her to a very suggestive place for dinner, such as the restaurant on top of one of the fanciest hotels."

"Not like our Italian restaurant."

"Nope. That was a platonic dinner, a place I go with my mother."

My belly sinks. He associates me with his mother.

"I will establish a bold level of attentiveness, and somewhere during the dinner I will progress to touching, sliding my hand up her—"

"I get it. I'm good. I understand."

"You asked."

"And I'm done asking."

We walk along for a few quiet minutes. The cold starts to get to me, even with his jacket, and my knees quiver. My nose runs and I sniffle. Yes, I'm totally worthy of his kissing-against-the-door act. Pathetic little thrift-store me with my runny nose and terrible timing.

"You're cold," he says. He lets go of my hand and draws me closer. "If you're ready to head back, I could throw you over my shoulder like I did at the wedding."

I hiccup-laugh. "That was terrible."

He grins, and in the lamplight, I'm almost knocked backward by his face, that strong jawline, the perfect teeth. And his lips. My eyes keep returning to that mouth.

He chuckles. "I think it was something like this."

Before I realize what he's doing, he's hoisted me on his shoulder. I smack his back with both hands. "Drew! You're going to wreck another hairdo!"

"Oh, it's going to get wrecked." He takes long strides, and I realize his hands are sliding up my skirt, gliding along the tights until he grips my butt.

That definitely didn't happen last time. "Where are you taking me?"

"Out of the wind."

I can't see where we're going, but it's not the direction of the car.

"This will do," he says.

I have no idea what he means until he turns around, and I see a park bench tucked along the tree line. There's a lamp beside it, but the bulb is out. It's noticeably less cold with the windbreak of the trees.

He sits down, pushing the dress up my thighs so my knees can separate and straddle him as he lets me slide down his chest to rest on his lap.

This is something.

Sitting face-to-face, my knees surrounding him, feels more intimate than the shed, because we are connected in so many places. My thighs press on his, and I'm situated directly on his crotch.

"So do you usually—" But I don't get the question out, because he silences me with a kiss.

And not just any kiss. A movie screen kiss, one of his hands behind my head, his thumb pressing against my throat. His mouth falls on mine diagonally, teasing my lips with the pressure of his.

His tongue runs along them until I open for him, and his breath mingles with mine.

He tastes of wine and cake. I wrap my arms around his neck and draw him closer. His fingers entangle in my hair, which has hopelessly fallen from the clips.

I feel weightless, lost, as if space exists differently on this bench. My entire body warms over as blood rushes to my skin.

His mouth continues to explore mine, but his hands begin to move. He unbuttons the front of his jacket, and his hands splay over my ribs.

They take in the curve of my waist and clasp my hips, rocking me against him.

I feel the hard bulge beneath me and tilt myself to increase the pressure where we connect.

He's got me. I get it now, the one-nighters. When you're here, you aren't going to say no to Drew Daniels.

I'm already completely willing to do whatever he asks. Naked on a bench in a public park? I might be down.

His hands continue their exploration, this time running up the front of the silky dress to cup my breasts. I suck in a breath. Drew has touched me before, and seen me, too. The unzipped coveralls gave him all the access.

But now everything is heightened. His magnetism is irresistible. Every touch makes me feel like I'm perfect and beautiful, everything he wants.

He breaks the kiss, sliding his mouth along my cheek and jaw and down to my collarbone.

I arch to him, wanting more contact, more everything.

I realize I am dressed terribly for a park bench in public. The dress has a back zipper, difficult to access under his jacket. I'm wearing tights and boots. There's no way for me to get to him.

As his hands run all over my body, I can tell he's drawing the same conclusion.

"I didn't think this through," he says.

"Me neither."

He wraps his arms around me beneath the jacket, holding me close. Our heartbeats slam against each other. I want so much more.

"Let's take this up again Friday night," he says. "When there isn't work the next day. The things I want to do to you might last until morning."

I shiver against him. "Okay."

He holds me a moment more, then shifts forward to help me down. I slide off his lap and stand.

We walk tightly together back to the car. I feel incredibly alive, and the cold doesn't penetrate.

So this is how the magic happens. Why women fall. He works them, makes their bodies sing. There's undoubtedly been a long line of them who've taken this walk with him. I'm not sure I'll be any different in the end, a hit-and-run, loot-and-scoot.

But I have one thing they didn't.

Three dates.

Chapter 24

DREW

I am playing with a brush fire named Ensley James.

Focusing on my veterinary work the next day is impossible with Ensley so close. We have a slew of annual exams, so I am tasked with entering room after room, facing pet owner after pet owner, smiling, talking, making chitchat while I do the part that I prefer, greeting their animals and making sure that they are healthy.

It's exhausting.

By lunchtime, I can't stand it. Even though the lobby is not ordinarily on my walking path in the back rooms of the clinic, I pass through just to get a look at Ensley.

When I pop out of the hall, Ensley's on the phone. Maria told me she loaned Ensley a pair of scrubs to see if she liked them, and sure enough, she's wearing a pale-blue set. I smile inwardly that they're blue. But they're not *navy* blue. I remember her saying *I look like death* when she wears that color.

I'm generally ambivalent about whether the receptionist dresses like the rest of us or wears street clothes. But I have to say, she rocks the scrubs. Even in my brief walk toward her desk, every asset that I felt in my hands last night seems accentuated by the soft fabric.

I have to clench my jaw and will my body to obey me as I pass by.

She's busily scribbling a note, the phone receiver in her hand, but she glances up. That moment our eyes lock is like an electric shock.

I've never felt this way merely by being in the same room as someone. This is voodoo.

I head into an exam room to finish out the circle. Apparently I'm just in time. Todd is muscling a nearly two-hundred-pound bullmastiff out the back door.

The owner is apologizing. "I'm so sorry. Calamity hates shots."

"Don't worry," Todd grunts. "We'll get him done."

I jump in behind to help steer the massive dog to the treatment space. It's going to be all hands on deck to tame the overweight beast who seems afraid of everything and keeps skittering about the floor, trying to get purchase with his claws. "Maria," I call. "We could use your help."

She sets down the folder she's writing in and hustles over.

I kneel on the floor in front of him, trying to connect with his warm brown eyes. He's scared, that much is clear. "You're okay, Calamity," I say soothingly, running my thumb across his brow. Massive strings of saliva drip from his mouth.

Todd folds over his back, holding his chest and front legs. "I set the shot on the counter. There was no way to do it alone."

Maria fetches it and closes in near the dog's massive hindquarters. She touches random spots, trying to get him desensitized so that the needle prick will be less noticeable.

"Look at me, you big lug," I say to the dog. "You're okay." I press both thumbs into the pressure points that will calm him.

"Going in," Maria says. She taps a few more spots, then inserts the needle.

Calamity's eyes go wide, and he erupts in a startled yelp.

I hold his collar with both hands, every muscle straining to keep him in place. "You're okay, boy. You're okay."

He pushes on his back legs.

"You out?" I ask Maria, not daring to look away from his face.

Maria steps back. "I'm out. We're good."

"Ease off him," I tell Todd. "Gently and slowly release the pressure, but keep a firm grip."

Todd does as instructed.

Calamity tries to push off again, but we have him surrounded. "You ready to go back to Mom?" I ask him. "Maria, treat?"

She sets the needle aside and moves toward the jar of oversize milk bones.

"It's a big treat for a big boy," I say.

She passes me the bone, and even though it's the size of my hand, Calamity downs it in two chomps.

"No exam on this one?" I ask Todd.

He holds on to the lead attached to the dog harness. "Just a shot."

I help them all the way to the back door of the exam room, and then Todd takes it from there.

I'm glad that's over. I'm about to head to my office when I realize I have Calamity slobber all over my hands. I pause by the sink, but only turn on the water before I catch a flash of pale-blue scrubs. Ensley.

I swiftly wash and dry my hands and head toward the hall. She's at the pharmacy, speaking to Vera about a question from a caller.

I step inside my office, thinking I'll get to some paperwork, but when she comes out, only inches from my door, an instinct takes over, and I reach out and grab her hand.

"Drew? I mean Dr. Daniels?"

I drag her inside the room and close the door.

Within moments, I have her pressed against the wall, my mouth on hers. I've been desperate for the taste of her since I woke up this morning.

Her mouth is all cinnamon gum, and she smells of hand lotion and pet treats. It might be the most perfect combination I've ever encountered.

Our tongues linger together, and I lean into her, wanting to feel every curve after the glimpse I got in the lobby.

I didn't get to touch her skin last night, not in the dress and the tights, so my hands slip beneath the cotton top, my fingers sliding along her ribs.

She sucks in a breath, her chest heaving against mine.

Front-hook bra. I can't resist. I snap it open and fill my hands with her breasts. The nipples harden and elongate, and I revel in the feel of them as my thumbs cross over the puckered buds.

I grind my hips against hers. We shouldn't have waited. I should've taken her right then on the bench, ripped those tights out of the way, and kept to my standard of one night only.

Even if I owed her two more dates, I could have done anything, something terribly public, something short. Kept it in my head that they weren't dates, they were random occasions we happened to be in the same place, just like work.

I want her to be like all the others. To flash with heat, to take her, and then to move on.

Stretching it out like this is painful. It takes up too much of my mental energy.

I want to punish her for these thoughts of mine, for making me ache when I normally never do. My mouth owns hers, pressing in, our tongues tangled, breath mingling.

But she breaks the kiss. "Dr. Daniels."

I kiss her again, shutting her out.

She pushes against me. "Dr. Daniels."

"You don't want this?" I growl at her.

"I do. I really do. But the phone. It's ringing. That's my job."

Shit. I take a step away.

She dashes around my desk and picks up the line. "Daniels Vet Care, this is Ensley. How can I help you and your sweet fur baby today?"

That's her spin on the way to answer. It fits her.

She glances up at me, then presses her hand to her chest. She's breathing fast.

"I see. I would be worried, too. When did it start?"

I run my hands through my hair. Her bra is still unfastened, the taut nipples poking against the fabric of her shirt.

I have to turn away.

This is torture. Of course it is. This isn't some random woman. It's Ensley.

I'm in over my head.

"I think Dr. Daniels is between patients right now. Can you hold for a second, and I'll see if I can get him?"

She places the call on hold, setting down the receiver.

"Anne Watkins is calling about her fourteen-year-old husky. Apparently, he hasn't been able to pee for two days. She's on line one."

I nod. "I'll take it."

She walks around the desk. I brush past her to take my chair. I have to focus.

Ensley pauses by the door, reaching beneath her shirt to fasten the bra again. I see a flash of her smooth belly and have to clench my fist.

"I should have left you alone," I say. "That won't happen again."

She turns to me, hand on the doorknob. "It *better* happen again."

And then she's gone.

Chapter 25

ENSLEY

Screw dating. I want to bang Drew Daniels in his office.

I stay away for the rest of Thursday, but when Friday morning rolls around, I've had way too many dreams of naked Drew to resist walking by his office every chance I get.

Fridays are only a half day of patients. In the afternoon, we have back-to-back surgical procedures.

This means I have tons of extra time to go wandering the halls.

It also means he's often in surgery.

I should wait. Not push my luck. We have our date tonight. There is zero doubt about what's going to happen.

But I want more. I want a preview of coming attractions. It'll be fun to start the foreplay hours beforehand.

In one of my infinite laps down the hall past Drew's office, he's in there.

I shouldn't be forward. I should let him do all the manhandling.

Right?

Hell no.

This girl goes after what she wants.

I step inside his office and close the door.

He watches me walk around his desk.

"Ensley." His tone is a warning.

"Hello, Dr. Daniels. My boss." Just saying it makes a hot thrill bolt through me.

He spins in his chair to face me, and screw it, I straddle him.

I don't need to make the next move. He's on me, his hand on the back of my neck, dragging my face to his.

I'm lost in his kiss again, my heart pounding, the ground sweeping out from under me.

His reaction is instant, and I press down into the delicious feel of his erection against the seam of my jeans.

This morning I raided Lila's closet and borrowed a shirt with a line of pearl buttons. And trust me, I thought this one through. I could picture him unfastening them one by one.

And now he's doing it, letting out a happy *"mmm"* upon discovering the front-hook bra again.

I want him to see me, to feel me. I want his mouth all over me.

He knows. He's got my number. Once my skin is bared to him, his mouth is everywhere. I clutch his head to my chest, his mouth surrounding my nipple. It's his office. The other employees are mere yards away in the treatment space. I didn't even lock the door.

I'm on fire.

Hell yeah, I'll quit my old job. I'll move here. I'll do this work for free, dammit, just for this.

The feeling is unbelievable. This must be what drugs are like. Heroin, speed. I don't even know the names of other drugs.

It doesn't matter. I don't need them.

I have Drew Daniels.

I'm so wet, my panties are clinging to me with how I press against him.

His hands grip my butt, rocking me up and down.

I gasp. "Please tell me someday you're going to finish the job right here on this desk."

He groans. "Trying not to do it right now."

"You said you would make me scream," I say.

"That's absolutely my intention."

But then there are voices in the hall. It's Vera and Maria talking.

He presses his face against my naked chest. "No screaming today. We can't keep doing this."

"Oh yes, we can. It's painful but so damn hot."

His eyes flash up at me. I love this vision of him, face buried against my chest. His rough whiskers chafe against my skin.

"Ensley James, you are going to kill me."

"What a way to go."

The voices recede toward the lobby. They'll soon notice we're both missing. With a reluctant sigh, I slide off his lap, swiftly clasping the bra and buttoning the shirt.

He watches me, his jaw set.

I open the door, ready for the ruse. "I'll get those files done and close out the register for the week."

He nods.

Maria walks up to the door and waits for me to leave.

"If I don't talk to you again, I'll see you Monday." I step aside so Maria can go in the office.

I keep my composure until I'm alone in the lobby.

Is this really my life? I've never felt like this before.

And I don't think Drew has, either.

Tonight, we'll get to do it all.

~

Both of my sisters help me get ready for date two. We've always been all up in each other's business, so Tillie sorts through my bras and panties to choose the right ones for tonight.

"Definitely the thong," she says. "Guys lose it over a thong."

"But it doesn't match the bra. He digs the front hook." I lift the pink one that has made Drew crazy twice now.

"Tillie's right, give him something different," Lila says. "I think I have a cute one. I can't wear my old bras anymore, anyway." She presses against her boobs. "Sore and swollen. I don't think I'll even look at another underwire for a year."

While she's gone, Tillie lifts the dress that I bought from a thrift store after work. It's designed to get his attention, shimmery gold with sheer long sleeves. The skirt is the same gold fabric at first, but it quickly disintegrates into a mix of solid and sheer strips that make you wonder how much of a peek you're getting when I walk.

I feel grateful to have found it. It's a size too big, but I made a swift hand-stitched alteration of it half an hour ago. One thing you get good at when you love thrifting is quick and dirty alterations.

"This looks like a dress for sex." Tillie plucks at the sheer sections of the skirt. "Maybe a thong is risky."

"It covers my butt. And I'm totally banging Drew Daniels tonight. It's a miracle it didn't happen on his desk."

She sets the dress down. "You're playing with fire, sister."

"I'm kind of enjoying the heat."

"At least you have an out. If it doesn't work past this weekend, you head back to Alabama. I'll already be there. I have to finish out my last shifts at the old job and pack my room."

I sit on the corner of the bed. For the first time, I realize that my failure here means that I will also lose my sister time. I'll be getting an apartment to live in by myself. And I will have lost Drew.

That can't happen.

"I won't fail," I assure her. "I'm pretty sure Drew's acting in ways he's not used to. I know I am. It's got to mean something."

"It means you both want to get laid," she says.

"Hell yeah," Lila says as she reenters the room, but she's empty-handed. "None of my crappy cheap bras would work. But I was thinking, do you need one at all?" She gestures at my chest.

"I'm not twenty anymore."

Tillie laughs. "Right. Because twenty-six is so much older."

I smoosh my hands against my boobs. "You don't think I'm sagging?"

Lila shakes her head. "Girl, you are not sagging a bit." She points at her chest. "These are sagging."

"They are not!" I say.

"While I love the comparative boob talk," Tillie says, "I think I'll go watch TV."

Lila picks up a pillow to toss at her. "You're jealous because you're a quadruple A."

Tillie tugs on her cropped shirt self-consciously. "I got passed over when God was handing out the boobs."

"You're fine," I say. "But I don't know if I'm no-bra material."

"Just do it. Get that boy candy," Tillie says.

Lila nods in agreement.

Oh, I plan to.

~

This time Drew's car is immaculate. I can smell the window cleaner and the rug shampoo, and a new bone-shaped air freshener hangs from the rearview mirror.

I don't hold back my grin. He did this for me. I sing the line inside my head. *For me. For me. For me, me, me.*

He's about to close the door when he leans in instead. "I couldn't say this in front of your sisters, but damn, I'm ready to tear that dress off you."

Sparks shoot through my whole body. "Be my guest."

Drew clutches the top of the door with an iron grip, as if he has to control himself. I love it. I arrange the strips of the skirt around my thighs as I sit down. His eyes are glued to my every movement.

I part them at the highest point to reveal a narrow band at the top of the glittery stockings. "Thigh-highs," I say. "In the event of park benches."

He closes his eyes, as if he can't handle the sight of them.

I settle back against the seat. I never feel this bold. I'm the awkward one. But Drew is drawing it out of me. I'm so alive, I swear I could wave my hands and move the stars.

He finally closes the door and walks around the front of the car.

And yeah, I see it. There's an extra bulge in those dress pants.

It's chillier tonight, so I have a fluffy white bolero jacket that covers my shoulders and arms. It comes together with a loop and button, which means it's covering the fact that I'm not wearing a bra. For now. As Drew starts the car and we head out of Lila's neighborhood, I wonder exactly when I'll reveal that detail.

Plus the bonus one under the skirt.

This man is mine. I can feel it.

It's been a long time since I slept with anyone. Tony Marini, almost a year ago. We dated something like six months before I figured out that he would never do more than call me on random Saturday nights for dinner and a hookup. When a month went by without even that, I finally went to the Enterprise Rent-A-Car where he worked and asked him, *What's the deal?*

He said he couldn't handle my newfound toxic positivity. It made him feel mean.

Whatever.

Tony was a normal temperament, otherwise. Compared to Drew he was practically a cheerleader. The vastness between my attitude and Drew's is at least ten orders of magnitude.

And yet, here we are.

We were more like each other when we were growing up. I had a lot of attitude. But maybe now we are so far apart that the opposites are finally attracting.

Chapter 26

DREW

I'm distracted all to hell by Ensley's outfit tonight. Damn. Her wardrobe is always electric, but that gold dress that falls apart into strips is something else. I almost don't want to take her anywhere but home. If any man looks at her for more than half a second, I'm going to smash a fist into his face.

"Where to tonight?" Ensley asks.

"An Asian fusion place."

"What made you pick that?"

I flip the signal to enter the highway. "A new experience for you. I thought we could make the most of the variety Atlanta has to offer."

"What does Asian fusion mean?"

"They base it in Asian cuisine, but add flairs from other countries, like Ethiopia or Brazil."

She frowns. "Will I be eating candied brains?"

A deep laugh bursts out. Ensley is good at getting those out of me. "It's always possible."

"I'd eat brains for you."

Would she now? I want to make a sexual quip about it, same as I might with any woman I was about to seduce into my bed, but I can't do it. Ensley's words aren't meant to be part of a ploy. She means it.

I manage to get out a curt, "You won't have to."

The restaurant isn't far, and we're seated in a secluded spot as I requested when I made the reservation. I should sit across from her to keep things easy while we're having dinner, but my body isn't paying any attention to logic. As soon as she's settled, I'm next to her, and my hand is already sliding up that silky stocking to finger the elastic.

We chat about work, and Sasha, and the kittens we rescued. The anticipation hangs over us as if dinner is just a formality, a framework to hang our next behavior on. It's like eating your vegetables to get the dessert.

We walk close together back to my car. I have no intention of breaking my touch on her until morning.

I intend to step aside to let her get seated, but my hand brushes her waist and I'm not waiting any longer to get this evening started. I press her against the door, claiming her mouth in ways that have already become a habit this week.

She wraps her arms around my neck. She tastes like the food we ate, heaping platters we shared. I sense when her resistance drops away, her body fitting against mine in the parking lot.

When our mouths are warm with each other's breath, I finally manage to step back. Time to move on. "My place, then?"

Her eyes glitter as she looks up at me and nods.

When she slides onto the seat, my hands are reluctant to leave her. I guide her knee into place, sliding down the stockings to her calf. "This will be my mouth in a moment."

She shivers in the gold dress. I know how she feels. We've had unfinished business for weeks.

It's time.

The drive home feels eternally long.

I try to see the neighborhood, then my condo complex, through her eyes. It's orderly, well kept, the white stone impersonal perhaps. Ensley would splash color everywhere.

I click us into my garage.

"Whoa!" she says. "Since when do places like this have private garages?" She stares out the window like a kid.

"It's an option. Most people use the covered parking."

"But not Dr. Drew Daniels."

We pull inside. Ensley bends down to take it in. "You could shoot a home magazine spread in your garage."

It's probably cleaner than most. I'll give her that. "I don't use it much."

She fiddles with the strips of her skirt as I shut the garage door. I wonder if she's nervous. If now that we're here, she's having second thoughts.

I don't normally have this moment. I don't bring women to my home. Our trysts happen at hotels, or occasionally at her place.

Ensley's different, my head warns.

Too late, I tell it.

Ensley still peers out the window.

"You okay?" I ask.

"Sure," she says. "Just taking in the spot Drew Daniels calls home." She flashes a smile. "And to spend time with my mother's namesake."

I head out of the car, and we meet by the back door. "You will get plenty of her here. She doesn't like to be alone, and she might be jealous of any attention I pay to you."

Ensley giggles as I open my door. "We'll have to find a way to share you."

We pass through the laundry room, and Ensley looks everything over, from the gleaming white washer and dryer to an overflowing basket of workout clothes, scrubs, and white lab coats. "Tomorrow's laundry day," I say.

"It's all good," she says. "You're neat."

I take her hand as we move into the kitchen. "Now you get to see where I truly live."

The kitchen is definitely not pristine. There are pots I didn't get to this afternoon. A dish rack next to the sink is piled high with washed and rinsed dishes that weren't dry enough to put away before I left. The sideboard is full of apples, bananas, avocados, and potatoes. "I like to keep things handy."

"So you cook?" she asks.

"Only on the weekends. I get in too late during the week."

She seems shocked. "But you do it."

"Sure. Something about the alchemy of assembling random things and making a dish appeals to me."

She wanders the kitchen, pausing to pick up a spatula or straighten a towel. Is she nervous?

I can cure that.

I fall in behind her. "I've been thinking about something." I circle her waist with my hands.

She looks over her shoulder at me. "What's that?"

"Making you come on this counter." I turn her to face me and lift her by the waist to set her on it. "Like this." I grab both her knees and whip them wide.

She sucks in a breath.

I step forward and our bodies connect. Then my mouth is on hers.

Kissing her has become familiar, like a favorite song played over and over again. In the shed. By the tree. In my office. In the restaurant parking lot.

Only now there will be no interruptions.

I slide my hands along her thighs, slipping my fingers in the gentle elastic of the stockings. There are straps that lead up, so I follow them to the bend of her hips, my thumbs slipping down between her legs.

But instead of finding a silky pair of panties, they press against warm skin.

My dick jumps into gear. Damn, that's hot. I let out a groan. "You haven't been wearing panties all night?"

Her breath feathers my cheek. "Nope."

The growl is next, because I'm not waiting one more moment for what I want. I slip two fingers inside her with one hand, circling her clit with the thumb of the other.

She cries out, so wet and ready. Her arms clutch at my shoulders. I remember this expression, this feel of her. I want to know the sounds she makes, the feel of her body when she loses control.

Nothing will get in the way.

Except, I hear the tiniest sound.

Ensley must hear it, too, because she goes still.

I pause, and we both simply breathe for long seconds. My hand is inside her, and her muscles clench around me.

I'm about to pass it off as nothing when she asks, "Where is Sasha? Doesn't she greet you when you come home?"

"Most cats ignore their owners unless they want something."

We wait another moment, and assuming it's nothing, I kiss her again, my fingers pressing inside her.

But the sound returns. The faintest mew.

I withdraw my hand from Ensley. "Okay, that's the cat."

"She sounds far away," she says. "Is she locked in a room?"

"I'll check." This has certainly never happened to me before. Cockblocked by a cat.

I help Ensley down and stride quickly through the living room. Both of the bedroom doors are open, and so are both bathrooms. I open all the closet doors. She isn't trapped in a room.

Ensley calls for her throughout the condo. I head for the treats, crinkling the foil bag. This always makes her come running.

But she doesn't.

Now I'm alarmed. Ensley comes up behind me. "I haven't heard her in a while."

"Me neither."

We hold still. Nothing.

We search and search. Under beds. Behind the sofa. I open drawers and go through the garage and even the car in case she hopped in when we came out.

I return to the kitchen, the only place we heard her. Ensley comes up beside me to hold my hand.

Then finally, I hear it.

Mew.

"I think she's in here somewhere," Ensley says.

I get down on hands and knees, listening.

And there it is again, the faintest meow.

"Open all the cabinets," I tell Ensley.

We swing all the doors, pushing aside pots and pans and plastic bowls. But no Sasha.

The noise, though, makes her cries louder.

"Is she in the dishwasher?" Ensley asks.

It's improbable, but I open it anyway. Empty.

"Is she under it?" Ensley asks.

I lie flat on the floor. "There's a gap here in the cover over the motor." I fumble with the metal shield and finally pull it off.

At first I can't see anything, then finally the barest light glints off a pair of wide, frightened eyes.

"How did you get back there, cat?" I ask. I reach in.

She can't move, but I get to her scruff and pull her out.

She looks pitiful. Her white fur is smeared with oil and grease.

"Is she okay?" Ensley asks.

I feel along her neck and joints and belly. "She seems fine."

She tries to lick herself, but I pull her head aside. "No cleaning this up," I say. "That's motor oil."

"Do you have some Dawn soap?" Ensley asks. "That will get the grease out."

"It's going to take a while."

She nods. "I'm up for it."

And she is. She covers her gold dress with an apron, and I strip off my shirt and jacket. It takes both of us to keep Sasha in the sink as we wash out the grease, then rinse out the soap so that it's safe for her to groom. The process takes hours as she keeps trying to escape, and her long hair is difficult to clean.

When we finally curl up on the sofa, the cat between us wrapped in a towel, it feels like we've been in battle.

"One cat can make a lot of trouble," Ensley says. She rests her head on my shoulder.

"She's definitely using up her nine lives." I want to kick myself after saying it, since Ensley's mom is dead, and this is her namesake.

But Ensley's eyes are closed. I tilt my head to look at her.

She's asleep.

I shift so that she's resting more securely. Sasha stretches out a paw and lays it delicately on Ensley's shoulder.

It's definitely not how I expected the evening to go.

But it's not bad.

Not bad at all.

Chapter 27

ENSLEY

The first thing I notice when I wake up is a terrible crick in my neck. For a moment, I can't quite get my bearings. There's a warm, fuzzy ball by my shoulder.

And I'm under a blanket.

And there's a rock under my head.

I shift to figure out what I've been sleeping on.

Oh.

It's Drew's chest.

He's out. I move slowly and subtly to take everything in.

I'm still in the gold dress. No shoes.

There's a blanket over us. That wasn't there before.

The fuzzy ball is Sasha, curled around my shoulder but lying under Drew's neck.

We're quite a picture.

I vaguely remember sitting down, bone tired after the search for the kitten and then the fight to clean her up.

We must have fallen asleep.

Me first, if Drew got a blanket.

It's nice, though. He's shirtless, like when we were washing the cat.

Which I don't recommend, by the way. We both had to coat ourselves in antibacterial cream because of the scratches.

But this moment might be worth it. Sasha senses I'm awake and opens a single blue eye. She takes me in, then makes a big show of closing it again.

I get it. Let's stay asleep.

But my neck is in a weird position. The more I think about it, the more I need to move. Pretty soon, my neck is screaming and even though I'm with Sasha and would like to stay here forever and ever, the gold dress is sticking to me, the blanket is hot, Sasha's fur is tickling me, and I have to pee.

Also, we did not have sex.

Damn it.

Does morning still count as date two?

I hear a jingling tune in the kitchen. It's my phone, and it's Tillie. Her ringtone is "Highway to Hell," a funny piano version she hates. I keep it just to irritate her.

She's probably wondering where I am. She's leaving today, heading back to Alabama to finish out the month and pack.

I'm supposed to be there to take her to the bus station, since I need the car.

Damn it.

I think I'll ease away from Drew and Sasha, as if I could extricate myself without them noticing. But the moment I move more than a couple of inches, Sasha yawns and stretches, digging her claws into Drew's chest.

He awakes with a start and picks up the kitten to set her on the back of the sofa. "Destroy that instead," he says, his voice gravelly with sleep. Then his eyes meet mine. "You're awake."

A hundred competing emotions hit me at once. Happiness, that we're here together this morning. Contentment, lying on his chest, his arms around me.

And disappointment, that we didn't connect the way we'd planned.

"Good morning," he says.

I wonder how many women get to hear the deep, rocky sound of his first words of the day. Probably a lot.

But only once.

"Good morning," I say, sounding more chipper than I normally do. I don't think it's the positivity mantras. It's Drew.

He smiles, an honest-to-God smile. "You wake up like sunshine."

"You're not so gloomy yourself." It's hard to imagine him yelling at a receptionist to the point that she quit. I mean, I can see him getting that way. I remember how he was the night of the wedding, and even that day I brought doughnuts.

But he's not that way right now.

I glance down at my crinkled gold dress. "This is going to be an epic walk of shame with no actual shame."

He grunts. "Sasha got all the attention."

I think I'll roll over, see if this morning will pay the dividends I was cheated last night.

But then my phone chimes again. "Highway to Hell."

"That's you," he says. "Who gets that ringtone?"

"My sister. She's headed back to Alabama today."

"And she wants you."

"I'm supposed to take her to the bus station." I stop there. I might incriminate myself about the job that still exists, the apartment I have to vacate, and the life I have back in Alabama.

"She doesn't have a car here?" Drew pets Sasha, who has settled on the top cushion of the sofa.

"We share one."

"Do you have time for an omelet before you go?"

Good God, a man who makes omelets after a night of not-sex. How do I say no to that?

But I have to check on Tillie. I can't make her miss her bus, and calling for a ride is expensive.

"Let me see what time she needs me."

I shove the blanket aside, grimacing at the vision of my own commando girl parts visible in the tangle of strips of my dress. I pull it down and don't look back at Drew to see if he's noticed. In the light of day, the dress seems tawdry and cheap. That's not what I was going for.

The phone sits on the kitchen counter, the very one where Drew had his fingers all up in my business. I have two missed calls from Tillie, plus a handful of messages.

Tillie: Still at lover boy's?

Tillie: Are you okay?

Tillie: I'm assuming you aren't dead in a ditch.

Tillie: Hey, call me. I have to leave at ten and Lila is puking.

The last message was an hour ago.

I punch through a call. Tillie picks up on one ring.

Her voice is terse. "I'm not saying you have to come see me off, but are you okay?"

"I'm fine."

"How was it?"

"It was something. The cat went missing. I'll explain later."

"Did you do the deed?"

"We didn't." I glance from the kitchen through to the living room. Drew is petting Sasha.

"What happened?"

"Sasha got lost, and we had to bathe her."

"Who the hell is Sasha?"

"Drew's cat."

"Like our mother?"

"Yeah, he named the kitten after her."

Tillie's voice is strident. "How did that pussy get priority over yours?"

It's a good question. "She got lost."

Silence.

"I can get an Uber."

"It's too much."

164

"Are you going to do the deed now?"

"He's making me an omelet."

"He cooks?"

"Yeah."

"Then marry him."

"Ha. Right, Tillie."

"I'm serious."

"I'll be there to take you to the bus."

I end the call.

Drew comes into the kitchen. I'm instantly distracted by his bare chest, his dress pants slung low on his hips. God, how did we not make something happen?

"Everything okay?"

"Yeah. Tillie was checking in."

He sets Sasha on the floor. "Let me feed her and I'll take you back."

I fumble with what words to say next, but he goes on. "This is pretty strange, right?"

So it's awkward for him, too.

"Maybe a little."

"We'll grab some breakfast on the way. We can get something for your sisters."

He's so courteous. I'd rather have the omelet. And sex.

But I only say, "Sure."

And that's what happens. We load in his car, stop for breakfast croissants at a bakery drive-through, and I make it in time for Tillie's departure.

I get a peck on the lips instead of a pecker in my parts.

And that's it. Date number two is all about the cat.

And the pussy getting all the attention isn't mine.

I have four days left.

And one date.

Chapter 28

DREW

Well, hell.

After dropping Ensley off at her sister's house, I spend an hour looking for places Sasha can get lost in, then shore them up. The dishwasher cover is tightened down so the opening is too small for even a clever kitten.

I find a few other spots where she could escape. A crawl space behind the utility room cabinets. A narrow gap beside the stove.

By midafternoon, I'm chopping onions and avocado, planning for a meal and wishing I was cooking for two instead of one. I could call Ensley over, maybe start the next date.

But what am I doing, really? She's an employee. And we're already acting every shade of inappropriate. Can I maintain any sort of relationship with her, even if it's only physical, and still be her boss? It's only a matter of time before Maria and Vera and even clueless Todd figure out what we're doing in my office.

And I know what I want to happen in my office. I can picture every delectable moment of it.

When did Ensley James get in my head?

The wedding?

When she showed up to save my clinic from the rash of bad receptionists?

But she's always been there, even when I didn't acknowledge it, even when I assumed I'd never see her again.

And now I know she was wishing I would save her.

Nobody ever looks to me for something tangible or steady. Not unless they have four legs and a tail. But she does.

My phone chimes from the other side of the kitchen. I set down my knife and walk over to it. Ensley has sent a text. She's back from dropping off her sister.

There's no denying how much my mood lifts at seeing her name.

I should hold back, not encourage her. I should keep our dates formal and contained.

But I don't.

Me: You remember how to get here?

Ensley: Maybe. You inviting me over?

Me: I owe you an omelet.

Ensley: So breakfast for dinner?

I almost type in *you* for dinner, but I control myself.

Me: It's the best dinner.

Ensley: Okay. An address would help, then.

I send it to her. Sasha hops onto the counter and sniffs at the onion, then backs away slowly as if it's the enemy.

"Not exactly your cuisine," I say.

She sits and peers up at me, looking like an innocent angel with her white fluff of fur. You'd never know that she completely derailed my night.

She delicately sniffs the air, not quite believing that all the smells on the counter are as horrible as the one she investigated.

I return to chopping, keeping my eye on her so that she doesn't unexpectedly bolt under my blade. I peel potatoes, creating fine julienne sticks. Hash browns will go great with these omelets. Now that I have a guest, I might as well go all out.

It's been a while since I cooked for anyone but myself. I can't remember when.

Back when I hosted guy nights, we ordered food and drank beer, watching sports and movies, occasionally playing poker. I certainly didn't cook for them.

When was the last one of those nights? I can't quite remember. Had I known the last one would indeed be the last? The gatherings definitely dwindled after I opened the clinic. The first year was pure adrenaline, late nights and weekends, too, between patients and finding a schedule and systems that worked, plus renovating parts of the building.

Then the years started racing. The guys all got married. Franklin was the last.

Sasha curls up on the dish towel. I turn on the radio, listening to a pop station of bubbly upbeat tunes, because I have a feeling that's what Ensley likes. She sometimes hums Lady Gaga at the front desk.

I wash the bell peppers and slice them into chunks. Food does what you tell it, mostly. Following a recipe is neat and orderly. Ingredients don't let you down, not unless you've made the mistake of letting them rot.

Unlike my life. Ever since that wedding, it seems half of my existence has a mind of its own.

I can't blame Ensley. I could have easily shot her directly out of my life. I didn't have to respond to her emails. I certainly didn't have to text or call her.

If anything, most of the moves have been mine.

I separate my onion, peppers, tomatoes, and potatoes into bowls to be ready for assembly.

It's too early to crack eggs, but I remove the chunk of cheddar from the refrigerator to grate by hand.

The idea that she's coming is nice. Something to look forward to. I haven't had a lot of that lately.

I'm so deep in these unfamiliar thoughts that I'm startled when there's a knock at the door.

Sasha opens one weary blue eye, miffed that she's been disturbed. I pet her head and walk past her to the front door.

I'm in completely unfamiliar territory here. I will not be following my usual playlist. Compliment, fiery kiss against a door, and sex.

I'm cooking. We're having a meal at my house.

I'm outside my norm.

When I open the door, she's there, wearing jeans and a long-sleeved shirt printed with a bright rainbow across it. She looks every bit the ray of sunshine she now endeavors to be. Her hair is pulled back in a wild curly ponytail, coiled tendrils around her face.

If she's wearing makeup, I can't see it, although her lashes are luscious and thick. And her mouth is a deep shade of raspberry that I can practically taste just by looking at it.

I want to devour her.

"Hello," she says, a bemused look on her face. I realize it's been several seconds of staring. "I parked in the space marked *V*. I assume that means visitor, not vengeance or vandalize."

And there she goes, making me laugh already. "Or vixen."

"Ah. Back to that." Her coy expression tells me she doesn't mind. "If so, I nailed my choice."

I move aside, and she steps in with a deep inhale. "I smell the fresh scent of chopped vegetables," she says. "This is not the smell you encounter in my house, hardly ever. It's all cups of Good Noodles and granola bars with me."

I refrain from making a quip about her diet. I never would, knowing where she came from, where a cup of noodles kept you from going to bed hungry.

I close the door, feeling awkward. I should kiss her or something. I've invited her here after seducing her multiple times.

But she's happy to wander the space, hands clasped behind her back. "Sasha hasn't gotten lost again, has she?"

As if on cue, the kitten bounds into the room and leaps onto the back of the sofa.

Ensley bends down to pet her soft head. "There you are, you little troublemaker. No hard feelings about the good scrubbing we gave you?"

The rumbling purr is evidence that she holds no grudges.

Ensley sets her purse on the side table and turns to me. "All I've had today is a cup of coffee and the croissant you bought this morning. My sisters took all the rest."

"Then I should get started," I say.

"I'm happy to help."

We head into the kitchen. "It sounds like you're not super familiar with kitchen work," I say.

She bumps her hip against me. "I can learn. And I have chopped a potato before. I used to dig them up from the community garden even though technically I wasn't allowed." Her eyes grow wide as she takes in all the work I've already done. "It looks like you have it well under control."

Even so, I give her the minor task of prepping the hash browns as I whisk the eggs and melt butter in the omelet pan.

"The oil is hot," she says.

I nod and take a moment to slide the potatoes into the pan.

She leans her elbows on the counter, chin resting in her hands. "I can't believe you have a special pan for omelets. I have a big one and a little one, and they have to do everything."

"What do you like to cook?"

"Good Noodles." She laughs. "That and baking cookie dough are ninety percent of my efforts. But I *can* cook. I used to make a great spaghetti sauce back in the day. I could stretch it for days if I got my hands on some tomatoes or even a cheap can of puree. I used to swipe basil off the bush at old man Ferrell's house."

"I'd love to try it sometime." I almost mention the lemon larceny as well, but decide to let it go.

When she doesn't respond, I drag my gaze from the melting butter to glance over at her. Her brows are pushed together.

"No cooking for me?" I ask.

She takes her time answering. "But this is date three already. I won't get a chance."

Oh, that. The decision to limit them seems a lifetime ago.

The butter bubbles, so I'm saved from having to reply.

I pour the eggs into the pan and begin sliding it across the surface of the burner.

"I can see you've done this before," she says.

I have to focus on the omelet, making sure it cooks evenly. Then there's the magic moment. I lift the pan off the stove and shake it well, ensuring that the egg isn't sticking anywhere.

And then with one quick flick of my wrist, the egg sails into the air, neatly flips over, and lands in the pan, uncooked side down.

Ensley claps. "That was amazing. Mine would've hit the ceiling."

"I bungled a few tries in the early days."

I add the ingredients to one half of the omelet before folding it closed. This part always happens fast.

The potatoes look done on the bottom, so I flip them with the spatula. The tops are golden brown.

"Do you like it hard or soft?" Ensley asks, and I whip my head around.

Her eyes are merry with mischief. "Got ya. I mean your hash browns."

"Crispy," I say.

"Same. Good to know we are hash browns compatible. I feel very sorry for the couples where one likes it hard, and the other likes it soft."

"I could always take a little and pull out early," I say, not realizing until I hear the words aloud that I've doubled down on the entendre.

Ensley erupts into giggles. "I'll exchange sexual quips with you any day."

"I believe that's what got us started with those dirty emails."

She nods. "And here we are."

I place the omelet on a plate and cover it with a second upturned plate to keep the heat in.

As I pour the second set of whipped eggs into the pan, I say, "If all goes well, they'll finish simultaneously."

Ensley bursts out laughing, and I realize I've done it again.

"I'm going to do it intentionally from now on," I say.

"I challenge you to an entendre duel," she says, picking up the whisk like it's a sword.

I shift the egg pan. "I think I might lose."

"But you're already two up on me."

"Then catch up."

She stares at the ingredient bowls.

"There's no sausage or pickle. You're making it hard."

I cough out a laugh.

She gazes up at me in confusion, then realizes what she just said. "I'm a natural!"

"As long as you don't say you want to park the beef bus in tuna town."

Her mouth drops open. "Drew! Ugh! I call off the duel!" She tosses the whisk in the sink, but we're both all smiles.

Soon, we're seated at the table, looking out the bay window onto the dog park at the edge of the complex.

Ensley groans with delight as she takes her first bite. "Perfection."

I cut a bite with the flat end of my fork, pleased that she likes it.

She sips her orange juice and stares out the window. "It's too bad you don't have a dog here. It looks like you chose this place with them in mind."

She's right. "I don't think I knew what I was getting into when I opened a solo vet clinic. Most veterinarians graduate and work at one of the large clinics before striking out on their own."

"Why didn't you?"

"The man who owned the clinic before me was one of my mentors in vet school. We had a conversation a couple of weeks before I graduated where he told me he wanted to turn his practice over to me. He thought I should take on a second full-time vet, since it was a big load to manage, but I didn't have anyone I trusted as a partner. So I just went at it."

"I understand Maria is a holdover from the old office."

"She is. That's why she knows the ropes so well. She has vastly more experience than I do."

"What about Vera? And Betty?"

"Betty worked for Dr. Adams, but retired with him. Mostly. She helps us in a pinch, as you saw. Vera I picked up when I took over. And Todd is pretty new. He's been there less than a year."

"And of course we know about your receptionist problems."

I grunt. "You've been amazing at filling that space. I feel confident with you there."

Her eyes cast downward, her fork twirling in circles on an empty part of the plate.

Maybe she doesn't want to talk about work.

"So what should we do next?" I ask. "Since this is our third date."

She glances up, lifting an eyebrow. My dick instantly jumps. Straight to that, then?

As much as I want to get to that, it feels sudden.

I point my fork at the window. "The woods along the edge of this complex are pretty, if you want to take a walk."

"I remember our last walk," she says. "In the park. To the bench."

The reminder doesn't make my anatomy any calmer.

Chapter 29

ENSLEY

So apparently we're taking a stroll.

We head out of Drew's apartment, following a sidewalk until it ends at a line of trees. The path picks up again in the woods, a narrow, winding trail of trodden dirt.

I'm glad I wore jeans.

"There's a pond up ahead," Drew says.

I worry about dumb things. My hair. Sweating too much, even though there's a chill in the air. But then Drew takes my hand, and suddenly everything changes.

This is a man who takes women to bed and dumps them. He has a system. Kiss against a door. Bang and feed. Or feed and bang. Then jump ship.

But he's showing me a pond.

He's out of his pattern.

We arrive at a clearing where the water shimmers, a swell of dirt at one end proving it's man-made, not natural. We're not alone. Other people walk their dogs, throw sticks, or just sit and talk.

Light filtering through the trees leaves bright patterns on Drew's face as we circle the space. We greet others with a hand wave as we pass. We're just another couple to them.

The earth shifts beneath my feet as reality starts to slide. We could be anybody. A longtime couple. Married. Nothing feels complicated here. Just a man and a woman on a walk like everybody else. No shed angst, no weird miscommunications, nobody with a secret job.

This is real life. Ordinary life.

And I'm spending it with Drew.

"You any good at rock skipping?" he asks.

"Rubbish."

"I'm pretty good."

"Skip it ten times, then."

He lets out a low whistle. "Challenge accepted."

"And we'll make it a bet." I'm feeling bold.

"All right. What are the stakes?" His cheeks have pinked up from the chill, his hair flying in the wind. He looks more handsome in a fitted black athletic shirt and jeans than I've ever seen him. I'm knocked off-center and reach out to hold on to a low branch of a nearby tree to steady myself.

"If you don't make it, I get a fourth date," I say, then hold my breath to watch his reaction.

But he doesn't flinch. "Done. And if I get all ten skips?" His head tilts, a small smile playing on his lips.

"You can pick your prize."

He nods. "It will involve you being naked."

Now we're getting somewhere.

"I accept." Then I hesitate. "Unless you mean right here."

"Nope." But he doesn't elaborate, instead searching through the crumbling rock for the right stone.

I watch him, knowing I'm in a win-win situation. Still, my heart thunders as he compares two choices of rock, then discards one.

We approach the water. Drew swings his arms a few times, warming up.

"One shot," I tell him.

"One shot," he confirms.

A few others standing around watch us curiously. A puffy Pomeranian runs to the end of his leash to sniff my shoes.

"Is he going to skip it?" asks the pup's owner, a man in a brown knit hat.

I'm always game for talking to strangers. "He is. And we made a bet on it," I say. "He has to skip it ten times."

This piques the interest of everyone in earshot, and soon we have a small crowd coming to watch.

"They put a wager on it," Brown Hat tells the others.

A woman in a green turtleneck says, "I bet it involves getting naked."

When my mouth falls open, she shrugs. "You two look like the type."

Do we? I glance over at Drew, but he's concentrating on the rock and angles.

Now everyone is very interested in the skip.

"Give him a warm-up," Brown Hat says.

"She doesn't have to give him anything," Turtleneck shoots back.

"I'm good," Drew says. He swings his arms a few more times, like a golfer before hitting the ball.

"Good luck," Brown Hat says.

"She'll get naked either way," Turtleneck says. "Look at him."

She's not wrong. Drew is the picture of manliness in his jeans, hiking boots, and black shirt. My chest tightens thinking that maybe, just maybe, he could finally be mine.

Drew's eyes take in the smooth surface of the pond. The afternoon sun beams down on the clearing, leaving a sparkle across the water. "Here goes nothing."

He flings the rock, and it hits the surface at a swift, low angle. It skips, and the people around us start counting.

"One. Two. Three. Four. Five." Their voices rise as the number increases.

"Six. Seven. Eight! Nine! Ten! Eleven!"

The stone finally sinks.

Brown Hat lifts his hand for a high five, and Drew slaps his palm. Turtleneck jumps in the air a few times. "He did it!"

"Nudity!" Brown Hat says.

Several others pick up rocks and send them skittering across the water to try their luck. Drew puts his arm around my waist. "I guess I need to collect my prize."

My body buzzes. "You won it fair and square."

I think he'll kiss me. His eyes are on my lips. But he only squeezes my waist and leads us back to the path.

As we walk through the woods, his fingers find the strip of skin beneath the edge of my shirt. My body kicks into gear at his touch.

His hand slides farther up, covering more territory.

My heart hammers. Right here in the woods? I might be game for that if we go off the path.

We pass an outcropping of rock and suddenly my arm is pulled, and we're surrounded by stone. His hands slip up my shirt, his mouth on mine. It's like all the times in the office, forbidden, sudden, hot, explosive.

Drew doesn't hesitate, pushing my bra up out of his way, hands teasing me, fingers rolling a nipple. I arch to him, pulsing with need. Finally, we're here, we can do more. We're free to explore.

He lifts my shirt and ducks down, his mouth replacing his hands. I clutch his head with my hands, pressing him into me. Above us, the light dances through the scant leaves.

I'm high, like a mountain climber reaching the summit. I knead the corded muscles in the back of his neck.

I want so much more contact, skin, all of him. I press back against the rock, feeling the bite of its roughness against my shoulders. It's new and wild, and I want to revel in every moment. I'm sparking with sensation, the breeze on my cheeks, my hair ruffling near my ear. Drew's hot mouth devours my skin.

"Come on," he says, his voice like gravel. He pulls down my shirt and takes my hand.

Soon we're running, flying down the path, dodging a family with a baby stroller, and breaking through to the building complex.

We pause only to fit his key in the lock, then we're inside, stumbling over each other, kicking off our shoes, kissing and holding on to each other as if we're engaged in the final act either of us gets before leaving this earth.

Sasha pokes her head up from her perch on the back of the sofa, but otherwise pays us no mind. Drew pulls me down the hall, past the kitchen, through the door to his bedroom.

He lifts my shirt over my head and sends it flying. My bra, too. Then I'm in the air, sailing toward his bed, propelled by his hands on my waist.

I'm barely down when he's over me, revisiting all the spots he's tasted and touched over the last weeks. My mouth, my neck, my breasts. Then my jeans are unfastened, and he tugs them down.

He whips off his own shirt, and then his mouth finds my thigh, lifting my calf to rest on his shoulder. He slows down, savoring this unknown part of my body, making his way up until his breath is hot on the pale-peach panties, chosen deliberately to match the dress I wore that first time we collided.

He grasps the lace edge with his teeth, pulling it down. His fingers tug at the waistband, and then they're gone, my last barrier.

There's no hurry. His gaze rakes across my body until our eyes meet. He watches me even as he leans down, connecting his tongue with my most tender parts.

I suck in a breath, but he takes his time, learning each hill and valley, each turn and fold. It's torture and bliss in equal measure. I grasp the comforter with both hands, holding tight.

He teases me, my body rising to meet him. Soon we move in tandem, his hands holding me up to him. He delves more deeply, feeling my rhythm. The tension gathers, and I forget everything but the sensations he draws from me.

The first flickers of lightning set off, like a bottle rocket sizzling into the night sky. He senses them and increases his speed and pressure, gripping me tightly, his mouth working harder, faster.

The collision is fierce, and my need reaches a fever pitch. I don't think I can take any more, my muscles trembling, but then, suddenly, it all lets go.

I shudder, crying out, tears squeezing from my eyes. The zigzags of heat and pleasure and relief and release consume me. I can't feel the bed or even Drew's mouth on me. Only the purity of the pleasure, the music in my body.

Gradually, I feel my fingers again, tangled in the bedcovers. And Drew's hair, tickling my belly. I settle back on the mattress, my breathing labored and fast.

Drew kisses the insides of both thighs. When I've relaxed, he moves over me, his mouth close to my ear. "Next time ask for twenty skips."

I laugh, so happy, so content. I feel my way along his broad shoulders, squeezing the bulging biceps. "I'm a good loser."

He lies next to me, trailing his fingers down the space between my breasts to my belly button. "An outie," he says. "I've pictured it a thousand times since the shed."

"My belly button?"

"All of you."

I like this. "Confession."

His eyebrows lift.

"When I dropped that jar of screws, I was planning to shake it to get your attention."

"Why?"

"So I could see if you were, uh, reacting to me."

"Ah."

"I didn't mean to drop it."

He kisses my forehead. "Why was that so important to you?"

"I didn't think someone like you could be attracted to someone like me."

"You think that's due to our history? Me being older when we were kids?"

"Maybe. Or because I thought I was nothing and you were everything." Now that's a confession.

His finger taps my nose. "You're perfect. You should have the world at your feet."

"Hardly."

He keeps touching me, his thumb grazing my hipbone, then his fingers dip between my legs again. "I'm happy to show you exactly how deep that attraction goes."

"Drew! Was that a sexual pun?"

He nibbles along my hairline. "Maybe."

His hand continues to stroke me, gently this time. The heat returns. He's ready for more. So am I.

I run my hands across his bare chest, following the curve of the muscles and pressing my thumb into the ridges of his abs. "You must work out a lot."

"I'm an early riser."

I glance down at his jeans. "I think you're rising now." I reach down to unsnap the band. The hiss of the zipper sends a shudder through me. This has been worth waiting for.

He releases me to get them out of the way, his blue cotton boxers not really containing him. I am not content with only a peek, so I push them down.

Good lord. That's about to go into me.

Chapter 30

DREW

Naked Ensley is everything I thought she would be.

All the facades are stripped away. She isn't trying to be pure sunshine. She's just herself.

And that's pretty great.

Watching her orgasm was about the best thing that's happened to me in a long time. She wasn't self-conscious or putting on a show. She gives herself over to the moment. Not everyone can do that. I'm not even sure I do.

Her gaze rests on my face as I stroke the length of her body. She's gotten my boxers off, her hands on me, too. It's the most intimate thing, especially during the day. There's no darkness to hide in. Everything is laid bare.

I lean over to kiss her, softly this time. That first time was about setting the mood, learning her, figuring out what she needs.

Normally at this stage, I'd be rutting it out, getting it done.

But I'm in no hurry.

Our lips flutter together. I sense the difference. It's more reverent than sex. It's connection. I avoid that, but with Ensley, it feels inevitable. There's too much history. And now I know how she's always seen me. Safety. The older, stronger figure who can help her, rescue her, even.

I'm not sure I can live up to that. But this moment makes me want to try.

She wraps her arms around my neck in a position that has become second nature to us. I haven't had any repeats, not in a decade, so it's new to me how easy it can be to fall into someone completely.

I bury my face in her hair as it curls across my pillow, smelling of shampoo and sunshine. Beneath that is the scent of her. I feel as if I've always known it. Maybe I have. I first met her when we were young. She's part of my history, my hometown.

And now we're here.

"Condoms okay?" I ask her.

"Maybe this first time," she says, then bites her lip. She doesn't expect there to be another time. And normally she'd be right. But now that we've come this far, I see she was right all along. Adding three dates to our decades of knowing each other was a tipping point.

But she was also wrong. The point of her dare was the assumption that adding extra dates to the mix wouldn't change who I am. I wouldn't set aside my old priorities because of her.

But I am. I already feel it.

The future yawns wide. I picture Ensley working at my clinic, the stabilizing force as other employees come and go. We're the power team, like so many couples who work together at many family businesses—doctors, accountants, restaurants.

I'm ready to make her mine in every way.

I don't keep condoms in my bedside drawer. I don't bring women here. "I'll fetch them," I tell her and head to the bathroom.

I catch sight of myself in the mirror as I open the drawer. It's the same me, just like before the wedding.

But I'm not the same. Not by a long shot. I have a woman here. And not just in my home. My clinic, too. She's everywhere. I can't set her aside. I won't.

I take the entire box and bring it to the bedroom. Ensley lies on her side, head propped on her arm, waiting. She's like a goddess, radiant skin still lightly tan from whatever she did for the wedding. There isn't a flaw on her.

"Can I put it on?" She spins around to sit on her knees, her breasts tipped with the light. Blood rushes to my groin, not that there was much left not already there.

I pass her the box.

She opens it with delicate fingers and rips the top off one package. Then her hands are on me, molding the latex to my skin, forcing me to hang on to my control.

Her eyes meet mine, and I lean over her, pushing her back on the bed. "I'm going to take my time with you," I tell her, and her breath catches.

I love how she responds to me, how her body blossoms pink where I touch her. I reacquaint myself with each part of her until she's writhing beneath me. "Drew." Her breath is ragged. "Please."

I slide into her gently, watching her face.

Her hands clutch at my waist, fingernails digging into my skin. I take it easy, seeing how she reacts, making sure there is no discomfort.

Her hips rise to meet me, and her body lets out a small shudder.

I plan to keep it light all the way through, but the way she sighs, matching my movements with her own, makes my blood rush. I increase my speed, braced on my arms over her.

She wraps her legs around me, and I'm no longer in control. I pound into her, reveling in each gasp and moan. She says my name over and over again, each sound of her orgasm another tightening of the connection that binds us.

Her muscles contract around me, her cries rising again. And that's it, too far. I unleash in her, every wild sensation converging where we join. For a moment, I'm lightheaded, like I passed through some other atmosphere.

Then she pulls me down on her to rest against her body. She clasps my head against her cheek. "Drew," she says, but whatever else she might have spoken is lost in the long rush of her breath. She settles for another simple, "Drew."

"Ensley." Our names are like revelations, like admissions. Like confessions. Something's happened here. Unexpected. Glorious.

I want it again. I don't want to ever go without it.

"Stay with me tonight," I whisper into her ear.

"But it's date three," she says.

"Then let date three never end."

She presses her hands against my cheeks. "May it never end."

Chapter 31

ENSLEY

I stay with Drew Saturday night and all day Sunday. We never properly get dressed again. I wear one of his big sweatshirts that reaches my knees. Panties aren't allowed. Or needed.

It's a lot. A lot, a lot, a lot.

But I have to go back to Lila's. I need clean clothes. And a breather. Drew Daniels can be intense.

On Monday morning, I brew a breakfast roast in Lila's ancient Mr. Coffee and stare out the window at the overgrown backyard. The weekend feels like a dream. Images flash through my memory. His bed. His shower. His sofa. Drew. Drew. Drew.

The only thing that bugs me, just a little bit, is something Drew said when I left. "Date three was epic."

It's almost as if we were still on the three-date plan.

Surely not.

But what if we are?

I hear Lila retching in the bathroom. Poor thing. I updated her last night, as well as texting Tillie. They hope I'll be staying in Atlanta, dating Drew, and working at the clinic. They seem excited.

Tillie thinks we can fit a blow-up mattress in the second room for me. We will have to put some of our stuff in storage, or give it away. It won't all fit here.

Somewhere down the line, Lila will need the space for the baby. For now, we can pool resources if we all cram into this rental. We can support her. *I* can support her. Tillie barely gets by.

I grab a can of ginger ale from the refrigerator and pull a sleeve of saltines from the box in the pantry. Lila's really going through it.

I wait in the doorway for her to rinse out her mouth in the sink. She sees me. "Thanks." She ties her hair back as she stumbles to the living room and collapses on the sofa. "Good thing this critter is only the size of a peanut. I'm not giving it any nutrients with all the puking."

I set the drink and crackers on the upturned milk crate that serves as a coffee table. "Did the doctor say when it will ease up?"

"Most people are better around twelve or thirteen weeks. I'm nearly there." Her stomach growls, and she reaches for a cracker. "So ridiculous. My stomach cleans itself out, then requires me to put something else in."

My phone beeps, signaling it's time for me to head out to make it to the clinic on time. "Call me if you need anything."

"Don't worry. I'm used to it." She nibbles on the corner of the cracker, resting her hand on the faded print of her sweatshirt over her belly.

I hate that she has it so hard. It's not fair. We had it so rough growing up, and here she is, barely getting by all over again and no partner to help.

My sister needs us, and it will be even harder when the baby arrives. She probably won't be able to work at all. Her boss at the pizza place is already threatening her shifts since she's taken so much sick time.

Between me and Tillie, we'll make it work. We vowed a long time ago to keep each other safe. I'm sticking to it.

I head to the kitchen to collect my coffee and hurry out to the car for my first day of working for a boss I'm banging on the side.

When I arrive, the first emergency of the day has already come in, a cat who ate a piece of fishing wire. When I pop into the back, Drew is on the phone, talking tersely with someone about X-rays and surgery.

The cat currently is not under any duress, lying on its side and getting pets from Maria.

Drew doesn't even look my way, intent on his conversation.

"We have another early work-in," Maria says. "They'll be here any minute."

Wow. We're moving fast. I hurry to my chair. The door to Exam 1 is open, and I can hear a woman crying. I flip on all my devices and push back to check on her.

An elderly lady with a thick fall of gray hair sits on the bench next to an empty cat carrier. This must be the owner of the tabby. Todd stands in the corner and gives me a shrug. "This is Mrs. Williams."

"Hello, Mrs. Williams," I say. "Are you all right?"

She looks up, her clear eyes rimmed with red. "I've killed Missy. I just know it. I should have put my craft things away."

I kneel in front of her. "Dr. Daniels is back there calling the best experts to help her. She was getting lots of love and attention and is not in any distress."

"What's going to happen to my baby?"

"Dr. Daniels will be in shortly to update you. He's conferring with some other veterinarians about the best course to take."

Mrs. Williams reaches out to hold my hand. At the connection, she breathes more deeply. "Missy is only four."

"We're going to take excellent care of her."

The seconds tick by. I know I should get ready to receive the day's patients and pull their charts. But this seems more important.

The back door to the exam room opens, and Drew steps in. He seems surprised to see me, but gives me a quick nod.

"Mrs. Williams, we're doing some X-rays on Missy to find the location of the wire. Once we know if it's gone down into her intestinal tract, we'll make our next move. You can sit tight, and I'll be back to you the moment we know more."

The woman lets go of my hand. "Will she be all right?"

He glances at me. I realize he's not sure what to say in this case, so I jump in. "We'll be right here with you every step of the way."

The door tinkles, signaling a client has entered the lobby. I excuse myself and hurry over to check in a woman with an angry cat missing several patches of hair. She sets the carrier on the reception desk. "Thank you so much for seeing me early. She's bleeding in at least three places!"

I peer in at the kitty, who gives me a hard look. "Did you get in a fight?"

"There's fur all over the yard," the woman says. "Not her color."

"Defending your territory, eh?" I ask the cat.

"There's some old tomcat they're fighting over," the owner says. "Beats me why they care one whit about him."

"I get you," I say to the cat. "You're all about your man."

She sits back on her haunches and calmly licks her paw. She seems more pleased than hurt.

I quickly check them in and sort through the file cabinet for her chart. "We'll get you right back," I say and send a note to the screens in the treatment space that the injured cat has arrived.

It's hard to focus. There's so much happening on Mondays. And the way my heart speeds up around Drew makes it even worse.

But I manage. The morning is a nonstop rush. I barely see Maria and Todd, much less Drew. We work straight through lunch. I get two calls from my boss Cindy that I can't take. Finally, I get a brief window between check-ins when the lobby is empty and I can rush to the break room to grab a sandwich. Lately lunch has been too short to even microwave Good Noodles.

I gulp it down, not even bothering to sit, as I call Cindy back. I'm not sure what she needs. I'm not due back until Thursday.

She answers on the first ring.

"Cindy, what's going on? You said to call?"

"Oh my gosh, Ensley. Are you sitting down?"

I glance at the chair. "No, should I be?"

"Remember when you got promoted to assistant head teller? Corporate said they were doing some reorganizing of the company due to the upcoming merger."

I vaguely remember that. "I thought the changes wouldn't affect us other than we might get one more teller."

"We were named one of the most efficient branches last week. I didn't bother calling to tell you on your vacation. But I've been promoted!"

"Really? A promotion! That's great." I'm happy for her, but surprised that she called me twice today for this. I shove another chunk of sandwich in my mouth.

"Here's the thing. The promotion is in Missouri."

I stop chewing. "You're being transferred from our branch?"

"I am!"

I guess this seals it. I mainly loved working at Farm to Market Bank and Trust because of her. If I'm left with Janet, I'm definitely staying here at the clinic.

"I'm going to miss you! When is your last day?"

"Wednesday. I was hoping you could come back a day early, if your sister can manage. I can't leave without saying goodbye."

I drop into the chair. "That's so sudden!"

"Well, I've known for a week. I didn't want to interrupt your break. I thought I'd be here until Friday, but they're moving the Missouri manager, too, so I want to catch her before she leaves her branch."

"Do we already have a new manager? I have a new boss?"

"Yes, he's been here today. He's got a different style from me, but I've told him how amazing you are. He's eager to meet you."

"Cindy, this is a lot to happen on my vacation."

"I know! The timing was bad. But there will now be an official head teller position, with many of the responsibilities I was absorbing. That could be you!"

"But I don't know if I want to be head teller for anyone else but you." What am I saying? I'm not even going back. Am I? Maybe I should talk to Drew. I need to be sure.

My safety net swoops out from under me. What if Drew thinks me working here is a bad idea after the weekend we just had? If we break up, am I out?

And now my old boss is gone, so I've lost the security in my position at the bank. I have no place to live in Alabama while I figure that out.

I don't dare simply quit my job and move in with my sisters. Tillie barely pays her bills. What if Lila needs more money to get by? I have to be able to feed her and the baby.

My hands start to shake.

The old terror comes over me, the one I spent all those positivity trainings working to keep away. I'm five years old. Mother isn't coming home from the hospital. Dad won't come out of the bedroom. Lila is crying. And the baby needs a bottle. Garrett leaves and doesn't come back. There's no dinner. No help. All the clothes are dirty.

No. I'm fine.

I'm an adult. I have options. I have skills. I will manifest a future that leads me into the light.

Be positive. Believe.

No. Forget that. Positivity doesn't pay the bills. Hedge your bets. Be safe. Be smart. Don't close any doors.

I draw a shaky breath. "I need to finish things out here in Atlanta," I tell Cindy. "If I can figure out how to be at the bank a day early, I will be there."

"If you can't make work hours, there is a happy hour afterward as a farewell," she says. "I can't imagine not getting to say goodbye."

I clench the hand not holding the phone into a fist to force the shakes away. "Don't you have to pack your apartment still?"

"They're packing me and moving me. They bought out my lease. I don't have to do anything but look for a new place while they put me up in an Airbnb."

"That's some star treatment." Some of the tension drains from me. I still have the bank job. I still have choices. I'm going to be all right. "What's the name of the new manager?"

"Milton. It's going to work out. I know it."

I have to believe her. Cindy wouldn't let me down. "Thanks, Cindy. And congratulations on the promotion."

I end the call. Everything's moving so fast. It's almost as if all my paths were leading me to stay here. I don't care if I burn a bridge with some random new manager. Maybe it's the perfect thing to happen.

As long as things seem all right with Drew.

That's what I have to figure out. And fast. I hold up my hand. No shakes. I'm tough. I'm resilient. I'm good to have this conversation with him.

I shove the last part of my sandwich in my mouth and toss the plastic wrap in the trash. I have to get back to my desk and think through how to approach him.

I whip around to rush through the door and run smack into Drew. Oh God. How long has he been standing there?

His voice could make boulders crack in half. "Who was that?"

I think fast. I can't lie. I won't lie. "My friend Cindy back in Alabama." That's true.

"It sounded like you were talking about your old bank job."

"I was."

His gaze pierces me. "Why would it matter if there's a new manager? Why is he your new boss?"

"We were just talking generally about it."

"And what do you have to *finish* here in Atlanta?"

I don't have an answer. There should be one. Why can't I think of one?

The flash in his eyes tells me he's figured everything out. My mouth goes dry.

"Drew . . ."

"You've been lying to me. You still work at the bank."

Oh no. No, no, no. I won't lie. "I was going to tell you."

"When? Before or after you fucked me?"

Shit. I try to gather my explanation. But everything sounds crazy. I wanted to see if we had chemistry? I took the job without quitting my old one just to try him out?

I stare at his polished shoes. How do I tell him I need to always know I will be safe? That I can always help my sisters?

But he isn't done with his accusations. "You wanted three dates. For what? To beat me at my own game? Give me a taste of my own medicine for all those one-night stands? Was that the whole point of having me confess something to you?"

I want to argue. To say the right thing. That I like him. That this fantasy of having him is coming true, and it's everything.

But then it's too late to say anything at all.

He spins around and is gone.

Chapter 32

DREW

I know I should calm down.

I know it.

But I can't believe this utter bullshit.

Ensley never actually took this job.

She just took time off from her real one.

She used her vacation to mess with my head.

And boy, did she do a number.

Three dates. An entire weekend.

Yeah, I fell for it.

How much of it was a lie? The whole I've-loved-you-since-I-was-a-kid story? Wanting to do something meaningful with her work?

I don't believe a word of it. Not now.

I shove papers around on my desk, disturbing Sasha, who lifts her head when a folder pokes her leg.

Sitting here isn't working. There are tasks to be done. Patients are coming in. I can't hole up in here. It's a Monday that's been a hell of a Monday.

I stand up, shaking my sleeves down, trying to pull myself together.

But the anger is right there, so close to the surface that it's barely contained.

At least I won't have to look at her again. She still has her old job. She doesn't need this one. She's out of here.

Maria pokes her head in the door. "New puppy exam in room two."
Her smile fades. "What's wrong?"

"I need you to fire Ensley."

She steps inside. "What? She's been doing great!"

"I don't care. Go out there and tell her to leave as soon as the last
person is out the door. Collect her keys. Change the passwords. Delete
her company email address. I don't want her to have any access here
at all."

Maria closes the door and leans against it. "Drew, you're not making any sense. Does this have to do with the two of you skulking around
here like illicit lovers? The entire staff knows."

Great. Just great.

"She never meant to stay, Maria. She still works in Alabama. She
took her vacation, and I guess wanted to screw with my head for a week.
She's due back there soon, and it might as well be today."

"Drew, that doesn't make any sense. Listen to yourself."

I'm absolutely fucking angry and I don't want to explain one more
thing.

"Maria, just do it, or I'll toss you out right behind her."

Maria glowers. "Don't threaten me, Drew Daniels. I've worked
inside these walls way before you got your inexperienced britches in a
bind with your surly ways. If you had a lovers' spat with Ensley, you deal
with it yourself. And don't think for a minute you can run this place
without me. Because you can't. So start acting like it."

She flings open the door and heads out. "And don't forget exam
two. It's your damn job."

I want to throw things. Every movie scene where some pissed-off
man has cleared everything off his desk runs through my head.

But it's not logical. I'm not being logical. Yes, Ensley needs to go,
and now. She was going to be gone, anyway.

And Maria's right. I shouldn't put it on her to do my dirty work.

I'll get it done.

I quickly head to the puppy exam, talk to the new owners, and shake the hand of another patient with an elderly cat.

Then I sit back at my desk and listen to a voice mail from the surgeon who extracted the wire from Missy this morning. She's recovering fine. That done, I perform a quick internet search for a different temp agency than the one I've used before. They never got back to me.

The new agency is great, and we have a pleasant phone call about the qualifications I'm looking for. The woman assures me they can have someone here tomorrow morning who can type and answer phones until they contact possible temp-to-hire receptionists who enjoy animals. They email the paperwork for me to fill out while we're talking, and I turn it right back in.

That much is done. The position will be filled.

I'll apologize to Maria and bring her flowers if I have to.

Now to fire Ensley James.

Chapter 33

ENSLEY

I don't know what to do. I check in patients like normal, my head spinning.

I have to make Drew understand.

I didn't want to hurt him or teach him a lesson. He's got it all wrong.

I wanted to be with him. I wanted to know him. And once I did, I needed to see if he had more in him than he's given anyone before now. If he had something more for *me*.

I think he does.

No, I *know* he does.

"Ensley?"

I look up. It's Mrs. Evers. I've never met her, but she called earlier, insisting that Drew see Bennie. She's been worried about him for weeks, and I finally suggested she come in. She needs reassurance.

Of course, now I'm concerned Drew will be impatient with her. He thinks she's a dog mom hypochondriac. And he's not in his best mood. I'm quite sure he's actually about as bad as he gets.

"I'll get you checked in," I tell her. "There's a bench near the window for you two."

Bennie is a brown dachshund. He seems perfectly happy, bouncing along on his tiny legs, sniffing at the ground.

Maybe Drew is right. The dog seems fine.

"He looks good, Mrs. Evers. Are you sure something's wrong?"

She picks him up, and he licks her face. "I know I call here a lot. I'm sure you all must think I'm a dotty old woman. But Bennie is my baby. Maybe he's fine, but I have to be sure. Wouldn't you rather be thought a fool than to miss something important?"

My throat tightens. "We're going to make sure Bennie is perfectly healthy and happy. I understand what you mean."

She sits on the bench. "Thank you."

I focus back on my screen. Mrs. Evers is right. You should be willing to look foolish for what's important. You can't care what anybody thinks. I send the notice that Bennie has arrived to the back screen, then switch to managing the flow of emails that have come in. If I stare hard enough, maybe I can figure out how to handle my situation with Drew. I care about him, and I think I'm somehow missing something important, something that's caused this huge misunderstanding between us.

But what?

I didn't want him finding out about my old job this way. Of course he's mad. But if I can get him alone to explain, I'll find the words. I have to.

Maria steps into the lobby to call Mrs. Evers into a room. Maria glances at me briefly, and I can see from the concern in her expression that she knows something is up. But she smiles at Bennie and leads the two of them in for the exam.

Todd pops out of the other exam room. "Dr. Daniels says to call Missy's mom to make sure the surgeon has talked to her. He says Missy's surgery went fine and to schedule a follow-up in three days here with us."

"Got it." I think he's done, and he knows nothing, but then he comes closer. We hardly ever talk, so my stomach drops that he's acting out of character. He knows, too.

"What's up?" I ask, trying to keep my voice level.

He raps his knuckles on the desk. "I probably shouldn't clue you in, but I have to."

"Okay." My heart hammers painfully.

"Drew's going to fire you. He told Maria to do it, and she told him to do it himself. Did y'all break up or something? Vera said she saw you two hanging out awfully long in his office and thought you might be dating or something."

My head spins. He's going to fire me. So that's it. There are no more chances.

Suddenly I can't manage that scene. I don't want it. Don't want to live through it. Don't need it. "Thank you for telling me."

Todd turns to go back to his exam room, but I say, "Can you hold on a second?"

He leans against the filing cabinet. "Sure," he says. "I'm waiting for the two Pomeranians to arrive. They're late."

"They are."

I check the schedule. Four appointments per hour straight through to five o'clock. That's a long time to wait for someone to come yell at you.

I draw in a breath and exhale slowly. "Can you tell Drew that he doesn't need to fire me? Once I check in the last person, I'll just leave. I'll put the keys in the drawer and sign myself out."

"Sure." Todd shrugs. "I wouldn't want to wait around for him to explode all over me, either."

"He already got me once today."

"Sorry. He can be a beast."

"Why do you still work for him?"

Todd shrugs. "I don't like the big chains. Generally, Drew and I get along fine. I leave him alone."

"Can you let me know when you tell him, and what he says?" I grip the handle of my chair. This conversation is so hard. "And I'm sorry if it puts you in a bad position."

"He can't yell at me any louder than he did at Maria. I'm surprised half of Atlanta didn't hear." Todd turns a treat jar in circles. He's uncomfortable, too. "I'll let you know."

"Thanks."

The man with the Pomeranians enters the lobby, and Todd comes forward to help untangle their leashes.

I return to my screen, madly trying to finish out anything that needs doing before the end of the day.

Because apparently, it's my last one at Daniels Vet Care.

Chapter 34

DREW

I'm trying to convince an eighty-pound Doberman to take a pill when I realize Todd has been hovering unnecessarily for the last five minutes.

"Just say whatever you need to say," I tell him, packing more cheese on the pill. Despite whining from pain, this dog could find a med pill in a haystack. I'll have to suggest grinding them up into a paste, because the owner will never get it done. I have the option of a needle, but I didn't want to take Todd or Maria out of their exam rooms.

But now Todd's here.

I tempt the dog with the cheese one more time while speaking to Todd. "You're still not talking."

Todd clears his throat. "Ensley knows she's fired. She's finishing things up and will leave her keys on the desk. You don't have to yell at her again."

The dog sniffs at my hand, but he's figured me out. He won't even eat the cheese off the pill at this point.

"Who says I yelled at her?"

"Anyone in the building at the time."

Todd has never challenged me before. I palm the cheese with the pill and hold on to the Doberman's collar so I can look at my tech. Is he under Ensley's spell, too? Maybe she's got a dozen men at her feet.

"Did she tell you to tell me?"

"Yes."

"And you told her she was fired?"

He stands taller. "I did."

"Did Maria tell you?"

"No. You were yelling. I heard."

I clamp my jaw tight. "Thank you for passing along the message. Now hold on to this dog. He won't take the pain pill by mouth, so I'm going to inject him."

"Is this the one that ran from the kitten and wound up in a cactus patch?"

The long black dog whips his head around to Todd as if daring to make fun of him for his predicament.

"Yes. He's scared of cats. The owner is worried about pain. He won't put down his paw, but there aren't any more cactus spines in him. He just needs to heal." I'm glad we're back to normal territory. I don't want to talk about Ensley.

Todd grips the dog's harness. Even on three legs, this one has the muscle to escape if we're not ready.

I open the cabinet and extract a bottle and a fresh needle. "I hope this does the trick, since he likely won't take the prescription. Maybe the owners have figured out a method that works by now. Be sure and ask."

When the shot goes in, the Doberman lets out a plaintive howl.

"He's kind of a wimp, isn't he?" Todd says.

"Pretty much." I cap the needle. "You can take him back. They shouldn't need to talk to me again."

Todd leads the Doberman to the door. "It's going to suck not having Ensley. She was pretty great."

That again. "I have someone arriving first thing in the morning. It will be fine."

Todd looks doubtful, probably imagining me yelling at the new receptionist.

But I'm turning over a new leaf. I will take deep breaths. I will not raise my voice. I will control my urge to come down hard on people.

Just as soon as Ensley James is out of my life.

Chapter 35

Ensley

Tillie waits for me at our apartment Monday night. I couldn't stay in Atlanta after getting fired. Lila assured me her friends would look after her, and it's only a week until Tillie is there permanently.

Tillie wraps her arms around me. I want to be mad, but I just cry and cry. I'm sad that I had to leave my sister. Sad that my boss, Cindy, is going to be gone. Sad that Drew wouldn't give me a chance to explain. Sad that the job I liked is no longer mine.

She strokes my hair and wipes my face with a damp washcloth, like I used to do to her when we were little. I may have been five when Mom died, but Tillie wasn't even a year old. I was the only mother she knew. I did my best to act like our mother after she was gone. I had Tillie and Lila to care for. Sometimes I swear most of my memories of my mother are my own actions, mimicked and amplified over the years from what I once knew.

"Will you go back to the bank tomorrow?" Tillie asks.

I shrug. "If I feel like it. But Wednesday for sure. It's Cindy's last day."

We watch Hallmark movies, even though I scarcely pay attention. It's helpful, focusing on a screen, letting Tillie comfort me. I'm grateful that she doesn't work Monday nights.

We take Tuesday to be together, getting our nails done and hitting the thrift shops. I find a pair of brown boots even cuter than hers and am glad I can wear something that doesn't remind me of Drew. I shove the gold dress into the back of my closet.

"You going to look at the one-bedrooms?" Tillie asks. "We should both be packing."

It's Tuesday afternoon, and I'm in denial that everything has gone belly-up. "Let me see if the leasing agent is in the office."

"I'll go with you."

We walk arm in arm to the apartment's main office, but it's locked up, a sign on the door saying they'll be back in an hour.

"Come to the bar with me," Tillie says. "I'll make you Blue Hawaiians until you fall off the stool."

"But I'll be a liability."

She pulls me close, pressing our foreheads together. "Nope. You'll just be my sister."

"And you're quitting there, anyway."

She grins. "Exactly."

But when the time comes to go, I can't make myself leave. I end up staying home, a pitcher of Blue Hawaiians on the table. I drink and scroll through my old texts with Drew. I want to delete his contact, but I can't. After half the pitcher, I go to the Daniels Vet Care website and stare at his photo in a white lab coat, stroking the screen as if I can feel his jaw.

And I can. Everything about him is sharply familiar. His chest, his arms, the way he looked down at me when he hovered over my body. Tears come again so I drink faster, watching true crime shows instead of Hallmark because I don't want a whiff of romance.

But even murder makes me think of Felicia and her red wine–stained dress. Then the rain, and the shed, and Drew, Drew, Drew, Drew.

Thankfully, the booze does its job, and I fall into a fitful sleep.

~

I'm a little hungover when I arrive at Farm to Market Bank and Trust the next morning, but it's manageable.

Cindy envelops me in the biggest hug. "I couldn't wait to see one more Ensley outfit before I go."

I step back and strike a pose as if I'm my usual bubbly self, even though inside I feel like I'm dying. I chose an eighties throwback in honor of Cindy's coming-of-age—a distressed denim miniskirt, a black cowl sweater, and fat black suede boots that sag like the jowls of a bulldog.

Bulldog. Vet clinic. Drew.

I shake it off.

"You nailed it!" Cindy says. "I had those very boots!" She marvels over my wrist full of black plastic bracelets and the giant bow in my hair. "You couldn't muster a side pony, though, even for me."

"Some things need to be left in their time period."

Janet side-eyes us as she drops the tills in the drawers. That's weird. She never had vault-and-till privileges before.

"Come meet Milton," Cindy says, swishing in her new navy suit. She's obviously upping her wardrobe with the promotion. Normally, she wears slacks and oversize silky blouses. Still. Navy. Blech.

We head to the safe deposit box room, and I run my hands down my miniskirt nervously. I'd been thinking about Cindy when I got dressed and should have thought about first impressions with the new manager.

When we enter the space, a tall, lean man in a stark black suit stands with arms crossed, watching another young woman struggle to open Box 304, which we've known for ages has been bent and impossible.

"Just get it open!" he booms. "Good grief, woman. Can't you do anything?"

Cindy straightens her jacket, her face neutral. She's got her poker face on. That's not good.

"Milton, this is Ensley James. I told you about her."

He turns to me, his round glasses shaded gray even though we're indoors. He looks like the villain of a James Bond movie.

I wave. "Hi! I'm Ensley."

He looks at me over the frames of his glasses. "The prodigal employee. Finally decided to grace us with your presence?"

Oh boy. I glance at Cindy, who motions for me to step closer to him. I feel like Dorothy facing the Great and Powerful Oz.

Only he's a skinny jerk.

"I cut my vacation short by a day to be here," I say.

"Oh, she wants a trophy," Milton says. "I'm anxious to see this stellar work ethic I've heard about."

Gosh. "But who is this?" I gesture to the new girl.

"I'm—" she says, but Milton cuts her off.

"She's temporary unless she does better," Milton says. "Thirty-day trial period and all that jazz."

The woman deflates. She's wearing the most beautiful blue dress with yellow flowers, and I already want to be her friend. "And your name is?"

"Helen," Milton says, his face pinching as if it's a dirty word. "And she can't even open a safe deposit box."

My compulsion to help this poor woman with her gorgeous dress supersedes my need for self-preservation. "Oh, that one has—"

"She'll get it," Cindy cuts in, and I can barely contain my shock, standing open-mouthed. We've never been able to get 304 to open. It's completely bent out of shape. Why is Cindy letting Milton humiliate Helen?

Cindy takes my arm and leads me out of the room. As soon as we're back in the main area connected to the lobby, I whisper-yell, "What the hell, Cindy?"

She flashes a wan smile. "He might take some getting used to."

"Like a soul-sucking maniac!"

"He's not that bad."

She's in denial. She doesn't want to think that she's leaving us to be miserable. "Helen is very nice," she says.

"I like her style."

"I knew you would. You two can form an alliance and make it through."

Janet sneers at us as we approach the customer service bays. "Meet Milton?"

"I did," I say, wondering what her angle is. Why doesn't she hate him?

"He gave me vault privileges," she says. "That's head teller work."

I whip around to look at Cindy. "But I'm assistant head teller!"

"It will be fine," Cindy says. "It's a reorg."

God. If Janet gets promoted over me after I've been assistant head teller all this time, I will die.

The only good thing about the first day back is Helen. She's resourceful and finds a flat-head screwdriver to jimmy open 304. Milton seems annoyed that she got it done. "It's still mangled," he says dryly, as if that can possibly be her fault since she only arrived two days ago and 304 has been busted since 2010.

Thankfully, Milton does not show up for Cindy's farewell happy hour, citing "important events."

I'm glad. We drink at Tillie's bar, and she keeps us at happy hour prices long after seven. We're all teary, and even Janet manages a few nice words. Helen turns out to be hilarious and a cheap drunk, so I worry less about the impending doom of a day of work without Cindy.

I keep Drew from my mind by sheer will, forcing him out whenever a thought of him pops in, right up until I curl into my covers that night.

And then I'm weeping again, lost, a big hot mess. I wasn't able to afford therapy, not ever, none of us did, but I saw a high school counselor a lot when my grades slipped because Garrett left home, leaving me with yet another hole in my life.

Each loss is every loss, she'd told me, and the words had taken hold.

So it wasn't just Drew I'd lost. It was the feelings that young girl had for the boy who came to play football with her brother, who hauled her screaming after getting caught stealing from a lemon tree, and whose mother gave her warm cookies and kicked off an obsession with cookie dough as safety.

Even more than that, though, it's about my mom. And the dad I had before she died.

And the hope for Lila, who's stuck now.

And tomorrow I have to face my first day at my old job without my best work friend.

I'm done being positive.

Life sucks.

Chapter 36

DREW

The new receptionist arrives promptly at seven thirty the next morning.

Abigail Fullman is in her midforties, an avid rock climber, and looks like she could bench-press a pony. She breezes into the lobby, looks around, and immediately says, "This could be cleaner," before I can even introduce myself.

She's not quite what I expected after a rash of twentysomethings, but it's a good thing. She'll have the mettle I've been looking for.

After only the barest introduction to her desk and log in, she asks me for the janitor closet and fishes out a spray bottle and rags. "I'm sure the animals will piddle mercilessly, but it should start out cleaner than it is." She immediately starts spraying the benches down.

When the first phone call comes, she plucks the portable receiver off the base and answers with a chirpy, "Daniels Vet Care, how may I help you?" while spraying the windows behind the chairs where the cleaning service tends to skimp.

Maria moves next to me, the day's patient folders in her arms. "Look at that."

"I know."

"I'll make sure she can check everyone in and file things correctly." She plunks the pile on the desk.

"I'll get the back ready for dental day."

Maria nods, watching the woman clean. She doesn't seem perfectly pleased, but I'm ecstatic. The new agency clearly has a better depth of personnel. This terrible period of revolving receptionists will end soon. I will be an absolute peach and give Abigail no cause to go.

But even the word *peach* bouncing into my head takes me back to the night of the wedding, the bridesmaids' puffed skirts, and Ensley thrown over my shoulder.

This delivers an entire onslaught of visions of Ensley. In the shed. Talking up the sommelier. In my kitchen. On my bed.

There's no need to rush my prep. I have a half hour before anyone will check in. I pivot on my heel, head to my office, and close the door.

Sasha scoots in with a flash of white fur, hopping onto my desk.

I don't want to sit there feeling miserable, my head in my hands.

But I do.

And what's worse, it's for nothing. It's not like I forced her to leave. She'd been planning to go home all along.

～

When the last dental patient is in his kennel, twitching out of the anesthesia under Maria's watchful eye, I check back in on the receptionist.

I pause at the end of the hallway to watch her work.

The lobby is clear at the moment, a lull after the dentals before the normal appointments begin. Abigail is on her hands and knees by the bench, scrubbing at the floor like there is no tomorrow.

She's mumbling something. I come up on her quietly until I can make out her words.

"Disgusting, vile mutts. Pissing on the floor. Stupid cats, scratching the vinyl. Stupid animals reeking of shit and stink and licking their own butts. We should drown the lot of them."

Heat rises in me, spewing forth like a science fair volcano. I have no control over the volume of my voice when I boom, "What the hell did you just say?"

Abigail jumps to her feet. "Dr. Daniels! Oh! I was cleaning up after the animals who were here earlier. Some nervous accidents, the poor things."

The glass rattles as I say, "Drown the lot of them?"

Her jaw drops. "I mean, what I meant was. Oh." She glances left and right.

"Why did you even take this position?"

"I. Uh. Oh. Haven't had a placement in a while." She clutches the floor cleaner bottle like a shield.

"Get. Out."

She scrambles to the desk and jerks open a drawer. "Yes. Of course. Good luck."

She snatches her purse and pulls her jacket off the back of the chair.

I stand unmoving in the middle of the lobby as she moves as far from me as she can to escape through the door.

Maria barrels down the hall and into the room. "What on earth?" She watches Abigail hustle to her car. "What happened?"

"She was wrong for this place." I cross the lobby to cut through an empty exam room to the back.

Maria doesn't budge. "Who's going to answer the phones, then?"

I have nothing to say to that. I don't know.

I sit at my desk. Should I call another agency? Call back this one?

I turn to my screen to do another search.

There has to be someone out there who can work with me. Someone who isn't impossible.

Todd stands in the doorway. "I don't speak up much about things happening around here."

"So don't start now."

He frowns. "We could cut and run, you know. The entire staff. We don't because we see how much you love these pets. You'd jump in front of a train for one."

I clamp my jaw to avoid yelling. "And your point is?"

211

"If you can't treat us like the lowest of the animals. Like the baby bunny you stayed to watch being born." He gestures to Sasha, curled up under my monitor. "Like this stray kitten you decided to keep." He blows out a rush of air. "Then you need to have a smaller, solo practice out of your house or something. Because when you treat someone like Ensley worse than a dog, it's a problem. Not with how you love dogs. But with how you don't love humans."

Speech done, he raps his knuckles on the door and leaves.

Who knew Todd was an orator? I should fire them all, but I catch myself. What's with this burn-it-to-the-ground mentality? Where is it coming from? Why can't I control it?

I know exactly what it is. Of course I do. It has nothing to do with Ensley. It goes so much further back.

But I won't think about it. I won't let those thoughts intrude one bit.

And to make sure it all goes to the same place, I picture the memories of Ensley, shove them into the same part of my brain that holds all the rest of it, and slam the damn door.

Chapter 37

ENSLEY

I don't want to go to work after Cindy's gone.

I didn't drink much at the happy hour, but I definitely have a crying jag hangover. Those are the worst. Puffy eyes, red nose, and lingering despair.

And of course, it's the first day of hell with Milton as my boss.

On Thursday morning, he tries to line all of us up in a row like soldiers at basic training.

The banking reps bug out almost immediately, claiming they have calls from corporate. Milton can't do much about it, and he takes out his frustration on the tellers.

Helen, Janet, and I stand in front of the wall of windows looking out on the drive-through lanes, waiting for Milton to get through his spiel about punctuality, accuracy, and self-discipline.

Janet nods the whole time, eyes big behind her round glasses, her cheek-length bob swinging back and forth like she's found a new religion.

She's sucking up. And it sucks.

Helen stands at attention, shoulders back, head up, arms at her sides. I half expect her to say, "Sir, yes sir!" She's probably terrified.

Milton pauses in front of me, taking a long, smirky look at my red-and-white-striped top and bright-green pants. "Are you an elf, lost from the North Pole?"

"The clients here like to come into the lobby and see what I'm wearing. It's been my thing since I got here."

"Not anymore. Professional dress. Navy blue. Black. White shirts preferred, but beige and tan are fine."

Good lord. I don't even own any neutrals. I can't afford a whole new wardrobe.

"Is this okay?" Helen asks. Her dress is a dark burgundy.

"Borderline," Milton says. "This is a respectable establishment where customers trust us with their money." He turns to me. "Not a competition for most outlandish costume."

The clock hits eight, which is when the drive-through opens. The first car of the day pulls up into the commercial lane.

Milton steps away from me. "Janet, I want you to handle the business transactions coming through."

I can't stop crying out with an explosive, "What!"

Janet turns to greet the customer. I have to shut my mouth while her microphone is on. As soon as the chute is activated, though, I finish what I started. "That's the job of the assistant head teller or the manager!"

"Or the head teller," Milton says. "I'm putting Janet in that position on a trial basis. I'm under the impression that Janet was underutilized with the previous management."

I want to sputter and spit.

"Helen, you fill the lobby desk with pens and deposit slips." Milton gestures for her to leave.

Now it's just me standing in front of him. Another car pulls into the drive-through, this time a regular lane.

"Well, go on," Milton says. "Do your job. Or did you forget after a week off?"

I was here yesterday, doing it, but I don't snap at him again. Instead, I take the farthest position from Janet and say hello to the new driver in the lane.

Mercifully, once the day gets underway, the customer traffic is enough to keep me busy. Milton trains Helen on using the check scanner and cash counter, berating her for every mistake. He's given her the crappy one that gets stuck. When he's called to the lobby for a problem with the ATM, I switch out the machines so she'll have a better one.

"You okay?" I ask her.

She shrugs. "He's better than my last boss."

Janet swivels on the stool by the drive-through. "Girl, same."

My head feels like it might explode. "Cindy was great!"

Janet shrugs. "She was your friend. Now you have to work like the rest of us."

"I did work!" Oh my God! This is outrageous.

It's time for the first lunch shift, and I take it, stomping to the break room like an angry toddler. When I open the fridge, I shift the tape on Janet's zone out of sheer spite.

But doing it only makes me think of Drew. And then I'm down yet another unhappy rabbit hole.

Milton comes into the room, and I tense up immediately. Please don't eat now. Please, please. There's only one table in the space.

But he heads to the coffeepot and fills his cup. "Don't take one minute over thirty." He taps his watch on his way out.

I'm blissfully alone. I unzip my lunch bag and pull out my Good Noodles to heat. There's also a granola bar, and I hold it in my hand, thinking of Cindy and her mushroom cauliflower. And my sister, sick in her bathroom with a baby on the way. And Maria and Vera and Todd.

Another crying jag threatens, but I force myself to buck up. "You're a ray of fucking sunshine, Ensley James," I say aloud, then laugh. "Nah. Just be you." It helps to cut myself some slack, and I heat my noodles. I'm blowing on them when Janet comes in. "Hurry up," she says. "I'm starving, and I can't be off the line while you're in here. Helen doesn't know anything yet."

"Why can't Milton cover? We never needed more than one person on the station at this time of day."

Janet repeats my words in a whiny simper. "We never needed more than one person befooooore."

Whew, that's mature. I breathe in the steam from my noodles and pretend she isn't there.

She gets a cup of coffee, and I wonder what the heck that's about. Janet's never drunk coffee a day in her life.

Until Milton.

Gross. She's trying to be like him.

I pick up my phone to check messages and spy a text from my brother, Garrett. Headed over tonight to help Tillie break down her bed and shelves for the move.

A wave of grief takes over. I'm not only stuck in this horrible new version of my job, but my sister is leaving me.

The losses keep coming.

~

I lie on the sofa staring at the ceiling until Garrett shows up with Tillie to start packing. I know I should do the same, but I can't seem to force myself to do it. It's admitting defeat.

"Hey, sis. Good to see you're lazy as always." He kicks the bottom of my shoe, which is sticking off the end of the cushion. He's tan from working outdoors in construction, wearing a flannel over a T-shirt and grease-stained jeans. He's probably the best-looking of our whole brood.

I give him the finger.

"Let her be," Tillie says. "She's mourning your old friend Drew."

Garrett pulls a screwdriver out of his pocket and kneels in front of the empty bookcase Tillie's taking with her. "Still pining for him after all these years?"

I flash a murderous look at Tillie, but she only shrugs. "No, she was seeing him in Atlanta last week while we were there with Lila."

Garrett looks up from the shelf he's taking apart. "How did that happen?"

I refuse to speak, face crabby and arms crossed over my chest, so Tillie keeps going. "They were both in Franklin and Ronnie's wedding. I told you they got married finally."

Garrett sets the first shelf on the carpet. "So you had a wedding hookup?"

I can't let that one go. "No."

Tillie grabs an empty box from the corner and heads for the hall. "I'm going to fill this while you two catch up. Garrett, tell your sister Drew isn't worth the hassle."

Garrett turns to me. "Drew isn't worth the hassle."

"What do you know about anything?" I pick up a pillow, intending to throw it, but he holds up his arm.

"So tell me. I haven't talked to Drew in years."

"He's a veterinarian," I say. "He has his own clinic."

"Damn. That was fast."

"He bought it off a guy who was retiring, so he didn't have to build it out."

"How did you two end up going out?" He bumps the round end of the screwdriver against a shelf to knock it loose.

I wait out the noise before answering. "He was having trouble keeping a receptionist on account of his terrible temper and grumpy attitude, so I helped out for a few days."

"That's a weird thing to do for someone you barely know."

Yeah, the story doesn't tell easy. I already know this.

Tillie's head appears around the corner. "She's leaving out the part where they kept getting naked."

"We weren't naked!" Except, I guess, we were at the end. "We had some weird chemistry going on. I wanted to be around him, see where it led."

Garrett shakes his head as he neatly stacks another shelf on the first one. "I reckon it wasn't easy for him to live up to the pedestal you put him on when you were a kid."

He doesn't have to tell me. I already know.

"He fired me in the end. I guess I didn't understand him after all. Seems like all he wants is a one-nighter."

"I'm not surprised." Garrett examines another shelf, splintered on the end. "He always said he wouldn't get into relationships. Said they weren't worth it."

"Right." I sit up on the sofa. "Because all his guy friends got sucked in by women and stopped hanging with him."

Garrett pauses in turning a screw. "He said that? Because that wasn't his reasoning in high school. I was there when it happened. And I don't blame him."

Wait. Garrett knows something more?

"What happened?"

Garrett taps his screwdriver on his hand. "I don't know if I should be the one to say it."

I circle the coffee table and sit next to him. "Garrett, please. Drew broke my damn heart. We—well, things happened. I thought I was going to move there and be with him. Then he overreacted and fired me and that was it."

"Overreacted to what?"

"That I still had a job here. He thought I'd already quit."

"He always had a temper. It came in handy on the football field. He imagined the other players were his dad, and he would tackle the hell out of them." Garrett turns back to the shelves, but I take the screwdriver from him.

"What was wrong with his dad?"

His eyes meet mine, and I see all the versions I once knew of my brother. The little kid, only a bit taller than me, racing through the house. The sad, silent one after Mom died, trying to hold himself together. The lanky adolescent, desperately trying to be good enough to get a football scholarship, and falling short.

I love him. I don't blame him one bit for escaping our house the way he did. We all would have done it if we could.

He's the best man I know, and he's torn about some secret that could unlock what I don't know about Drew.

"The story might help me," I say. "It's not like I'm going to see him again. I want to work out what happened in my head so I can move on."

Garrett runs his hands along the shelf and sighs. "All right. His parents were always this perfect couple. Cookies after school. Kiss on the cheek."

"I only ever met his mom."

"I was over there a lot. And it looked pretty good to me. But then one day our sophomore year, Drew shows me this box he found in the garage. It's full of letters from women, and some of them recent. His dad's got a whole string of them, all thinking he's leaving his wife for them."

"Oh no."

"And that's not even the worst of it. Old man Daniels catches Drew with the stash. And what does he do? Makes him stand guard at the garage to make sure his mom doesn't come home while he was banging those chicks in their own bed!"

"What?"

"And as soon as Drew did it once, then his dad had the threat of telling his mom that Drew was in on it. It was the worst damn thing the bastard could have done. So Drew had to keep doing it. Hiding his dad's hookups from his own mom."

My heart sinks. No wonder he's miserable. "That's terrible."

Garrett holds out his hand, and I pass him back the screwdriver. "So that's the whole dirty business. He might have made up some other excuse to you, but that's the real deal. He never made anyone a girl-friend. He said he thought he might be like his dad, and he couldn't stand it. I guess the one-night thing makes it easy. You can't cheat on someone who isn't yours to begin with."

I sit by Garrett while he finishes the shelves, and I don't move when he heads to Tillie's bedroom to take apart her bed so that it will fit in a friend's truck.

Poor Drew. This is terrible.

But he can be his own person. He can control himself. He's thirty years old. Surely he knows that.

Doesn't he?

I simply have to talk to him. Shock him with what I know.

I have nothing to lose.

Chapter 38

DREW

The latest receptionist, Tatiana, pops into the surgery bay on Friday.

"Why are you interrupting?" I ask, forgetting I'm trying to improve my tone. Tatiana furrows her brow at me, her long ponytail of black braids swinging.

"Dr. Drew, stop snapping like you're the last turtle in the pond. I have to give you messages, and if you can't handle an interruption during a basic neutering job, you need to get yourself a more seasoned vet all up in here."

Todd, who is assisting in the surgery, bites back a smile.

"Fine." I turn back to the dog. "What is it?"

"Nope," Tatiana says. "You ask nicely."

This is the receptionist I deserve. I know it. "Can you please convey to me your message?"

"I'd be happy to, Dr. Daniels. Your friends Franklin and Ronnie are here to see you."

I didn't expect that. "Tell them I'll be there in about ten minutes."

Tatiana spins around, heading back to the lobby. It's her second day, and it's pretty clear she's more in charge than I am.

"Those your friends who got married?" Todd asks.

"Yeah."

And it's odd that they're here. They should barely be back from their honeymoon cruise. They've been totally out of contact.

But they probably know about Ensley now. I guess this confrontation was unavoidable.

I leave Todd in charge of watching the beagle come out of anesthesia, and shuck my white coat on the way to my office.

The moment I walk in, Ronnie stands up and says, "Drew Daniels, who do you think you are?"

Yep, they know about Ensley.

"Welcome back."

Ronnie charges up to me, all four feet, eleven inches of her, and pushes on my chest. "You had sex with my best friend! And then you fired her! You're a monster, and I should have thrown you out of my wedding myself!"

"Babe, babe, let's discuss this like adults." Franklin draws her back against his chest. "Ronnie had about seventy messages from Ensley when we hit land. We put the story together."

I clamp my jaw to avoid roaring. My voice is measured as I say, "Then you know she lied about living here. About taking this job."

Ronnie wrestles away from Franklin to stab me in the chest again. "She thought she was helping. You were the ass who assumed she wanted to work for you. She didn't know what to do."

"Oh." I think back on that first day. Ensley had seemed flustered when I said she was hired. I thought she was overwhelmed that I took her on so quickly.

Ronnie pokes me again. "When she thought you two had a chance, she found a way to be near you until she could figure things out. Of course she didn't quit her old job. You know how she grew up. She wasn't going to risk being hungry and homeless if you dumped her. And that's exactly what you did! Thank God she was smart enough not to put her future in your hands!"

Even though I want to argue with Ronnie about the nature of firing Ensley, I'm stopped by one thing she said. That Ensley wouldn't have risked her job without knowing she was safe.

Damn it.

Of course.

Shit.

"Yeah, I see you putting it together." Ronnie pokes me again for good measure. "And you had to go and break her damn heart."

"Nobody's heart was broken," I say. "We only had three dates."

"And how many do you usually do?" Ronnie asks. "Oh wait, you told her straight up. One. One damn date. And she got three! She was so happy. She's crushed on you since she was twelve years old! You're her big blind spot! Oh! I wish I'd been here." She turns and pokes Franklin in the chest. "And you wouldn't let us have a satellite plan!"

Franklin knows better than to argue. "Sorry, babe."

Ronnie turns back to me. "She thought you two were the real deal."

Had she? Hadn't I? I only know I saw red when I realized I'd been lied to. And I hadn't even seen her again. She'd left like she told Todd she would, locking the lobby door at the end of the day and slipping out the back without a word to anyone.

Ronnie stands on her tiptoes, not that it gets her much closer to my face. "So what are you going to do about it, Drew Daniels?"

"I don't think I can do anything," I say. "She left. She didn't say goodbye. We haven't talked."

Ronnie pokes me again. "Not good enough. It's grand gesture time. I want to see you climbing a fire escape."

"Doesn't she live on the ground floor?" I ask, but Franklin gives me a throat-slicing motion over Ronnie's head. "Of course," I add.

"Show up in a limo. With roses. And give a big speech in front of a crowd."

"Babe, I think you've watched too many rom-coms." Franklin is hushed by Ronnie's arm slashing through the air perilously close to his face.

"Ensley deserves it. She had my back at my wedding when everyone else just stood there. She has everybody's back. And I bet she was the best damn employee you ever had."

I take a step back, but Ronnie is unrelenting, walking forward so that I can't escape her. "You will put yourself on the line for her. You will."

"What if she doesn't want to have anything to do with me?"

"Then you get to feel just a fraction of what she's going through. It's what. You. Deserve." She punctuates each word with a stab in my chest.

"Okay, we've said our piece," Franklin says. "Let's go get some ice cream."

"Fine." Ronnie's face doesn't change, but she lets Franklin guide her toward the door. "But if you don't do your part, I'll be back. I think she should quit you, but I'm not the one who can tell her to ignore her own heart."

I'm certain hearts have nothing to do with it, but I hear what she's saying. I sit down on my chair, elbows on my desk.

Sasha has been watching the entire exchange from a high perch on the file cabinet, but she jumps down, winding herself through my arms. The motor of her purr helps me calm.

There's too much going on in my head to sort this now. I have work to do. My life doesn't slow down for personal problems. There's a rap on the door, and I prepare myself for round two of Ronnie's onslaught, but it's Tatiana.

"The second surgery canceled. The dog was throwing up through the night, and she didn't feel it was a good day to do the neutering."

I nod. "Thank you. Reschedule it."

Tatiana gives me a look.

"Please reschedule it. Thank you."

"That's better."

I shake my head. Tatiana has my number, that's for sure. Between her and Maria, I can't even talk loud without a reprimand. It's fine. I ought to know how to behave by now. I'll get it right. Until then, they are right to treat me like a toddler.

But the cancellation means I have a blank space in my schedule, a small breather I can use to figure out what to do about Ensley.

Email her? Text her? Do I reach out at all? Despite Ronnie's threats, I could let this go. Let Ensley go.

Sasha meows and sits prettily, her long white tail curled around her paws. I could send a picture. Take this full circle.

I open the drawer and pull out my cell phone. I don't keep it on me during surgery. There are two notifications. One is from Franklin, warning me that Ronnie wants to visit and she's pissed.

The second, well. Damn.

The second one is from Ensley.

I can barely swallow over the lump in my throat as I click through to read it.

Drew. You are not your father. Having one-night stands with lots of women doesn't mean you are destined to be a cheater. You have choices. You can make different ones. Call me when you get your shit together.

I try to think how to reply. I type word after word, then delete each one. I take pictures of Sasha, thinking I'll use her anyway.

But it doesn't seem right.

I know who can tell me what to do. The only person who can really understand where I came from, what's made me into *me*.

I scroll to the top of my contacts and press the button for *Mom*.

She answers on the second ring. "Drew! I haven't heard from you since Ronnie's wedding. How was it?"

Now that's a loaded question.

"It went fine."

"Was Felicia as terrible as everyone thought she'd be?"

"Worse."

Mom's laugh trickles through me like raindrops on thirsty dirt. "You're calling me during the workday. That's not usual."

I hesitate. What do I want to ask her? What is love? How did she still believe in it after everything Dad did?

When it all blew up, she told me she'd known all along, which helped alleviate my guilt. Only when she learned that Dad was blackmailing me did she finally decide to leave him. I lived with her until I graduated and left for Georgia Tech.

I don't speak to my father. Probably never will again.

"Baby? What's wrong?" Now her voice is dark with concern. "Did something happen?"

I clear my throat of any emotion. "How did you get past what happened with Dad?"

"What do you mean? The divorce? Going back to work?"

"No, emotionally, I mean. You've been dating. How do you trust anybody?"

"Well, I figure there can only be so many really bad characters." Her voice lightens. "Surely I won't get quite so unlucky twice."

The harder question is on the tip of my tongue, but I don't know how to ask it.

"Why are you asking me now? I always got the impression that you never wanted to talk about it."

"I, well, I met someone."

"Did you now? You've never mentioned a woman before."

"I never really dated before."

There's a small silence, then she says, "I had a feeling that might be it."

I try to speak, but my throat is closed down. Damn, there's that stupid emotion. I force myself past it. "I think I might be like Dad."

"No." Her voice is hard-edged and firm. "You are not like him at all. The capacity to love, truly love, isn't in him."

"I only seem to care about the animals."

"And that should tell you all you need to know. Love isn't limited that way. If you can love anything, then you can love, period."

"I'm not so sure."

"Well, I am. And I'm your mother, so you have to listen to me."

I bark out a quick laugh. "Probably so."

"You going to tell me who she is? Her name at least?"

"You know her."

"Part of the old crowd, then? Did you see her at the wedding?"

"I did. Ensley James."

Another pause. "Does she know how you've always felt?"

"Mom."

"I know, I know. She was too young for you. But I know why Garrett was your best friend. I know why you always went there instead of coming here. To see her. Help her family out. Even back then. It's always been Ensley."

"Is there anything you don't know?"

"There are things I wish I didn't."

We're quiet again. She waits me out. She's good with silences.

I clear my throat to be sure it will work. "She was thinking of moving here to be with her sister, but I wrecked it."

"Can it be fixed?"

"I don't know."

"Are you going to try?"

"Maybe. Any ideas?"

"Show her you know who she is. Meet her where she's at."

I do know who Ensley is. And she told me what she wanted from me. Said it plain as day.

"Thanks, Mom."

"Let me know how it turns out. And if you end up here in Alabama, I'm only a mile from Ensley's childhood home."

"I know, Mom."

"Give an old lady a visit."

"I will."

"Good luck, baby."

I only sit there for seconds before the image of what I need to do is in my head. Mom had a favorite romance movie when I was a kid. I thought it was cheesy and horrible.

But I bet Ensley doesn't.

I know exactly where I'm headed and what I'm going to do.

Chapter 39

ENSLEY

Thank God it's Friday.

I wait for Milton to leave the teller area for the vault before taking my position at the drive-through window. I've avoided him all morning, although he did seek me out to berate me for letting the pen stock get low in the lobby. I'll fill it up after this line of cars dies down.

Pens. I'm reprimanded over pens.

Helen has trained up and manages the lobby window while Janet and I work the cars. Fridays are always busy with customers cashing their paychecks for the weekend.

I smile and count cash and fill the pneumatic tubes, over and over. I miss being at the counter, but since my wardrobe is now the same as a funeral director's, there's not much to see, anyway. I can't believe I've been forced to wear navy blue.

I'll have to shop this weekend to get more drab things. The money I got from working for Drew dropped yesterday, so I have a bit extra.

My designated lunch period finally arrives, the last one of the day, and I'm starved. As soon as I enter the break room, I greedily pull out my phone to see if Drew has responded to my text this morning. It's not likely. I should have done it last night after Garrett left. But I'd filled screen after screen with thoughts, and it took sleeping on it to decide which one was best.

Nothing yet. But there is a note from Cindy asking how it's going. I write her back.

Me: A nightmare. I have to wear navy.

Cindy: There's a couple holes in some other cities.

Me: Like where?

Cindy: Memphis. Savannah.

Me: I don't know anyone there.

Cindy: I didn't see Atlanta on the list.

I never told her about Drew going up in flames.

Me: It's fine.

Cindy: I'll give you the best reference ever. Just let me know.

I send a message to Lila, asking if she's doing all right. I do this multiple times a day, now that she's alone. Tillie won't get there until Monday. I still have to go to the leasing office and find a new apartment in the complex. I'm down to mere days on this one.

Too much.

It's all too much.

Maybe I need a huge fresh start.

I wait for my noodles to cook and scroll through links for job sites. I click on one and type in *bank teller*.

It assumes Alabama based on the geolocation, but then I get an idea and change it to Atlanta, Georgia. If not for Drew, for my sisters.

Several line up, all requiring me to sign up before I can look closer. I glance around the room, making sure nobody's coming in to see what I'm doing, then quickly register for the site.

Gosh. There are a lot of openings. You can upload your résumé and have them send you a list, but then one catches my eye.

Farm to Market Bank and Trust.

Not Atlanta, but Marietta. It's a town just outside Atlanta on the same side of the city where my sister lives. Cindy probably didn't recognize it.

Me: Cindy, there's a spot in Marietta.

Cindy: Where is that?

Me: Just outside Atlanta!

There's a pause. I start gulping my noodles. Lunch is almost over.

Cindy: It's entry level. You'll take a cut.

Me: But I will live with my sisters. I can afford a cut.

Cindy: You want it? I'll put you in for it.

Me: I want it!

Cindy: I'll email you some paperwork. We'll make this happen.

My heart absolutely sings. It will be a bit of a commute, and less money until I can work my way back up. But I'll be with my sisters.

And not so close to Drew that I think about him all the time.

Of course I'll think about him all the time.

The thirty-minute mark hits, so I quickly toss my trash and hurry to the teller booths, silencing my phone. I can't wait to tell Tillie and Lila, but I'll make sure the paperwork goes through first.

I give Milton a bright smile as I sit on a stool at the windows.

"It's quiet out here," he says. "Go wipe down the plants in the lobby. They look dusty."

Janet sneers at me.

I swivel on the seat. "Isn't that what the cleaning staff—"

"Are you questioning your superior?"

This isn't worth it. I'm as good as out of here, but I'd rather not get fired before we can get my transfer through. That might look bad.

"Sure, Milton. I'll do it."

I open the janitorial closet and find a clean cloth and a spray bottle. Milton stands close to Janet, and I start to wonder if something's happening between them as she gazes up at him.

Don't do it! I want to tell her. Not with your boss!

But I can't stop others from making the mistake I did.

Distance is important, I realize. Maybe established couples can work in the same office, but a new romance is too volatile. The highs and lows are too much. And if it goes belly-up, well, there goes your job.

I know better now.

I pop into the lobby. It's empty for the moment, so nobody gets to witness the teller having to clean the plants. But Milton is right about them. They're dusty. The cleaning service has been missing them.

I try to find some peace in the task. I'll be doing lowly ones again anyway, once I'm in Marietta. I can be humble.

The door opens behind me, sending a bright swath of light across the plant. I turn my back, hoping it's not a regular who expects me to be in colorful clothes behind the glass.

I spray a low leaf, thick and green. I'll make this the cleanest, brightest plant in the lobby. I'll be happy with my lot until I can make the change I need. I don't need to fake being positive. There isn't a mantra for this. Just honest work and hope.

And fresh-baked cookies. I'll make a cookie for every leaf I have to clean.

A pair of shoes stops by my knees. They're brown and shiny. The khaki pants are cuffed, and I think I see a smattering of white cat hair on them.

Something in me knows Drew has these same shoes, and that the cat hair is Sasha's. But it's a Friday afternoon, and he's at his vet clinic three hours away. It's surgery day.

But the shoes don't move.

Then he speaks, low and gravelly and unmistakable. "Nobody makes Ensley James wear navy blue."

Milton comes out the door to the lobby, but I barely register him, or how Helen and Janet have come to the glass to see what's happening. I look up and he's there, his white shirt rolled up his forearms, his tie loose at his throat. He seems harried, like he's had to come here in a rush.

"Drew?"

Milton's voice cuts through the lobby. "Sir, we can take care of you at the window. She's cleaning the plants."

"So Ensley James is cleaning the plants," Drew says, each word coming slowly and deliberately, like a mobster trying to make sure he has his facts straight before ordering an execution. "If your best teller is dusting the foliage, then you must have made her do it. And it's true that shit floats to the top."

Milton sputters as Drew grabs my hands and lifts me to standing. "Ensley, I failed on the one thing I vowed a decade ago when I was your brother's friend. I swore I would help your family. I'd be part of what kept you all safe. I got the opportunity to make good on my promise, and I let you down."

I squeeze Drew's hand. "But your father—"

Drew shakes his head. "You were right. My father isn't me. I can do better." His smile is small, but it's the best Drew can do. "It's time to get you out of here."

He scoops me up in his arms, and Helen lets out a cheer. "You go, Ensley! Get your man!"

"This is highly inappropriate!" Milton is sputtering again.

I wish Cindy were here to see this. She'd be whooping it up. But she's already made my escape possible. And so did I. No matter what Janet might say, I did a good job here. Customers loved me. And I was able to be friends with my boss. *That's* what has gotten me a transfer. Me. My work. My attitude.

I link my hands around Drew's neck. "Where are you taking me?"

"To Atlanta. I won't let you feel anything but safe ever again."

"So you're rescuing me?"

He pulls me more tightly against his chest. "Isn't that what you always wanted?"

"I have news for you, Dr. Daniels," I say. "I already got myself a job in Marietta so I could live with my sisters."

"What?" Milton shouts. "You didn't give notice."

Drew carries me to the door. "Consider this her notice."

Helen runs out with my purse and jacket. "Don't forget these!" She piles them on my belly. "Good for you!" she whispers.

She opens the door for us, light blasting into the lobby one more time. Drew carries me out to his car. "So you got a new job?"

I tweak his nose. "I already saved myself. And I'll be able to help my sisters."

He sets me down by his SUV. "I'm glad. They're important."

"Do you remember what Julia Roberts said at the end of *Pretty Woman*?"

He shakes his head. "I don't watch romantic movies. Other than my mom's favorite."

"*An Officer and a Gentleman*?" I venture.

"How did you know?" He unlocks the door.

I gesture back toward the bank. "Hello! The factory scene."

"She may have made me watch it more than once." He leans against the side of the car. "So what did Julia Roberts say at the end of *Pretty Woman*?"

I lean into his chest up on tiptoe so that I'm in kissing range.

"She saves him right back."

Chapter 40

ENSLEY

Six months later

It's happening. It's happening.

I shove my phone in my pocket and whip my headset off. "Carrie!" I call across the room. "Carrie!"

The other tellers turn to me, saying their spiels to the line of cars. Of course it happened on a Friday afternoon, when we're end-to-end with cars lining up to deposit paychecks.

Carrie turns from the cash drawer where she's counting out twenties to replenish our stashes. "Is it time?"

"It's time!"

She shoves the drawer closed. "I'll take your spot. You get to the hospital." She squeezes my arm. "Tell Lila it will be horrible, but in the end, that baby will be worth it."

I nod, passing her my headset. Carrie has been my boss since I moved to the Marietta branch, and she's wonderful. She lets me wear whatever I want, and once again, clients come in to see what my daily outfit is.

I've been able to go to Lila's prenatal appointments with no fuss about time off. And when her scumbag boyfriend tried to show up around the seventh month, I was able to take a week to get her through the dark days after he said she was a fat sow and left her a second time.

Men are the worst.

Except Drew, of course.

I snatch my bag from the cubbies in the break room and push out into the brisk fall air. The baby is coming! I put through a quick call to Drew's cell phone.

He picks up, a minor miracle, although the clinic is definitely less harried since Tatiana took over as office manager. She's got the whole space humming so well that Maria took a two-week vacation over the summer.

"Is it time?" he asks.

"Yes!"

"I have one last patient, then I'll be up there."

"You sure? You'll probably be sitting in the waiting room by yourself."

"I'll do the food runs and make sure you all have what you need."

"Okay. See you there."

I start my car. Tillie is with Lila, and they've already left for the hospital with her packed bag. My own bag is in the back seat. I have Good Noodles and granola bars, soft warm sweats to stay comfy, and treats for Lila. Plus the first baby gift, which Tillie and I bought together, a precious swaddling blanket and matching hat for her first pictures.

I get stuck in traffic and smack my hands against the steering wheel. Tillie texts that they've checked in and Lila will be in birthing room 407.

I'm still on the freeway when Drew texts to say he's on his way. Good grief, I'm going to be the last one there.

If I don't make this baby's birth, I'm going to be so mad!

But I needn't have worried. When I arrive in the room, Lila is getting settled in her gown and Tillie is starting up the labor playlist.

"Drew went to get coffee for all y'all," Lila says. She looks perfectly fine, like nothing's happening at all.

I drop my bag on the floor. "Are you actually in labor?"

But then it happens. Lila clutches her belly, her breath coming in huffs. I rush to her side and hold her hand like we practiced in her birthing class. Tillie takes her spot near her shoulders, massaging the tension there.

The nurse pops in. "I see your team is all assembled. Where did Dad go?"

The three of us exchange glances. I'm about to correct her when Lila squeezes my hand. I instantly know what she means. It's nice to feel like this is a normal situation. There is no need to tell anybody about the real dad until it's time to sign the certificate.

"He's getting coffee," Tillie says. "This is Lila's other sister, Ensley."

"How lovely you're all here. I'm Candace, and I'll be here through the night. Are you comfortable enough? We've paged your OB and let him know labor has started."

Lila nods, huffing in and out.

"Good." She writes her name on the whiteboard. "I'll be back to do the next set of vitals soon. Call me if you feel anxious or have any trouble."

When she opens the door, Drew is there, holding a to-go tray of coffee cups. "Ensley, you're here!" He leans down to kiss me, but I hold him away until the nurse has cleared the door.

Drew looks at me inquisitively. "Is there something I don't know?"

"The nurse thinks you're Dad," I say. "We're going to let her keep thinking it. So don't freak her out by kissing me."

Tillie bursts out laughing. "You know this ruse is going to bite us in the butt."

"Shush," Lila says. "And put your attention on me. I'm the one having a baby." Her contraction must have ended, because she's talking normally again.

"Asshole isn't going to show up, is he?" I ask. "Drew makes a much better father figure."

Tillie throws me a look, but I ignore her. "We need to know."

Lila shakes her head. "I lied about the due date, just in case. He thinks it's October. I don't want him here."

"Good for you," Tillie says.

"We've got you," I tell her.

"We really do," Drew says. "Just call me Dad."

"I'm going to laugh when they try to take pictures of you two and the baby," Tillie says.

"I will like that picture just fine," Lila says. "Thank you for being here, Drew. The jig will be up when my regular doctor arrives, so you'll be free to avoid the icky parts. He knows about he-who-will-not-be-named."

Drew sets the coffee on the side table. "I'm here for whatever you need me to do."

The hours are long. Lila gets an epidural and sleeps between contractions. I crash next to Tillie on a foldout sofa. Drew mans the rocking chair, fetching ice or drinks or food as we need. I'm so glad it's a weekend so he can be here.

Around two a.m., I awake with a start. More people fill the room.

"We're going to fetch Dr. Hendrix, the obstetrician on call," the nurse says to Lila. "You're ten centimeters. We'll be turning down the epidural so you can push."

Lila's eyes go wide. "Does that mean it's going to hurt? I don't want to turn the epidural down!"

I try to shake away the sleepy cobwebs. "I think they told us that in birthing class."

Lila seems to panic, her hand pressed to her chest. "I don't want it to hurt!"

Nurse Candace glances over at me. I stand up and take Lila's hand. "You can do this. We've got you."

But when the next contraction hits, Lila screams. "Noooo. I don't want to do this alone!"

Nurse Candace swivels, eyes landing on Drew. "Come on, Dad, get in here. Mom needs you."

Drew doesn't miss a beat, kneeling next to the bed on the opposite side and taking Lila's hand. "I've ushered a lot of babies into this world," he says. "You're doing way better than the mice."

"Don't they eat their babies?" Lila cries between panting.

"Not usually," Drew says. "But it happens."

"Okay," Nurse Candace says. "Let's focus on *this* baby. Which we are not going to eat!"

A tall man in scrubs enters the room at that very moment, pulling his mask over his mouth and nose. "What is this I hear about eating the baby?"

Even Lila laughs at this. "Drew is a veterinarian," she says. "And I don't want to hurt."

"Let's see where we are." Dr. Hendrix situates himself at the end of the bed. "Lila, I'm here until your regular doctor arrives. He's been paged, but things might happen fast."

"Please don't let it hurt," Lila begs.

He reaches beneath the blue paper sheet. "How about if I told you it would only hurt three times. Can you do it, to get the baby out and meet her?"

Tears stream down Lila's face, but she says, "I can do that."

The doctor watches the monitor. "Here comes the contraction. Give me a big ol' push, Lila. Big one."

Lila lets out a long guttural groan, her eyes squeezed shut. Drew catches my gaze across the bed. I know what he's thinking. Should he be here?

I cast my gaze down to where Lila has a death grip on his hand and meet his eyes again.

He nods. He's in it. He will be part of this birth story.

The push plays out, leaving Lila breathless and panting. "Two more?" she asks.

"Two more," Dr. Hendrix says.

Of course, it's not two more, but on the fifth one, he announces, "I can see the head!"

Lila seems bolstered by this. She pushes harder. "I want to be done!"

"Here she comes." Dr. Hendrix gestures to the nurse.

I catch Drew's eyes. He's watching me, too. I know he's ushered a lot of creatures into the world, but it's his first human birth.

There's a small cry, and we both look to the doctor. He lifts the baby, red-faced, covered in white. A nurse quickly wraps the baby's lower half, and they place her on Lila's chest.

Tillie starts blubbering behind me. "Oh my gosh oh my gosh oh my gosh."

Drew and I are released as Lila wraps her arms around the baby. Tillie snaps shots with her phone, her face blotchy with tears.

My face is wet, too. Lila brings the baby up to her neck, eyes closed. She looks ethereal, as if she's won a great battle and the calm has come.

The doctor steps around us, placing his stethoscope on the baby's back while she lies on Lila.

Drew moves to my side of the bed, almost taking my hand before remembering the nurse thinks he's Dad. I'm so proud of him for going along with it. He cares about all of us.

"Baby looks good," Dr. Hendrix says. "We're going to give you a few minutes together, then we'll take her for her assessment."

Lila nods. The room quiets as people leave. Drew turns his back while the nurse cleans Lila up. I can't help but smile as I watch him. All up in the sisters' business. It's part of the deal.

When it's just family in the room again, Drew draws me against him, and Tillie sits on the edge of the bed. "Did you finally decide on her name?" I ask. "You wanted to wait until you saw her."

Lila nods. "Rosalina James. Rosie."

"It's lovely," Tillie says. "You feeling okay?"

"I think I'm high or something," Lila says. "I feel weirdly great."

"The pain is gone," Drew says. "I see it in every species."

We fold up the bed into a sofa again. It might be the middle of the night, but we're done sleeping. Drew and I sit close together while Tillie keeps taking photos of the baby to send to Garrett and presumably our dad. It's his first grandchild. Maybe seeing his daughter as a mother will jar him out of his twenty-year funk. It's probably the only thing left that could.

"What's your position on kids?" I ask Drew. "Was this too scary?"

"Not at all," he says. "But I have a long way to go before I'm father material. You, though. You'll be a natural."

He's right. I will be. I mothered my younger sisters for their whole lives. And even if times were hard, we stuck together. So I totally believe in my ability to bring little humans into the world.

And I'm also going to be the world's best aunt.

I sit close to Drew, enjoying the strength of him beside me, even as the neonatal nurse arrives with the rolling cart, puts the identifying bracelet on the baby, and takes her away.

Lila almost immediately falls asleep, and Tillie carefully leaves her side. "I'm going to go take pictures," she says, tiptoeing out.

Then it's just us, and I rest my head on his shoulder.

"I have one more confession," he says, his lips against my hair.

"Really? We haven't had one of those in a while."

"I know." His voice has gone husky.

"Well, spit it out."

He clears his throat. "Remember that time you were watching me in the window, and you fell and broke the lamp?"

My cheeks flush hot. "You remember that?"

"I do."

"That's embarrassing."

He squeezes my arm. "Don't be embarrassed."

"Why not?"

"Because that was the day."

"The day?"

He leans forward so he can look at me. "That was the day I noticed you. That I really saw you."

"You saw me?"

"Yeah. You were young. It was not something I would have pursued. But I saw the strength you had in keeping the family going."

"I did my best."

"I fell in love with you right then. And I didn't forget you. You were always in the back of my mind. It was so pure, that love I felt. I held on to it even though I couldn't show it in any obvious way. I knew that my dad—that the things he did, were something I'd never let happen to you. Because you deserved everything. No one should ever dim that light in you. Especially not me."

I'm quiet. I never knew that Drew thought about me. That maybe he'd loved me all these years. "And then we got to the wedding."

"I was terrified. Because you landed in my lap. And I was not the man who could ever protect you. Not where I was then."

"But you learned."

He draws me closer to him. "Yes, I learned."

He kisses me. Not the frantic one in the shed, or the crazed ones in those early days in his office. Or even the ones that led to that first weekend we were together.

It's a kiss of comfort. Of knowing each other.

Of safety.

Of trust.

"I love you, Drew Daniels," I whisper against his mouth.

"And I love you, Ensley James."

We gaze at each other, reveling in the same love we've known for months now, when the light snaps on.

Nurse Candace stares at us, her mouth a line. "Well, this is disgusting." She walks right back out, muttering, "She just had his baby. Kissing her sister."

Lila's eyes pop open, and when she sees us in our embrace, she shrugs. "That's our family. Keeping it screwed up."

"It is," I say to her. "It really is."

Epilogue

ENSLEY

Wedding bells peal as Drew and I wait in the church's foyer for the ceremony to begin. Drew is best man, but he's left the groomsmen's dressing room to wait with me for the moment when Maria and Vera usher in the unusual members of the wedding party.

"They're crazy," I say.

"Completely crazy," Drew concurs.

"What are the odds this works perfectly?"

"Zero. There is no chance."

Oh boy. I should have worn flats. I check my sparkly silver platforms. They perfectly match my belt and a tiny hat positioned in my hair. My dress is coral, long-sleeved for a February wedding. It has fringe hanging off the bottom. It's smashing. I found it for twelve dollars at a thrift store in downtown Atlanta.

But this is no outfit for what is about to happen.

Wedding guests arrive, sign the guest book, and enter the sanctuary. When the door opens, organ music pulses into the foyer, then fades again as it closes.

Drew checks his watch. "They should be here any minute. My understanding is Vera and Maria go in first, get everyone situated, and then Todd comes out with the groomsmen."

I nod. "I'll be backup."

"You're going to stay up front to help if things go south?"

"I should have worn flats."

Drew nods, his mouth pressed tight. "This is going to go south."

Several old ladies are startled when the ruckus begins. They glance back at the exterior doors and hurry into the sanctuary.

As if that is any kind of escape.

Drew and I rush forward to help.

Seven dogs on leashes.

Seven.

There's a border collie, two Labradors, a boxer, a Yorkshire terrier, and two pugs.

Vera looks harried, her pink dress already askew from managing the dogs. "Now this is what I call a blended family."

Maria shakes her head. "Their house must be insane all day long."

The dogs go in random directions once they're inside the foyer, sniffing at everything. The boxer is about to lift his leg when Drew extracts a clicker and punches it three times.

The dog lifts his head, and Drew pulls out a treat. "No peeing," he says, and feeds the dog.

The other dogs rush to Drew's feet, begging for treats of their own.

"Don't overdo it," Maria warns. "I only got half of them to do their business in the grass."

Drew is right. Zero chance of this going perfectly. But Todd and Tatiana insisted their wedding day wouldn't be right without their fur babies.

"Why didn't they do an outdoor wedding?" Vera says.

"Catholic mass," Drew says. "Tatiana wanted it."

Vera shifts the leashes, which have gotten tangled while Drew gives each dog a treat. "And how long will it be?"

"Close to an hour." Drew holds out a finger to the collie, who is trying to jump over the back of the boxer to get another treat.

"I'll be there to help," I say, but Maria looks skeptical.

"In those shoes?"

Dang it. I'm the worst about practical footwear.

"I think I'll walk you in," Drew says. "You're going to need all hands on deck."

"Thank you," Maria says. "We probably should have gotten more help."

A family with two teen boys arrives, and Drew has them open the doors wide for the dogs.

The music swells, and the guests turn to see what's happening.

The dogs have settled and look more or less organized as Maria and Vera walk them down the aisle. The boxer heads for an old lady, about to lift his leg, but Drew clicks again.

The boxer turns his head. By then the other dogs are leaving him behind, so he trots to catch up.

Zero chance of success. Full zero.

I can't believe the church is allowing this, but apparently Tatiana's father is heavily involved with the parish. The concession was that the dogs would be contained.

So on the right side of the front of the church, there's a portable fence, the sort that normally corrals small children. It's decorated with white satin bows and pink roses.

I follow the group, only hurrying forward when the three of them have trouble getting all the dogs in the fence.

The boxer immediately leaps onto the top rail, biting the roses off the bows.

Oh boy.

There's no way they are truly contained. Only the terrier is too small to jump the fence, although the pugs would have to get a running start.

Vera and Maria settle in chairs on either side of the enclosure, wrapping the leashes around their arms. Drew heads up the aisle to meet the groomsmen in the back, and I take a seat on the pew closest to the dogs.

Maria shakes her head at me, and I know what she's thinking. These dogs are too wild, too untrained for an event like this.

But they're doing it.

Todd's mother and father arrive and sit in the opposite front pew. Then Tatiana's mother walks in, led by her son, who looks to be in his midtwenties. They sit on my pew, close to the center. She glances at the dogs with a pinched expression. She's clearly not a fan of this idea.

The music changes, and the back doors open. Todd enters in his tux, followed by Drew and two groomsmen I only met last night at the rehearsal.

The dogs go wild at the sight of Todd. He stops by the fence and pets each one, feeding them a treat. Maria grimaces, checking on the poop bag dispenser attached to her belt.

I have to work very hard to contain my giggles.

The bridesmaids arrive one by one, all wearing pink satin gowns.

A little girl in a pink dress walks down the aisle dropping rose petals. White ribbons are woven into her sleek black braids.

The guests let out a collective sigh at the cuteness.

She makes it to the front and stands by Todd.

Then the music swells, and the priest enters, gesturing for us to rise for the bride.

The movement makes the dogs bark and leap. Maria and Vera stand up, trying to calm them down. I move forward, too, kneeling in front of the enclosure, trying to keep the boxer inside.

Tatiana begins her walk up the aisle with her father. Todd has eyes only for her, but I notice that Drew is watching the dogs.

Maria and Vera are holding back the Labs, and I have a grip on the boxer. The pugs are fairly quiet, but the terrier yaps his head off.

Oh boy.

Tatiana appears at the front of the aisle, and I know the moment the dogs spot her. The boxer lunges. I have him by the neck, but the pressure on the fence makes the flimsy setup start to lean.

The Labradors sense their escape and push forward.

Everything happens in slow motion.

All three big dogs surge ahead.

The fence topples and comes apart, scattering roses. The dogs race away, coming to the ends of their leashes.

Vera and Maria are pulled from their chairs, fighting to keep their balance.

Drew hurries forward, trying to extract his clicker from his jacket.

Todd holds out his hand, shouting the dogs' names.

But Tatiana is unflappable. The dogs surround her, jumping and yipping.

She kneels and kisses each one, wrapping the leashes around her wrist. By the time she's done, all seven dogs are calm again, and they are the ones who end up walking her up to Todd as her father sits next to her mother.

"Told you they wouldn't stay in the fence," Tatiana says.

Todd laughs. "I will never doubt you again."

The priest does not look pleased, but the ceremony goes on. Maria and Vera shrug it off and sit next to me. Tatiana's mother pats her forehead and neck with a handkerchief, clearly in distress about what just happened.

The dogs are more or less content to sit near Tatiana, even during the extended homily by the priest.

But when he tells Todd to kiss the bride, and the audience begins to clap, that's it. The dogs are done.

They jump and bark and take Tatiana's arms in opposite directions. Todd grabs at the leashes.

The wedding coordinator opens the back doors for the bride and groom's exit, and the smell of food from the reception in the adjoining hall filters in.

The dogs catch one whiff, and they are off, taking the bride and groom with them.

The organist fires up the recessional music, but Todd and Tatiana are already gone. The bridesmaids and groomsmen look at each other, not sure what to do. After a moment, the priest says, "On to the reception!"

Drew stays behind to pick up the scattered roses and stack the fencing. I head over to help.

"Zero chance," he says.

"Absolutely zero."

Drew places the broken flowers and petals in a pile on a pew. "They'll be back in a minute for pictures."

"Should we wait here?"

"Might as well."

We watch as the room empties until it's only us near the altar. Sun streams in through the stained glass.

"It's lovely here," I say.

"Do you like church weddings?"

"Mom sure did," I say. "She felt happy in big beautiful churches like this."

"Does it sometimes feel like she is here?"

"It does right now."

He watches me, and our gazes hold. "This is a pretty tight secret," he says, "but Tatiana is pregnant. That's why the wedding came so quickly. She's planning to leave the clinic when the baby arrives."

"Oh no! You'll have to start over with an office manager."

Drew takes my hand. "I know that based on how things started, you decided that us working together was a bad idea while we dated, and by then Tatiana had taken over anyway. I didn't like you getting stuck at the bank again, but you seemed to like it this time."

"I do like it. It's fine. It's honest work."

"But do you still want something more meaningful? And when you worked at the clinic before, did that count? Did it make you happy?"

I think I'm starting to see where this is going. "I did love it there. Even if I managed to get stuck up in a tree." I squeeze his hand. "And we still haven't broken in that desk of yours. I was promised a certain action on top of it."

"You'll get that for sure."

"You mean if I work for you again?"

"Yes. I miss you there. And maybe it would be different this time."

"You mean you won't kiss me against the wall anymore?"

"Oh, I'll definitely kiss you against the wall at every opportunity. But I have something to address the dating part of your concern."

He reaches in his pocket and pulls out the clicker and frowns. "It's here somewhere." His hand dips inside again, and out comes a baggie of treats.

Then a spare poop bag.

"What are you looking for?" I ask.

His lips are a grim line. "Okay. There it is."

"Drew?"

He opens his palm. "I brought this."

I suck in a breath. It's a diamond ring. "You carried it all day?"

"Weeks, actually. Waiting for the right moment." He looks around. "Since everything started at a wedding, I figured another wedding would be a good time to take the next step."

He drops to one knee. "Here's what I know. This place makes you think of your mother. And since she can't be here, maybe this is exactly the right place to ask my very important question."

Tears smart my eyes. "And what is that?"

"Ensley James, I love you. I've loved you since you were twelve years old. So this is a long time coming. Will you do me the honor of becoming my wife?"

He looks so handsome in his tux, just like the last time, almost exactly a year ago at Ronnie's wedding. The colors stream behind him through the glass, and over his head I spot a depiction of the Virgin Mary looking over the manger.

Maybe Mom is here somehow, making sure I'm standing this way and seeing this window.

I bend down to lean in close. "Yes, Drew Daniels. I will marry you. On one condition." His lips are breathlessly near mine. I'm eager to kiss them, but not yet.

"And what's that?"

"We *elope*."

His smile is big and genuine, a sight I once never thought I could see on this grumpy veterinarian's face. And when he leans in to seal our decision, I know that somewhere, my mom is clapping her hands with delight.

And the twelve-year-old version of me is right beside her, jumping up and down, because every single one of her dreams is about to come true.

ACKNOWLEDGMENTS

I had so much help on the journey to writing this book.

Huge thanks to the all-star vet techs Clint Lienau and Jenny Rookey for their help with the behind-the-scenes doggie and kitty antics at the clinic.

And Sammi Dyer—wow. You were painfully sworn to secrecy after beta reading this book. And how wonderful that you and hubby reconnected decades after he was *your* childhood crush! I had no idea you were the perfect person to be the first reader until you told me.

Huge love to Lindsay Zappone. The baby bunny born in this story is in honor of your sweet bunny Harper, a much-loved fur baby who crossed the rainbow bridge in 2022.

Huge thanks to my agent, Jess Regel, for getting this book out into the world, and to my editors, Maria Gomez and Lindsey Faber, for making it shine.

Then there's the Austin Java Writing Group, whom I've met every week for almost twenty years. There is no writing friendship like our writing friendships. We have forged an unbreakable bond since first meeting at NaNoWriMo in 2005. (You even found me a husband!) Our original crew: Audrey Coulthurst, Chris "Fool" McCraw, Ivy Crawford, Enrique "Henry" Gomez, Rebecca Leach. And the ones who came along the way and fit right in: Amber Lee Jonker, Helen Wiley, Hannah Bauman, Delia Davila, Lori Thomas.

And the friends who became part of our writerly support: Casi Clarkson, Lisa Merry, Irma Kramer, Jen Kramer, Jimmie Bragdon, Max Clontz, Nawal Traish, Lindsey Wilson.

I'm grateful to my comedy writing friends who were part of my search for the perfect rom-com story structure: Jennifer Bailey and Mike Wollaeger. And thank you to *Onion* founder Scott Dikkers for coming to our Clubhouse rooms and advising us, and also for your brilliant books on comedy writing that we dissected endlessly.

I can't go without a shout-out to my friends on Clubhouse who cheered me on every single day in sprint rooms during this draft, including Vanessa Hollis, Aparna Verna, Bart Baker, Celeste Barclay, RJ Gray, Marlayna James, Jordan Barnes, Rachel Lithgow, Aubrey Spivey, Rachel Ember, April Floyd, Koek Ros, Paul Guyot, Ngozi Robinson, Julie Kenner, Carmen Swick, Jami Albright, Jayne Rylon, Hannah Byron, Stephanie Berchiolly, and probably several more I met and bonded with after these acknowledgments went in to the publisher.

I also want to mention my core romance writer friends, who have been by my side for over a decade: Julia Kent, Blair Babylon, Olivia Rigal, Marina Maddix.

And Pippa Grant, your advice was always priceless.

My family probably averts their eyes whenever they catch sight of my steamy book covers, but their support in my life has been core to my success: Dad, who always boasts about my authorly endeavors. Wesley, whose lively ideas often make their way into jokes in my books. Elizabeth, who inspires me every day about facing adversity with grace. Emily, whose work ethic and sheer smarts make me proud, and whose savvy got my books on viral videos on TikTok. And of course, Kurt, my husband. Every love story is our love story.

EXCERPT FROM *TASTY MANGO*

Chapter 1

I've always pictured this moment.

Me, in a little black dress.

My hair swept into a perfect chignon.

An exclusive restaurant filled with elegant diners.

China clinks. Crystal glasses gleam on linen tablecloths.

Seated opposite me is the ideal man. Tall, dark, handsome.

Custom suit. Gold cuff links.

He's charming and witty.

Wildly successful in business.

And he only has eyes for me.

It could have been the greatest first date of my life.

Except.

My belly is too big to let me pull up to the table properly.

The baby is kicking like crazy for me to eat something—*now*.

And a funny trickle of wetness is forming deep in the recesses of my panties.

And *not* the good kind.

Am I peeing myself?

"Havannah, are you okay?" Donovan McDonald pauses, his water goblet halfway to his lips. He's a gentleman, so he's not drinking wine, since I can't.

His eyes are on me, his thick brows knitted in concern. His gaze dips to the table's edge, where I'm hunched, trying to hide my bump. I'm desperately trying to appear like a normal date from the chest up.

"Perfect!" I say, keeping my voice as chipper as possible, wondering if a wet spot will show on the dress. I really want to sneak away to the bathroom to see what's going on.

God. This is horrible.

Of course, it's mid-June, so I don't have a wrap to tie around my waist. Just my foolishly tight dress that fit fine at six months pregnant but is snug at nine.

I shift on the chair, making sure my legs are hidden by the table-cloth. I spread my knees in hopes that I can air-dry.

Pregnancy is a beast.

But I have a few days to go until I'm due, and I hear first babies are always late. I've vowed to be nothing but chic and put together on this date. He'll see my elegance, my poise—

Uh oh.

Another squirt of wetness slips out.

How can this be? I peed right before I came. I'm not coughing, or laughing too hard, or sneezing.

I push my cloth napkin under the tablecloth and shove it up under my dress. Sorry, fancy restaurant. I'm stealing this. It's an emergency.

The waiter approaches. "Your salads."

He sets two perfectly arranged wedges in front of us, artfully cut on a square plate with a fan of tomato slivers.

At the smell of bleu cheese, Junior kicks hard enough to make my belly jump. Another bit of water slides out. He must be aiming for the bladder. So that's what's happening.

I let out a sigh, relieved to have figured it out. I squeeze my thighs around the cloth napkin and pick up my fork.

"This looks amazing," I say.

"You look amazing," Donovan says.

Our gazes meet over the vase of roses in the center of the table. He is such a hunk. His dark eyes sparkle. His beard is neatly trimmed. Everything about him is absolutely perfect.

And he's here with *me*.

I'm fine. We'll have a lovely dinner. Then he'll leave again and think about me on his travels.

This will work.

"How is the new financial manager working out?" he asks.

I cut off a sliver of lettuce, despite Junior's insistence that I eat the entire thing whole. I'm a *delicate flower*, baby. Don't make me look bad.

"Magnolia says he's great. I'm more of the branding expert." I slip the tiny bite in my mouth.

Donovan's grin disarms me completely. "I guess we shouldn't talk shop on a date."

A date.

It hits me one more time.

I'm on a date with a billionaire.

Junior kicks again. He couldn't care less about the man. He wants the food.

I go to stab more salad, but my plate is empty. I've inhaled it.

A waiter rushes by, the white cloth tucked into his belt flying behind him. His movement disturbs the candle near my water glass, and a waft of smoke reaches my nose.

Oh, no.

The tickle is small at first, and I try to suppress it.

Not a sneeze. No, no, no. Not when I'm already leaking.

Donovan's gaze is resting on me. He's smitten. I can see it.

But he's also paying close attention. I can't squeeze my nose or take preventive measures. That wouldn't be elegant *or* chic.

The tickle becomes an itch, then expands to a burning need to sneeze. My eyes water slightly.

Donovan's hand snakes across the table, heading toward mine. "I'm so glad we got to do this."

The moment is here! We're connecting! Me and this perfect man! I reach for him as well.

But I can't hold back the sneeze.

It takes over my face, my lungs, my upper body. I inhale in a big "Aaah" then release in an alarming "Choooo!"

The candle goes out.

Several diners turn.

But Donovan's hand doesn't move. His lips quirk with a smile he's trying to hide. "Bless you."

He might say something else, but I can't pay any attention whatsoever.

My legs feel warm and wet. *Really* wet. Like, to my ankles.

A weird sound sets off a panic. What is that? Rainfall? Water spilling?

My glass is still beside my plate.

Then realization dawns. It's water hitting the floor below the table. Below *me*.

I'm soaked. My legs are drenched. I can feel it in my *shoe*.

I can't seem to stop myself from abruptly standing up. My chair kicks back, then falls behind me.

Donovan leaps from his seat. "Havannah?"

I stare down at my bare, dripping legs. The soggy cloth napkin falls to the floor with a *splat*.

There's no hiding it now. I have to say it.

"My water just broke."

ABOUT THE AUTHOR

JJ Knight is the *USA Today* bestselling author of romantic comedies and sports romance. She's a fierce mama bear for all the humans under her care: biological, adopted, and those in need of mom hugs. Her books portray characters who learn to push through hardship to find love and belly laughs. For more information visit www.jjknight.com.